STEVE BEAULIEU PRESENTS:

IT'S A BIRD!
IT'S A PLANE!

A SUPERHERO ANTHOLOGY

TABLE OF CONTENTS

This book is lovingly dedicated to a man whom none of us knew but who changed our lives forever.

Adam West—you *are* Batman.

You are the hero we all wanted and Gotham deserved. Thank you for the memories. Thank you for the laughs. And thank you for igniting the flames of our imaginations.
September 19, 1928 - June 9, 2017

FOREWORD

SUPERHEROES OF A SORT, have long been staples of literature, and I'm not just talking about comic books, either. I'd venture to say that the modern superheroes—those with the extraordinary super-human or supernatural powers used for good—are better examples, but it could be argued that figures from the Bible such as David (he of the Goliath-slay-ing fame) and Samson (he of the locks of strength) are early visions of what modern day superheroes would become, though the term superhero didn't come into usage until the early 1900s. And I'm sure there are even earlier examples of superhero-type characters—let's forget about the pantheons of gods peppered throughout history—appearing in both written and oral stories. I'm no historian, mind you, but I'd be willing to lay down a day's pay on that.

Among those predecessors, we find the likes of Robin of Locksley, better known as Robin Hood, whose tales, for me, were the earliest literature I read (*gasp*...I didn't read comic books as a kid, only when I got older) in which a central figure was hero-ic, relieving the wealthy of their wealth and easing the burdens of the poor by distributing that wealth to them. Not necessarily the best way to go about being a superhero, I'd say, but a good example of how certain central themes can be found that run through most superhero tales, modern and otherwise.

The collection you're about to read illustrates and highlights many of those persistent themes: the oppressed overcoming oppression; good facing off versus evil and triumphing; the indomitable will of the human spirit coming to the forefront, despite seemingly insurmountable obstacles and circumstances, oftentimes tragedies. These stories have it all, everything you expect from a superheroic tale, with enough twists and turns—some blindsides, fair warning—to keep you satisfied.

Chris Pourteau leads us out of the gate with his story "Geek Gurl Rising," a quick but powerful tale of an ordinary girl blasting through preconceived notions and doing something amazing. The perfect primer to get you, the reader, in the right frame of mind for the remainder of this collection.

Patricia Gilliam's "Anna" is next up. A haunting story set in the world of her *The Hannaria Series*. This classic alien on earth story is sure to please fans of the series as well as new readers unfamiliar with the previous works.

Rhett C. Bruno's "The Roach Rises" comes next in the lineup. This gritty, noir-esque vigilante hero tale examines what happens when one man thinks he's outlived his usefulness as someone heroic.

"Cleanview," by Hall & Beaulieu, sees a lowly janitor privy to the inner thoughts of a superhero he considers the most powerful man on the planet.

Christopher J. Valin gives us "Photo Op," the next tale in our quest for superheroic adventure, in which an aging superhero takes on a rather unusual mission to protect his secret identity.

In Kevin J. Summers' "The Paladin," a young crime fighting superhero is born from the tragedy of the loss of a loved one to the seedy underworld of the big city encroaching upon their small town. But does he go too far in seeking and exacting his revenge?

Alexia Purdy brings her tale "Mercurial" to the collection. In it, a young nurse discovering her powers confronts an aging, perhaps over-the-hill, superhero who's let life get the better of him, so much so that he may have lost his way—and his ability to carry on with the work he was destined to do.

Andy Peloquin's "One Last Time" introduces us to a mild-mannered office worker who wins the superhero lottery and is transformed into the city's protector—but for how long and at what cost?

Josh Hayes offers up "Hero Worship," a story about a jaded and bitter man who holds superheroes in contempt.

C.C. Ekeke gives us "An Ordinary Hero," a subtle but nuanced story about a day in the life of a superhero's significant other which takes a twist

3

when the unexpected happens. How he handles it may just make him a superhero, too.

Next up is Jeffrey Beesler's "The Spotlight." A young girl confronts evil and things don't quite go as planned.

The collection is wrapped up with "Fade," by Josi Russel, which tells the tale of a woman whose superpower isn't what she wished it were. But it's a unique ability that comes in very handy.

We've all been in situations where we wished we had a superpower, a way to fight back against some wrong being done to us or to others, a way to make the wrongs of the world right again. While we don't find that we're suddenly imbued with the ability to fly or to summon superhuman strength in these situations, many of us have found that within ourselves is an inner strength of will that can be tapped into to help us get through the tough times. I've used this superpower many a time myself, as I'm sure many of you, dear readers, have.

Inside each of us is a superhero waiting to be unleashed, waiting to be freed to right the wrongs of the world around us, even if only in an infinitesimal, minuscule way. I encourage each of you to read these stories and take inspiration from the heroes who you find inspirational, then pay that forward into the world around you. The benefits may not be that of adulation from the public, or huge monetary rewards or the like, but I can guarantee you that those you help will see you as the hero you are.

I do hope you enjoy these stories as much as I have, and I hope that you'll unleash the superhero inside of you to make all the positive changes in the world that you can.

WE'RE ALL SUPERHEROES AND WE CAN ALL MAKE A DIFFERENCE!

1 June 2017

Todd Barselow, *Acquisitions Editor and Publisher*

Auspicious Apparatus Press
Davao City, Philippines

GEEK GURL

RISING

CHRIS POURTEAU

NEVER LET THE RATS in the experiment know you're watching them, thought Carrie Conrad, peering over the top of her book at the Fearsome Foursome. The clock above the school stage showed five minutes to fifth period and an hour's worth of freedom. *Almost time for the lunchtime ritual. But I'm ready for them this time.*

Teen talk about music and hair and what someone said about someone else echoed around the lunch room. At their table in the middle of the cafeteria, Brad Magnuson, his girlfriend Stephanie Seward, and that other hangers-on couple, *what're-their-names*, snickered and gestured toward Carrie's table. There was a kind of no man's land around the Foursome, a reverent, empty space reserved only for those who were summoned to approach.

Carrie gripped tighter the tome she was reading and watched them work themselves up, gathering their courage. Most of the time, she felt invisible at Rosecranz High. And sometimes feeling that way, like she didn't exist at all, hurt more than anything. But sometimes, on days like today, she wished she could go unnoticed by everyone, be just another face in the crowd.

The process preceding her harassment by the Foursome had begun to fascinate her, though. She enjoyed predicting each stage, as if observing the behavior of rats in a lab experiment. Ticking off the preliminaries like boxes on a list made Carrie feel powerful, like she (not they) controlled what was about to happen. It almost made the inner pain that always followed worthwhile.

There it was, Carrie noticed, the first glance her way from Stephanie, a kind of scouting mission. Brad's eyes followed his girlfriend's, as everything he did followed Stephanie's lead. *Like a dog following his favorite scent*, Carrie thought. Brad might be the king of Rosecranz High, but Stephanie was his queen bee, and school rumor wasn't shy about how freely her honey flowed. And the court jesters, the hangers-on couple, were always there to giggle encouragement. All eight eyes of the Fearsome Foursome were on Carrie, now.

Brad rose and adjusted his football uniform, then Stephanie stood up.

The football hero and the cheerleader. How original.

Leave it to the brain trust to wear their school uniforms for Halloween Day. *At least the court jesters put some effort into dressing up*, Carrie thought, finally remembering their names. Richard was a cowboy, his girlfriend Cassidy a Goth with fake piercings.

As the four walked over, Carrie focused on reading her book. *Never let the rats in the experiment know you're watching them.*

"Hey there, Scary Carrie," Brad said as they walked up. He held his helmet under one arm and Stephanie clung to the other, exuding perkiness. "Whatcha reading today? More comic books, little girl?"

Carrie ignored him. *Take that!*

"Doesn't look like a comic," Brad said, his gaze assessing the large, thick book. "Shakespeare. Huh. Sounds about right." He made a show of looking her up and down. "No costume today? I figured you, of all people, would've come in costume. Like, Wonder Girl or Bat Thing or whatever."

"Are you kidding?" Stephanie said. "She's *in* costume. Now, hmmm, let me see if I can guess...I know! You're Geek Girl, Queen of the Nerd Patrol!" Somehow the cheerleader queen managed to focus on Carrie while slinking against Brad like a cat marking a couch. Looking down her nose, Stephanie continued, "Same thing she wears every day, Flash."

The court jesters tittered.

"Where'd you get that name anyway?" Carrie asked, not deigning to look at them.

"What name—Flash?" Brad asked.

"Yeah."

"So—Brainiac ain't so smart after all,"

11

Stephanie snarked. "He's only the fastest running-back in Rosecranz history!" She bobbed up and down with excitement.

"Oh, yeah," Carrie said. "I forgot."

Zing!

Cassidy the Goth girl made a what-a-*moron* clucking sound.

"Got a date for Sadie Hawkins yet?" asked Richard the cowboy in a tone that said he already knew the answer.

Carrie sighed dramatically, then looked him dead in the eye. "Not yet, Dick."

Cassidy dropped her boyfriend's hand and loomed over the table. "Don't call him that! How many times do I have to tell you?"

"Call him what?" Carrie asked, returning to Shakespeare.

"Dick!"

"Call who Dick?"

"Di—Richard!"

Carrie stared over the edge of her book to see the light dawning in Cassidy's eyes that she'd just been had. The Goth-grey makeup flushed a darker color. Cassidy clenched her fists.

"Careful, you're starting to look not dead, thou craven reeling-ripe horn beast," Carrie said.

For a moment, only the dull hum of lunch room gossip could be heard.

"What'd you just call me?"

Carrie lifted the thick *Riverside Shakespeare*

she was reading. It was heavy, but lifting it in front of them made her feel powerful. "Try reading something besides *Teen Vogue*."

Stephanie moved to Cassidy's side. "You think you're so smart, but you're not. You're new here, and you just better watch—"

The bell announcing the end of the last lunch period sounded, transforming the buzz of teen conversation into a drone of disappointed moaning.

"You unmuzzled ill-nurtured pigeon-egg," Carrie said without looking at the book. "Forsooth, your words do tax my ears as a pox does the skin."

Stephanie gaped, flummoxed. Carrie could see the wheels turning as the cheerleader tried to identify the insult she was no doubt sure had just been levied against her.

"Come on," Cowboy Dick said, tapping Flash's arm. "Coach'll have our asses if we're late."

As students rose, their chairs scraping, Stephanie struck a hand out, batting the *Riverside Shakespeare* aside. Carrie grabbed after it but missed, and the big book slammed to the cafeteria floor.

"Forsooth that, you little bitch."

Something else, a magazine spilled from between the Riverside's pages. Carrie gasped, her stony defiance crumbling into embarrassed horror.

Cassidy giggled. "Hey look! Scary Carrie's getting married!"

Now it was Carrie's face that flushed, red as a

beet, as the foursome stood ogling the *Brides* magazine on the floor. Its cover with a beautiful blonde woman in a beaded white dress was bright and vibrant against the Elizabethan illustration on the cover of the *Riverside Shakespeare.*

"She wasn't reading Shakespeare! She was planning for Prince Charming!" Stephanie's voice carried over the din of exiting students, and eyes from all quarters sought out Carrie on the floor as she scrambled to recover her magazine and its Renaissance camouflage.

"Good luck with that!" Flash said as others gave Carrie a wide berth, like she might have the plague. "Come on, peeps. Can't keep Coach waiting."

Cassidy looped her arm into her boyfriend's and, with a last kick at Shakespeare, headed to class with her friends. Flash sneered and led Stephanie away as she threw another joke over her shoulder about Carrie's manless future.

Still sitting on the floor, Carrie watched them go. She reached over and picked Shakespeare up. Unlike earlier, the book felt cumbersome now, like her arms had lost all their strength to lift it. With half-glances both pitying and grateful they weren't Carrie Conrad, the last of the students passed by. None stopped to help her up, and their coldness made Carrie feel like crying. Instead, after a moment, she got to her feet, carefully folded the bridal magazine inside the *Riverside Shakespeare*, and headed for her refuge.

At least it's fifth period, she thought. Thank God for that.

• • •

To Carrie, walking into Rosecranz High's library always felt like walking into relief itself.

It must be what Superman feels flying to the Fortress of Solitude. Or Batman coming home to the Batcave. Like retreating to a secret place, a personal space where you could set aside the worries of the world and relax and just be who you are, far away from the madding crowd.

Not that the library was secret from anyone. But it was hers more than anyone's who came here. Anyone but Mr. Johns, maybe. He was her favorite teacher, although he wasn't, technically, a teacher at all. But his balding head, thick-rimmed eyeglasses, and signature bowtie had become touchstones of sanity for Carrie since moving here with her parents barely a month before. She'd sought out the library on *day one* and made it her sanctuary, her treasure chest of other worlds into which to escape from the real one.

Rupert Johns looked up from the stack of books he was checking in and smiled pleasantly. "Hi, Carrie. Fifth period already?"

"Never soon enough," she mumbled more to herself than him. Carrie walked to her favorite table, the one closest to the stacks. She loved the smell of the books on the shelves. Mr. Johns had once described it as the scent of knowledge waiting to be reborn, and that had sounded just about right to Carrie. Setting down her backpack, she tried to re-turn the librarian's smile. But his expression in re-turn showed just how lopsided her attempt must have been.

"What's wrong?" he asked.

Carrie gave him a look like he was crazy. "What? Nothing. Why?" Her words fired like bullets.

He set down the book he was checking in. "You've been crying."

"No I haven't!"

His head tilted to the side, and Johns gave her a calm but quizzical look. "The Rat Pack again?"

His voice sounded concerned, but she could also hear a steely support in it, the even tone of an ally who empathized from experience. Bullying by Magnuson and his entourage had become an all-too familiar point of discussion during her visits to the library. And, Johns had confided, he'd been bullied in high school, too.

Carrie quickly wiped her hands across her cheeks. "Yeah." No sense denying it now. And it felt wrong to be untruthful with Mr. Johns. He'd been there for her since she'd started her junior year at Rosecranz, introducing her to Shakespeare and Charles Dickens and Edgar Allan Poe. He'd been her Alfred, her Professor X, her Gandalf, her guardian of the gateway to other worlds. He'd been her one reli-able friend.

"The rats didn't perform the way I wanted

today," she said. "But I'm sure we'll have another chance tomorrow to perfect the experiment."

"Did you try the Shakespeare strategy we talked about?"

Carrie perked up. "I did! They had no clue!" A proud grin spread across her face.

"There it is!" he said, reflecting her expression and returning to his inventory. "Sunshine always clears away the clouds." Then, somewhat more seriously, "Time's ticking, kiddo."

"Don't remind me," Carrie groaned. She had an hour before sixth period, an hour to center and gird herself for the rest of the school day. Unpacking her books, she quickly buried the Brides magazine under the comics she'd brought for the day. *Wonder Woman. Captain Marvel. Power Girl. Jessica Jones.* Last came the *Riverside Shakespeare*, which thumped the table like an anvil.

"Reading anything good lately?" Johns asked, nodding at the booty she'd unloaded.

"I'm halfway through *Henry V*. I'm not sure if I like Prince Harry or not. But I like Falstaff!"

Johns nodded. "Sounds familiar. How about in the comic-book department?"

"The new *Jessica Jones* is pretty good. Better than the Netflix show even! The new *Wonder Woman* is cool, better than they have been. Story's finally getting interesting."

Closing the last book he was checking in, Johns placed it on the stack of re-shelves. "I was always a

Marvel man myself. More complex characters, people with real problems. DC's heroes were always so two-dimensional. Except Bruce Wayne, of course."

"Right," Carrie said. She scanned the comic covers on the desk. All of them touted strong, if idealized, women—powerful, dynamic, and kicking ass. She loved devouring those stories and picturing herself tossing Wonder Woman's lasso or turning the unwanted hand a thug placed on her backside and throwing him through a store window like Jessica Jones.

But if she were honest with herself, Batman was her favorite hero. He didn't take crap from anyone, and he had no special powers to make him *super* —other than uber-intelligence, athletic prowess, and willpower. Prone to anger and violence, he was as human as heroes came. Carrie could relate. *Except for the athlete part*, she thought self-consciously.

"I've got a surprise for you," Johns was saying. "And like I said, clock's ticking."

She shook herself back into social mode. "A surprise?"

The librarian was trying not to smile and made himself busy with a new stack of returns.

It's a gift! Mr. Johns got me something! Oh my gosh!

"It's back in the stacks, in Pooh Corner," he said as he stamped quite deliberately.

Suddenly excited, Carrie headed for the part of the library farthest away from the rest of the school, a secluded corner she'd dubbed Pooh Corner. She loved to sit on the floor surrounded by the stacks and read during fifth period, to breathe in the musty aroma that seemed to hang in the air around her like a cloud of imagination. Carrie thought of the Corner as the place where books were born in the library because that's where Mr. Johns kept his new acquisitions until they were assigned a Dewey Decimal number and placed in their permanent homes on the shelves.

She turned at the last row of books that led to Pooh Corner and nearly stepped on a black mask some student must have dropped earlier in the day. A Robin mask, the thought came to her, though really it was just a cheap, plastic mask from the Halloween store. She ignored it and approached the new acquisitions stacked vertically in the very place where she always sat on the floor to read. Her eyes went wide as the multicolored covers teased their inner treasure.

On top, a collection: *Batman: From the 30's to the 70's*. Carrie reached out slowly and picked it up, savoring the moment and feeling the weight of future adventures in her trembling hands. An older version of Batman and Robin from the 1960's graced the dust jacket. They stood, ready to leap into action, perched on a rooftop with the moon spotlighting them from behind. Carrie opened the heavy collection and saw images of the Dark Knight and his ward she'd never seen before, some almost comical in their simplicity. She flipped the pages quickly, drinking in the Dynamic Duo through the ages, and between black-and-white story panels, color cover collections leapt off the page at her. She was seeing Batman evolve from his very first story, right before her eyes.

"Oh, Mr. Johns," she whispered.

She set the Batman collection down and saw *Ultimate Spider-Man: Volume One* was the next title in the tower of books. Carrie scanned down the spines of the volumes below it and found a trove of other colorful Marvel and DC titles, not yet tagged for the library's shelves, pristine and perfect. Mr. Johns had ordered all of them for her, she realized. A whole encyclopedia of comic collections. He'd ordered them for her.

She sat down in her place in Pooh Corner and began to examine them, one at a time and slowly. It would take her at least the remainder of fifth period just to appreciate them all, and many more wonderfully luxuriant hours beyond that to read them. She'd be lucky to even touch all their covers before she had to go to sixth period.

Crack!

Carrie jumped at the loud noise. It had sounded like a car backfiring, like a pop and a bang happening at the same time. She knew the chemistry lab wasn't far from the library and wondered if an experiment gone wrong might cancel classes for the rest of the day. Carrie angled a hopeful ear.

Boom!

A second backfire, deeper and more resonant and sounding closer. Wait, how did someone get a car inside the school?

Carrie heard a door slam open. She heard blinds clatter against glass. The door to the library had blinds. She heard screams beyond, from the cafeteria maybe.

What in the world?

"What are you—oh my God!"

Mr. Johns?

"Shut up! Just shut up!" The voice was shrill—frightened and thrilled at the same time. "Come out from behind there, right now!"

Carrie heard the rustling of fast feet at the front of the library. She set down a hardback *Ultimate Fantastic Four* and pressed against the wall of Pooh Corner. Something was very, very wrong. A *smack!* and Mr. Johns cried out.

Mr. Johns!

"Is there anyone else in here? And don't lie to me!" The voice held a strange lilt, as if the man speaking had sucked on helium balloons.

Carrie's heart kicked into overdrive. A moment passed, an eternity in which she waited for Mr. Johns to speak the truth of her presence. He always spoke the truth. Instead, she heard *shuck-shock*—the sound of a pump-action shotgun.

"No! It's just me!" Mr. Johns sounded scared. Terrified. "Why are you doing this? Who are you?"

IT'S A BIRD! IT'S A PLANE!

"Get up!"

Carrie glanced down at the superheroes scattered on the floor around her. Her gaze fastened on the *Batman* collection she'd seen first on the top of the stack, with the Dynamic Duo poised on the rooftop.

I wish you were real. I wish you were here.

She heard feet moving, coming toward Pooh Corner. Carrie glanced around desperately and had the absurd thought that if she stacked the collections up high enough, she could hide behind them.

"Move!"

Mr. Johns appeared at the end of the row of books. He threw his eyes at her, then quickly looked away again. She'd seen his desperate apology there, a half-second glance railing at his inability to protect her.

Oh, no.

Then a shorter man appeared and pressed the barrel of his shotgun into Mr. Johns's back, forcing him against the stacks that lined the back wall of the library. He was slight, not tall at all, shorter than Mr. Johns, even. He wore a trenchcoat and ski mask, all black, and a heavy jacket—no, a flak jacket like she'd seen in *Call of Duty*.

The gunman in the trenchcoat looked right first, down the row away from Carrie.

She closed her eyes, waiting.

Please don't see me, please don't see me, please don't see me!

22

She opened her eyes, afraid to look but needing to look at the same time.

Trenchcoat glanced left and directly at her. She saw Mr. Johns wince in his certainty of what was about to happen, knowing he was helpless to help her.

Carrie watched the eyes behind the ski mask rake over Pooh Corner. She stared straight at them as they stared back, seemingly not at her but *through* her. After a heartbeat that lasted forever, the lilting voice said, "Okay, come on, then."

The shotgun motioned for Mr. Johns to move, and the awestruck librarian headed back toward the front of the library. Trenchcoat followed, mouthing threats and promises of death if Johns didn't do exactly as he was told.

Her mouth open wide, her mind disbelieving, Carrie sat, shaking. Her palms were sweating. What had just happened? Why hadn't the gunman seen her? She looked at the floor and the pile of hardback comics scattered around her, searching in her mind for an answer that made any kind of sense at all. Her eyes stopped short when they spotted the cover of the *Ultimate Fantastic Four.* The heroes were there, each of their powers on display—Reed Richards's elastic Mr. Fantastic, The Thing's rocky skin and huge fists ready to pummel, Johnny Storm's flaming body, and ... his sister, Sue Storm Richards, her upper half clad in the familiar blue of the Four's costume, and her lower half—her lower half turning transparent as she became Invisible Girl.

No. No way.

It didn't make any sense, no sense at all. Carrie couldn't turn invisible. *Especially* when she wanted to. Flash Magnuson and the rest of his entourage had proven that again at lunch. But Trenchcoat hadn't seen her, had he? Could she—no, that just wasn't possible.

Was it?

I mean—why didn't he see me? He looked right at me! I—

The alert from the school's public address system sounded three long, grating notes. A voice she guessed was the principal's began to speak, hastily urging teachers and students to shelter in their classrooms until further notice. His tone was calm but shaking. Three more buzzing alerts followed, then silence.

Carrie had heard about things like this. Gun-wielding killers, teens with a grudge against the world, coming after those they blamed for whatever the hell it was they blamed them for. And now a man —no, a boy, she thought, making the connection with the high tenor of the voice behind the ski mask—had come to Rosecranz High and taken someone she cared about hostage. The only person here who had ever cared about her.

She looked down at her hand and saw it was anything but invisible. Its shaking was all too apparent, and her palm glistened with the sweat of fear.

And yet, what had happened had happened. Trench-coat hadn't seen her.

And he'd looked right at her.

Carrie slowly clenched her hand into a fist and held it tight until her knuckles turned white.

I'm coming, Mr. Johns. Don't worry. I'm coming to save you.

• • •

The police would be coming too, that much she knew. Carrie peered around the end of the row to Pooh Corner, down the library's main aisle toward the empty reception area. She heard the rattle and bang of the aluminum blinds as the main door opened to the cafeteria. Then she heard Trenchcoat bark a quick, "Go!"

They were leaving the library. She took a step forward and felt something give underfoot. Carrie looked down and saw the cheap, plastic mask she'd almost stepped on earlier. She stared at it, thinking, *Invisible Girl* doesn't wear a mask. Then her rational mind chimed in, *But I'm not Invisible Girl!*

She was no hero. This was no comic book.

But what had happened had happened. Trenchcoat hadn't seen her. And if she put the mask on, would she be embracing this new reality, what-ever it was, too fiercely? If she actually allowed her-self to believe, would she try to grab the magic so tightly that it slipped through her fingers?

She bent down and picked up the mask. The police were coming. And if things escalated, if

Trenchcoat got crazier, Mr. Johns might get hurt. Killed, even. That much she knew.

Batman wears a mask. Spider-Man does. One way or another, most heroes wear a mask, she realized in a moment where a truth you've known all along becomes a sudden, profound revelation. *Either as their hero selves or as their secret identities, like Clark Kent and Kara Danvers and Diana Prince wear glasses.*

Glasses were kind of like a mask, right? The way heroes hid their secret identities to protect themselves and the ones they cared about from evildoers. Like Mr. Johns had tried to protect her when he'd told Trenchcoat he was alone in the library.

Maybe instead of chasing her new reality away, wearing the mask would actually cement it into place. At least long enough to save Mr. Johns like he'd tried to save her. Stretching the rubber band around her raven hair, Carrie put the mask on.

Walking quietly, wishing her steps could be invisible too, she approached the door with its aluminum blinds. There were screams in the cafeteria as lunch staff scrambled to find cover.

Boom!

More screams drowned out by the buckshot from the shells hitting a wall across the lunch room. The blast had come from her left. Carrie caught a glimpse of the gunman's long coat as he turned the corner and disappeared deeper into the school.·

Please don't see me, please don't see me, please

don't see me! she chanted again as she slipped out of the library. Had that been what had invoked her invisibility before? Carrie had no idea, but she figured saying a little superhero prayer couldn't hurt.

More screams from the corridor to the left. She hurried her steps to follow.

"Everybody on the floor!" Trenchcoat piped in a breaking voice. "Right now!"

Her heart pounding in her chest, Carrie chanced one eye around the corner and saw the door to the chemistry lab standing open.

Boom!

The shot and the screams that followed confirmed it. Trenchcoat and Mr. Johns and a classroom full of other hostages were in the chemistry lab.

"Do as he says. Just do as he says."

Mr. Johns's voice.

He's okay! I still have time to save him.

She heard stools scrape the floor as the students complied. Another voice—Coach Kirby?—said something macho.

"Just do it, Lee, for the love of God!" Mr. Johns pleaded.

"Oh, Coach Kirby, you just do whatever you want," Trenchcoat said in an ominous, even hopeful, tone.

Somewhere outside the school, echoing and distant, Carrie heard the first sirens. The police were on their way. As far as she knew, no one had been killed—yet. But when the police got here, if it was anything like she'd seen on TV, if the shooter feared for his life....

Mr. Johns.

Carrie invoked the name of every superhero she'd ever read about. Wonder Woman, Jessica Jones, Captain Marvel, Power Girl, Supergirl, Super-man, Spider-Man, every Avenger—old roster and new—every member of the Justice League, especial-ly the Caped Crusader. She saved the Fantastic Four and Sue Storm Richards for last, picturing the blonde-haired heroine transforming into the trans-parent outline of Invisible Girl on the page of a comic book. In her mind, Carrie imagined them all standing around her as she chanted again, *Please don't see me, please don't see me, please don't see me!*

She crept toward the chemistry lab. Her face was sweating under the plastic mask, her hands shaking again. She touched the cold frame of the doorway and, shivering, peeked around the corner.

Trenchcoat, somehow seeming even shorter than before, stood in the middle of the room, lording it over the hostages. Mr. Johns was sitting on the floor directly in front of him, with Coach Kirby and the other students scattered around the room as if holding class sitting down.

She saw Stephanie Seward staring at the door-way, a look on her face like she was calculating whether or not she should make a run for it. Carrie gaped back at her, mouthing, *Please don't say any-thing.* But, like the gunman in the library, Stephanie seemed not to see her. Her eyes just kept roving hungrily over the doorframe and her escape beyond.

Oh my God. It's working. She can't see me.

The sirens were louder now. Trenchcoat must have heard them too. He was getting fidgety, like he didn't have a plan beyond this moment. *I have to act fast*, Carrie thought. Before his desperation turned into a feeling of *nothing-left-to-lose.*

His back was to her, the gun held loosely at his side. She could creep up behind him and knock him out before he could hurt anyone. Quiet and stealthy, like in *Assassin's Creed.* All she needed to do was....

Wait, knock him out with what?

Carrie stared down at her empty hands. She had no weapon. And if she tried clobbering him with just her fists, she risked the gun going off and Mr. Johns getting hurt if she didn't knock Trenchcoat cold on the first try. Standing in the doorway, she looked around for possible weapons. Bunsen burners lined the long shelf to her left at the back of the classroom. Books and backpacks sat on desks above the students cowering on the floor, arms wrapped around one another. Flash and the rest of the Fearsome Foursome were huddled in a group together near the center of the room. Stephanie was whispering to her boyfriend.

"Hey! Shut up over there!" yelled Trenchcoat.

But Stephanie kept whispering, insistent. Flash, his football helmet on the desk above him, just shook his head.

IT'S A BIRD! IT'S A PLANE!

The sirens, numerous and nearer now, were a symphony of wailing banshees, rising and falling all around them.

"I said, shut up!"

"Please, leave them alone," Johns begged. "Don't hurt them. It's not too late to—"

"Shut up!" yelled the gunman, voice climbing in register. Like the shriek of a teenage girl screaming at her mother. Flash and Stephanie shrunk in on each other as Trenchcoat advanced. When the shotgun came up, Richard and Cassidy crab-crawled away from their clique mates.

Carrie moved into the lab. She hated Flash and his girlfriend, but she didn't want them to die. Maybe if she could distract Trenchcoat, make him look somewhere else, she could make *them invisible too*. It was an impossible thought—not really a thought at all, more like an impulse—but today had already proven itself a day for making the impossible possible. Carrie reached out and tipped a burner over at the back of the lab. It clattered to the desktop, then rolled onto the floor.

Trenchcoat turned, the shotgun trained on the space where the sound had come from. But no blast followed. Absolutely sure now that he couldn't see her, Carrie danced around the gunman as he moved to investigate the noise. She dashed forward and knelt in front of the king and queen-bee of Rosecranz High, wrapping her arms around them.

Stephanie startled at the touch, then the light

30

of recognition dawned in her eyes. Flash's mouth opened.

"Be quiet," Carrie whispered. "Don't say a word."

"Where'd you come from?" Stephanie asked. "Why're you wearing that mask?"

"That's *lots* of words! Shhhhhh!" Carrie saw Flash look behind her and knew the shooter had turned back around.

"Where are they? Where'd they go?" Trench-coat strode back to the middle of the room, his eyes darting this way and that as he looked under desks. "You'd better come out right now!"

Carrie didn't know what to do. The gunman was yelling, threatening, gesturing wildly with the shotgun, and it was only a matter of time before his anger got someone shot. Someone like Mr. Johns.

Thunk!

They heard the metallic sound of a door slamming open against the wall down the hallway.

The police were here.

Oh no, too soon.

"Scary Carrie, what are you—?" Stephanie began.

"Shut up, thou hasty-witted harpy!"

On instinct, Carrie had drawn that arrow from her quiver of Shakespearean insults. Stephanie, eyes wide, shut up.

Boots squeaked on the polished floor outside the classroom, coming closer.

31

"They shouldn't have done that," Trenchcoat said. "And now it's too late."

Carrie looked over her shoulder to see the gunman turning his shotgun on the person closest to him in that moment.

Mr. Johns!

The librarian threw his arms around his head in a hopeless attempt to protect himself.

She had milliseconds. She had to act.

Carrie sprang from the floor and grabbed up the football helmet from the desk. Superman, Power Girl, Hulk, Jessica Jones, Thor, Supergirl, and the Thing—all the strongest, mightiest heroes she could conjure filled her head as with one, mighty blow she bashed Trenchcoat across the back of the skull.

"Unghh!"

Boom!

There was a shattering of Bunsen burners from the lab's back wall as the buckshot hit. The shotgun clattered to the floor, and like a heavy sack of bones and blood, Trenchcoat collapsed beside it.

The blast from the shotgun died on the walls. Officers rushed in from the corridor, guns at the ready. Carrie stood over the shooter, Flash's helmet still in her hand.

"Carrie?" Mr. Johns looked up from beneath his elbows, and said her name as if, by speaking out loud, he could prove to himself he was still alive. "Carrie Conrad?"

Trying to catch her breath, Carrie smiled with

relief.

I did it! I saved him.

The police moved quickly, kicking the shotgun out of arm's reach and pulling Trenchcoat's hands behind his back. Carrie stepped out of their way as they worked to haul the comatose gunman up. One of the officers yanked off the ski mask.

Gasps erupted around the lab. The shooter's long, blonde hair fell around her shoulders.

"It's a girl!" a student said.

"I think I know her," said another.

"I know her ... Melinda Payne," Kirby said. His face had gone white. He sat down on the stool behind his desk and took a long, slow breath. "She was just in here yesterday, begging me for a better grade."

"I can't believe it's a girl," a boy said.

Somehow, some way, it didn't surprise Carrie at all that Trenchcoat was a girl. In fact, it seemed exactly as it should be. *A girl villain for a girl hero*, she thought simply as she watched the officers drag her away. Thinking that made her glow, inside and out.

The look on Mr. Johns's face as he rose from the floor gave her pause. Then Carrie realized why he was staring so oddly at her and took off the mask. His lips stretched into a mirror image of her smile, proud and radiant above the familiar flare of his bowtie.

"I know it's not exactly school policy," he began as he opened his arms, then grunted from the impact of Carrie plastering herself against him in a bear hug. "Thank you, Carrie," he managed quietly. "Thank you for saving my life."

• • •

It was Monday before Rosecranz High re-opened. Many a parent had to hear many a teenager complain that they'd only had to miss one day of school. The attack had happened on a Thursday.

The police had interviewed the witnesses, of course, including Carrie. Trenchcoat, a.k.a. Melinda Payne, was a senior and had taken rather personally the fact that her grade point average had proven insufficient for the college of her choice to accept her. Earning a failing grade from Coach Kirby had been the final nail in her academic coffin. You might think her reaction to that bit of news a tad extreme, but then, you don't know Melinda's parents or her own deeply ingrained fear of academic failure.

"A typical teen," someone joked in the teacher's lounge, "albeit with a shotgun."

No one thought that was very funny.

At lunch on Monday, Carrie moved tables twice before realizing her fellow students refused to let her sit alone. They yammered at her with excited enthusiasm. Some even hugged her, which made her uncomfortable, especially when the boys did it. Still, she accepted their gratitude for stopping Melinda with a kind of quiet grace and hardly insulted any of them in her mind with the help of the Bard.

One boy asked sheepishly if she had a date to

Sadie Hawkins yet, and she stammered out a no, prompting him to get down on one knee and offer himself for the honor. Carrie turned a bright red as the lunch room held its breath but finally stammered out a yes, drawing thunderous applause from her assembled peers. She'd never been so glad when the fifth period bell rang, not even on the worst day of teasing by the Fearsome Foursome.

When she walked into the library, she found Mr. Johns standing at the counter, quietly stamping returned books as always.

"How's the hero—pardon me, *heroine*—of Rosecranz High?" he asked, beaming broadly.

"Popular," Carrie said, though her tone had a bit of *the-dog-that's-caught-the-car* in it. "It's..."

Mr. Johns set his stamp down and waited patiently.

"... *uncomfortable*," she said finally.

"Feeling a bit at sea?"

Carrie nodded, finding her favorite table. "I just want to sit here for an hour and be normal again." She set her backpack down and began unloading it. There was the Riverside Shakespeare, of course (those insults had come in handy), the brand-new issue of *Brides* magazine, and the comics she'd never gotten around to reading last week—*Wonder Woman, Power Girl, Jessica Jones, Supergirl*, and one of the comic collections Mr. Johns had ordered for her, the *Ultimate Fantastic Four* featuring Sue Storm Richards on the cover.

"That's quite a haul," Johns observed as he walked over.

Carrie took in the array of adventures on the tabletop. "It is. Oh, hey," she said, looking up, "I never thanked you for ordering all the collections. They'll keep me busy till I graduate!"

"Only a year?" he teased, then winked. "So, what are we reading today? *Wonder Woman? Romeo and Juliet?*"

"Not *Romeo and Juliet!*" she said quickly. Sadie Hawkins was looking scary enough. The only thing worse would be not having a date, she'd decided right after she'd gotten one.

"I was wondering, have you ever thought of writing something, Carrie?" Johns asked. "A comic book of your own, maybe? You know, the best writers are voracious readers. It's how they learn their craft. All it takes to be a good writer is that and practice and a great imagination."

Imagination, Carrie thought. *It's the most powerful superpower anyone could ever have.* That much she knew. Imagination, she was convinced now, was what had helped her become invisible and save Mr. Johns. And had it helped her conjure the strength to knock out Melinda with one blow, too? Carrie wondered in that moment what else her imagination could help her do.

"Seriously," Johns said, "you should think about writing a superhero comic. You've already got the hero part down!" His eyes sparkled with the idea.

"Maybe so," Carrie said, her mind's eye seeing visions of her future life and its infinite possibilities. "Maybe I'll write a book someday. Maybe I'll even write a comic book about superheroes." Her gaze found the *Ultimate Fantastic Four* again, and she smiled at Invisible Girl on the cover.

Or maybe I'll become one.

A Word from Chris Pourteau

I hope you enjoyed reading "Geek Gurl Rising" as much as I enjoyed writing it. I've been a comic book geek for as long as I could read (1977 and 1978 seem to have been my big years, if my boxful of comics is any indication). I seeded some Easter eggs for readers in my story as a nod to what those comics meant to me growing up. (For example, Carrie Conrad's name is a nod to Stan Lee's alliterative naming convention—Reed Richards, Peter Parker, Bruce Banner.)

As with Carrie, comics opened my imagination to the possibilities of what *can be* while firmly grounding me (via their multi-paneled morality plays) in what heroes *should be*. Without those comic books growing up—my favorites were *Batman* and *Spider-Man*—I doubt I'd be a writer today; or, even, a lover of reading.

If you'd like to let me know what you think of "Geek Gurl Rising" or if you just want to say howdy, feel free to email me at c.pourteau.author@gmail.com. If you'd like to find out more about me or read more of my stuff, sign up for my monthly newsletter. I promise not to spam, and I'll send you free stuff.

To give you a sense of my eclectic writing habits, my first novel, *Shadows Burned In* (a family saga, near-future, psychological thriller), won the 2015 eLite Book Award Gold Medal for Literary Fiction. In 2015, I edited and produced the collection

A SUPERHERO ANTHOLOGY

Tails of the Apocalypse, which contains short stories set in different apocalyptic scenarios and feature animals as main characters. My own contribution, "Unconditional"—which was well-received when it was published on its own earlier that year and more or less generated the idea for *Tails* as a result—is part of the collection. You can check out my catalog of fiction on Amazon.

ANNA

PATRICIA GILLIAM

THREE MINUTES and forty-nine seconds—not enough time to evacuate the entire hospital or move the device. Maybe enough time to disarm it. Removing the front cover panel isn't difficult, but my hands are shaking. I can't concentrate like this. It's all the noise. Kids crying. Patients asking questions their doctors can't answer. Floor upon floor of phone conversations, medical monitors, movie gun battles, breathing machines, news feeds—

I have to focus. I recognize the bomb's configuration, but its components are more advanced than anything I've ever encountered. I can't risk everyone's lives on the small chance I'll figure it out in time.

I leave an electrical room, passing two fire alarms in over-crowded waiting areas to find a third in a vacant hallway. Pulling it leaves a tacky layer of tamper dye on my fingertips, but I hide my hand in my jacket pocket and return without being stopped. People seem more irritated than concerned by the lights and blaring noise, but at least some of them begin to exit. I hope they make it—need to convince myself that I made the right call.

One minute and twenty-seven seconds left when I make it back. Timers haven't changed too much, and I gain manual access on my first attempt —resetting it to its maximum of 99 hours and 59 minutes. It maintains this for two seconds before returning to its original countdown. I search for a wireless transmitter nearby, but it could be any-where. I need to disconnect the device's receiver, but the closest access panel is sealed shut and adhered to the wall. Safely going through the front would take me several minutes—time I've already spent.

Thirty seconds. I should run—maybe drag one final group out with me—but I'm too frustrated. I start pushing aside entire sections I shouldn't— areas that could detonate the bomb through pres-sure sensors—until I can see the receiver. I pry it free, and it clatters to the bottom of the casing. An-other reset of the timer. One second. Two seconds. The countdown holds this time.

Ninety-nine hours and fifty-nine minutes— more than enough time for everyone to leave and the actual experts to arrive. I exhale and rest against the opposite wall, laughing in relief despite the blue dye coating both my hands and the timer's controls. I could be discovered at any moment—probably blamed for everything—but I could live with that. Someone needs to know the truth about what happened to me.

I see the timer change again, but I'm not sure of the cause this time. Ten. Nine. No. No. No. No. Not now. I stand and scramble to get it back into manual mode. The reset seems to work again, but I don't want to trust it.

All right, new plan—I'll just continue resetting the timer and buy everyone a little less than two seconds at a time. Hopefully whoever finds me will believe me.

Seconds later, I hear hinges squeak and realize I forgot to lock the door on my way back. A white-haired man in lab coat smiles at me in recognition, but I don't know him. His glasses make his eyes look unnaturally large, almost comical, and they widen more at the sight of the bomb.

"Just keep guarding it! I'll get Fynn." He disappears before I can ask him anything.

Three more resets. The sequence is almost muscle memory now, and I've increased the frequency to once a second as a precaution.

A man in a dark suit appears in the doorway, but the old man isn't with him.

"Are you Fynn?" I ask, but he pulls out a gun and aims it at me without saying a word. "Listen to me! I'm preventing this thing from going off. You'll kill everyone—including yourself!"

His gaze remains on me, but he changes his aim to the device before I have time to react.

Everything goes bright and silent.

• • •

"Hey, try not to move." A younger man's voice says, and I hear the click of a radio. "This is Roebuck. We have a survivor near the parking garage—female, early-to-mid twenties."

My left eye refuses to open, and I have to blink several times for my right to focus. Roebuck crouches beside me and squeezes my hand. I squeeze it back.

"I'm about two minutes from you," a woman responds from the radio. "Med team is about five minutes out."

"Copy." He's trying to hide the panic in his voice but not doing a good job of it. "Lot of overhanging debris over here...may need to move her before they can treat her."

"What happened?" I ask. Pain shoots through my abdomen and chest when I ignore his advice and try to sit up. I slump back, small rocks jabbing me through my jacket. "Where are we?"

"Someone bombed the hospital about four hours ago. My name is Corbin Roebuck. I'm with the IBI. What's your name?"

I want to answer, but nothing comes. "I'm sorry. I can't remember right now."

"It's all right. We'll get it figured out." He forces a smile when a dark-haired woman arrives and crouches beside him. "This is my partner, Bethany Fynn. Beth, she's conscious but doesn't remember her name."

46

I've heard Fynn's name before, but we've never met. The pain has put my mind into a fog, and part of me just wants to close my eyes and never move again.

"Do you mind if I look at your eyes?" Fynn asks me, already clicking on a small light.

I resist the urge to shake my head. My neck hurts, too. "Sure, go ahead."

She shines the light toward my face and then frowns. "Can you see anything out of your left? There's swelling around it, and I don't want to make things worse."

"It won't open," I explain, and she moves on to my right eye. I can see the beam, but something makes Roebuck release my hand and back away. He seems confused, almost frightened.

"Guess that explains how she survived..." Agent Fynn doesn't seem fazed and starts speaking another language to me. I don't understand it.

"Sorry, I just know English," I reply, still concerned by Agent Roebuck's reaction. "What's wrong with me?"

By that point, a full medical team has arrived. Fynn asks for them to scan me.

"She needs emergency surgery." The medic sounds nervous. "I've never seen this much shrapnel in a living body. If she'd been human, she wouldn't have survived."

If I had been human? None of this makes any sense, and it doesn't help that Agent Roebuck keeps staring as if I'm some sort of monster.

A sharp ringing strikes my ears, and I scream out in pain. The medic with the scanner puts something to my neck, and I feel a sting followed by a coldness coursing through my veins.

I black out.

• • •

The smell of coffee brewing wakes me. Without thinking, I open my eyes and sit up. I can see out of both eyes again, and all the earlier pain has vanished. Part of me had expected to wake up in some government lab—if even I woke up at all—but this looks more like someone's living room. The couch is leather, and I'm covered by a hideous neon pink bedspread.

Someone changed my clothes to a matching navy sweatshirt and pants, and I don't see any of my original clothes nearby. I check my stomach, and there are no signs of surgical incisions or scarring. I push up my sleeves, and there isn't even a scratch on my arms or hands. A rapid pulse of blue light trails underneath my skin from my forearm to my wrist, startling me.

"What the hell?" I mumble to myself, but Agent Fynn hears me and walks in from the next room. "Sorry—hi."

"Hi." She smiles but is keeping her distance now. "Do you remember who I am?"

"Agent Beth Fynn with the IBI," I answer, and her posture relaxes. "Is Agent Roebuck here, too?

Tell him I didn't mean to scare him. To be honest, I'm kind of scared, too."

"He's just cautious around Hannarians—long story." She disappears for a few seconds but returns with two mugs of coffee, offering me one. I don't feel like drinking anything, but the warmth feels nice. "Has anything come back to you now that you've healed up—your name or what happened?"

I move the bedspread to one side of the couch and sit down. Even without coffee, there's a nervous energy coursing through me. It's difficult to sit still. "I know this will sound crazy, but I don't even remember being an alien. How long was I unconscious?"

It feels as if it could be weeks later, but Fynn is still wearing the same pant suit and shirt from the site and has dark circles underneath her eyes. She glances at her phone. "We found you about eleven hours ago. Our med team sedated you because you were in pain, and we drove you to one of our facilities for emergency surgery. It took maybe ten minutes for your body to stabilize after all the shrapnel was removed, and Roebuck and I moved you here as a precaution."

"Where are we?" The living area has large displays with realistic landscape animations instead of windows. "I just noticed your decorator has a sense of humor—different season per wall."

"This is safe house—safe bunker to be more accurate." She takes a sip of her coffee and points to the ceiling with her other hand. "There's a dairy farm about five stories above us—blends in with the surrounding landscape on satellite feeds, and the owners are retired agents. Even with your memory issue, we want to protect you as a potential witness—not hold you here against your will. As soon as we reach the Ambassador, we'll make transfer arrangements and hopefully locate your family. We've done everything we know to do for you from a medical standpoint."

I nod. "Thanks for saving my life. I'd like to help you, but I don't know what to do or where to start. I remember Agent Roebuck finding me and then you showing up. I think before that I was actually near the bomb—tried to disarm it, but nothing seemed to work. How many people?"

"Relief teams are still searching for survivors." She pauses, closing her eyes as if she's having trouble keeping her composure. "Nearly three thousand confirmed dead and rising. If you hadn't pulled the fire alarm, it would have been at least double that."

A short flash comes back to me, and I check for dye on my hand. There's nothing there. "How did you —"

"It was all over your clothes," she explains. "We found no identification on you—not even a human alias—and your biometrics aren't registered with the Ambassador's diplomatic office or our databases. How did you know about the bomb? Did you contact anyone else about it, or did someone contact you?" There's no accusation in her tone, but it bothers me that I have no solid answers.

"I remember seeing an old man with white hair out to here." I gesture out from my head, not feeling any less crazy for describing Einstein. "He seemed to know me—or at least thought he did—but I think he mistook me for someone else. He told me he was going to find help—find you."

Fynn seems confused but then brings up a photo of the man in her phone. "Is this him?"

"Yeah."

"His name was Dr. Lance Jacobs." She sighs and returns the phone to her jacket pocket. "He meant to find my uncle—not me. Just before the bomb detonated, they delivered a cure for the bioweapon victims in the quarantine ward. As far as motive for the attack, we believe several EIP terrorist cells wanted those victims dead rather than cured. The cure was never dispensed, but so far none of the bioweapon victims have been found alive. My uncle and Jacobs were located about five hours ago. Neither of them made it."

"I'm sorry." Another flash hits—the man with the gun. "I don't know if he was EIP or not, but another man shot the bomb just before it detonated. I thought he was aiming for me at first."

"Can you remember what he looked like?"

"Do you have a tablet with a drawing program? I think I could sketch him for you."

She returns with a small tablet, and I draw the man from memory—late thirties, shaved head, military build, and a nose that must have been broken and reset incorrectly. Other details surface that I didn't originally notice—that I shouldn't have noticed—but I add scars on his chin and above his eyebrows. I hand the tablet to Fynn, and she takes a photo of it instead of doing a file transfer.

"That gives us a start." She waves for me to follow her to an elevator. "There's no Internet or DMR access down here for safety reasons. If anything happens where you need to leave, there's this elevator and a stairwell near the kitchen. You're actually free to leave at any point, but please tell one of us if you do. We just don't want anything bad to happen to you."

"I wouldn't even know where else to go." My thinking feels clearer, but trying to force memories forward isn't working. "Unless I remember something, I'll be here when you get back. Otherwise, I'll come up and find you."

• • •

I wait a few minutes after Agent Fynn leaves before I wander around. The stairwell door is between two oak pantry cabinets, and I open it long enough to determine I'm on the deepest level of the bunker. If anyone else is on the other four floors, I can't hear them.

There's a large wall display between the living and kitchen areas, but it appears to be more for movie and music storage than communication. The cameras and microphone for video calls have been removed, which makes sense to me from a tracking standpoint.

I browse through the movie and music titles, hoping something will prompt my memory. I can remember entire scenes from some of the children's titles, and there's a sci-fi movie that catches my attention. I turn it on and lower the volume. The special effects are shoddy by current standards, but I remember it terrifying me as a child.

"Aliens are real, you know," a young boy says as he sits down beside me on a couch. He's brought us cereal but taken all my marshmallows for his trouble. He grins at my disappointment and then places a handful into my bowl, giving me more than him. "They're not like the ones in the movies, though. Hannarians are more like us—just scarier in a different way, I guess."

"Fan of the classics, I see."

I whip around and shove Agent Roebuck against a wall. My fingers clasp tight around his throat, and the pulse in his neck starts to race. I can't let go or back away. My own body won't let me, and I'm terrified I'm about to kill him.

Roebuck raises his hands in surrender, and his voice is strained. "Sorry—my fault! I thought you heard the elevator. Can you get control back?"

I take a deep breath and release him, backing away to the farthest corner of the room. It feels like forever before I'm able to speak again. "Are you okay? I'm so sorry. I couldn't help it."

"I think I'll live." He flinches as he rubs his neck but forces a smile. "Seriously, I've been through much worse with other humans. Are you all right?"

"No, I'm not..." I shake my head, and his smile fades as I start pacing. "None of this feels right. I don't know what happened to me, but I think I used to be human."

• • •

"Normally when a Hannarian goes missing, they contact us—not the other way around." Despite insisting that he's fine, Agent Roebuck puts a damp hand towel around his neck and talks to me from the kitchen. "Jernard answered my messages but said he didn't recognize you—told me he'd contact us back once Earth wasn't under impending attack by giant lizards. I couldn't tell whether he was joking or not."

"Jernard?" I ask. I don't know the name, but Roebuck seems to think I should. "Is he your Hannarian contact?"

"I stabbed him in the foot when I was seven, but I'd like to think we're on decent terms now." He enters the living room but stands in the doorway closest to the elevator. "He thought you might be one of the bioweapon victims who had turned sooner than the others, but that doesn't line up with what you told Beth. No one in quarantine was showing symptoms according to the last uploaded reports, and you obviously have a degree of control over your abilities. From what I understand, that doesn't just happen overnight."

54

"Did you sneak up on me on purpose—to test me?" I ask. He doesn't answer, and I feel a surge of anger. "Thousands of innocent people are dead, and you're wasting time on—"

"Helping you remember may be the best use of our time." His voice is calm, and he steps aside when I walk toward the elevator. "This is the fifth time we've seen this type of device in two years, but we keep hitting dead ends when it comes to tracing the components. Someone is making them specifically for these attacks—nothing else. The fact that you almost managed to disarm one—"

Almost managed...my stomach twists, and I feel sick. "Look, I can walk you through everything I tried, but it will only delay one—not stop it. Your techs need to design something to interrupt an external signal being sent to the timer. I might be able to help them with that—maybe recreate something they could test without anyone getting hurt."

"You could build one of those devices from memory?" He's staring at me again, and I realize I may have said too much. "I'm not an expert on amnesia, but how could you recall that and not know who you are? Beth and I will understand if you're trying to protect yourself or someone else, but we need to know the truth."

"I know I'm not a victim, Agent Roebuck—bioweapon or otherwise." Part of me feels as if I need to ask for a lawyer, but the IBI tends to stay five steps ahead on these things. I haven't been charged for a crime, but bringing me somewhere isolated works more to their benefit than mine. I just need them to understand that we want the same thing. "I came to the hospital to stop the bomb, but I can't remember how I knew about it. That's the truth. We need to be focused on preventing anything like it from happening again."

"You believe there will be more attacks soon?" Based on his tone, he thinks I'm aware of something specific.

"You don't?" I ask, and he sighs. "Look, I don't want anyone else to get harmed or killed—same as you. I just—"

We both look at the elevator door when it dings. Fynn is still holding her phone, and she shows something to Roebuck before she speaks to me.

"Can you remember if disarming bombs is something you do often?"

"You mean, like a hobby?" I'm confused, but she frowns at my response. "I knew the overall basics of what I was looking at, but this device was different—new to me. If I'd had more time, maybe I could have done more to try to stop it. Why?"

She hands me her phone where she screenshot a message. "This is an inventory of what the surgeons removed from you and what our experts were able to indentify—so far."

I scroll through the list and finally realize why she's upset. "Only a portion of the fragments were from the device today. The other pieces are older tech—probably multiple devices from the looks of it."

"Who are you?" she asks, and I shake my head. "We're running tests of the other components against all our open cases. If they match any previous attacks, we'll know soon. Do you understand?"

I take a deep breath, trying to keep my tone even. "I am not lying to you." I push up my sleeves again and show them my wrists. The blue light pulses have now become constant lines—resembling another set of blood vessels. "Take me to one of your labs. Run all the tests you want. Do whatever you have to do so you can focus on the people actually behind this!"

Another flash hits.

"You don't have to do this!" I'm shouting at the boy from before, but we're both older now—late teens. I chase him down an alleyway and grab his jacket's hood. "What if you're caught? What if you get yourself killed? I can't lose you, too."

"You think Mom and Dad died for some great ideology—freedom from the big bad aliens from up above?" he asks in a bitter tone, and he pries my hand free. "They did what they had to do to keep us alive—to keep us from starving. If I bail on this tonight, the EIP will kill me and try to use you next. I don't want that for you, Anna. Your mind could be used toward so much greater things. Just let me do this. Let me keep us safe long enough to find a better way. Please."

He's cradling something in his other arm—

57

something that shouldn't have existed in reality. Something I created.

"I thought it was a model—some sort of physics game," I try to explain, and I realize what's happened. "Dad's program shared my modifications, didn't it? The EIP thought you did it instead of me."

He turns away and continues walking. "The target is an abandoned warehouse that needs to come down anyway. The owners are aware of it—need the insurance money for some new project they can't afford. No one will get hurt."

"But it's a test of the design—and when it works the EIP will distribute it to their entire network. We can't let that happen!"

He stops and faces me again, angry tears in his eyes. "Go home, Anna! Now!"

I become aware of the IBI bunker again. Fynn and Roebuck are still blocking my path to the elevator, but there's a clear shot to the stairwell...where a few dozen armed IBI agents could be waiting on the surface. I have to fight an urge to run, knowing it won't do me any good long-term. I need answers from Fynn and Roebuck just as much as they need them from me.

"What year is this?" I ask. Roebuck gives me a skeptical look. "I'm serious. I thought I knew, but now I'm not so sure."

"It's 2300—will be 2301 in a little over a month," Fynn answers. "Why?"

"I think I know why I didn't flag your

databases." I slowly make my way to the couch to sit down, keeping my hands visible. "Your profiles are normally filtered by age, right—to save on search time? Some of the parts your surgeons found in me were over thirty years old. Run everything again with no age range set. I think you'll find me."

"Do you already remember something?"

I nod and wipe my eyes. It's more of a gut feeling than a memory, but I know my older brother is dead. "Nothing good."

• • •

Fynn leaves again, and Roebuck stays with me. We're both quiet for a while, and he goes into the kitchen and returns with a tray of turkey sandwiches. He leaves them on the coffee table, and my stomach rumbles until I take one. The taste is off from what I expect—too salty—but it's the least of my problems.

"My parents were both in the EIP." Roebuck sits down across from me and hesitates, almost as if he's afraid someone else will hear him. "Beth's uncle led an IBI team to raid their house when I was a kid —had no idea I existed. All I knew was that I had been alone for days, and there were strangers with guns in my house. So I did what I was taught—hid with the biggest knife I could find and defended myself when some guy got too close."

"What happened?" I can see scars on his face now, but they're faint relative to the man who shot the bomb.

"Well, it turned out Jernard had picked that day to do a ride-along. I was lucky—considering what could have happened—but he reacted and lost the ability for anyone to understand what he was yelling. I ran from him—tripped over an electrical cord and fell down our basement stairs. I woke up in a hospital—Beth's uncle waiting by the bed to tell me my parents had died in a failed attempt to kill Jernard's wife and son. Jernard still covered my hospital bills, and Beth's aunt arranged for my adoption by the Roebucks. That's basically how I got to here."

"Why are you telling me all of this?"

He breaks eye contact with me and looks down. "I know what it's like to believe your family connections will ruin any chance you have at a good life. It's still not easy for me, but the people who surround you can make a big difference. Regardless of what we find out about your past, the IBI has programs if you want out. You just have to make the choice."

"I'm not faking the amnesia, Roebuck. I try to think about certain things, and it feels like running up against a wall."

"I'm not saying you're lying." He makes eye contact again. "There are things I wish I could forget if I could. Maybe Hannarian minds can protect themselves as a survival instinct—no different than your body reacting to any other kind of threat."

"Is there any way to know if taking the cure will help me remember again?" I ask, but he shrugs.

"I don't believe I wanted to be like this, but in a strange way it makes me feel safer. I just don't want to hurt anyone else."

The elevator dings, and Fynn is back sooner than I expect. "We all have to go—now."

"What's wrong?" Roebuck puts his hand on his holster but doesn't draw his gun. "Are we compromised?"

Fynn shakes her head. "Rossetti's team in Atlanta just found another device."

• • •

"How much time do they have?" I ask. The three of us take the stairwell, but I've almost gotten too far ahead of both agents. I slow down. "I don't know if this is something I could talk somebody through over a video call. If they can get everyone out first—"

"It's at a power station." Fynn catches up to me, and I let her and Roebuck pass and then keep pace behind them. A worker found it during a routine inspection, but the timer isn't active. We don't know how long it's been there. Everyone except building security has been evacuated, but the biggest risk is to the grid—and whether this is the only device or one of several."

"Were any of the bioweapon victims flown to Atlanta?" I ask.

"I'm not aware of any. Why?"

"Motive," I reply. "The EIP leadership wouldn't do something like this without hurting themselves in the process. I think this might be someone else."

"A rogue cell, maybe?" Roebuck asks, talking more to Fynn than me. "Kressler didn't exactly make a lot of friends with the 'if you can't beat them, join them' approach. Some of the more radical chatter makes it sound as if he was working with the Hannarians—that his bioweapon would later lead to the spread of a contagious virus across the entire planet."

The name Kressler is familiar, too, but I still have to put things together through context. "If that's the case, you both could be at risk around me." If they're concerned, they don't show it. We reach the top of the stairwell, and a whiff of cow manure and dried hay almost overpowers me. "Sorry, I need to stop for a second. My eyes are watering…"

"Both of you stay here. I'll get the car," Roebuck says. Once I can see again, I notice both the stairwell and elevator shaft are covered by an emptied barn. "Be right back."

Fynn waits until after he leaves before she hands me her phone, showing me a photo of a gray-haired woman with deep burn scars on the left side of her face. "Your name is Anna Kressler. Your brother nearly killed you over forty years ago."

The memory isn't as strong as the flashes, but I remember leaving as my brother asked—then doubling-back to the warehouse once he believed I had gone home. I remember the pain and heat of the blast and cringe. "It was an accident…"

"He just accidently blew up a warehouse with you inside of it?" Fynn's tone turns angry when I hand her back the phone. "You were paralyzed from the neck-down, blinded in one eye, burned on almost the entire left side of your body—"

"By a bomb I designed—not Ron," I interrupt, and her eyes widen. "I was fifteen years old. Ron was barely seventeen. If I had never touched any of our father's programs, maybe the EIP would have left us alone. Maybe we both would have turned out to be better people. I don't know."

Roebuck pulls a small black SUV into the barn. Once he realizes Fynn and I aren't getting inside, he shuts off the headlights and opens his door. "Hey, I just got a message from Rossetti. The timer on the device activated without anyone touching it. They have about three hours."

I look at Fynn for a reaction. She hasn't told Roebuck who I am yet, but I'm not sure why.

"Do you have somewhere nearby where we can set up a live 3-D feed?" I ask. Fynn doesn't immediately answer. "I just want to show them everything I tried—try some other ideas if you'll let me. It will save them some time."

"There's the Des Moines office," Roebuck suggests, but he's starting to sound concerned. "Beth?"

"Let's just go." She opens the back passenger door, and I get inside—testing my door handle to see if I could get out if needed. It doesn't work.

"We sometimes have suspects in the back,"

Roebuck explains, and he pushes a lock control as Fynn gets inside. "Try it again." My door opens this time, and I know it's my last chance to run before things get any worse. The thought of watching someone else die using my instructions feels worse than if I could be there in person. "It's not exactly against IBI protocol, but we don't recommend riding with the door open."

I hesitate. "Could a Hannarian ship get me to Atlanta in time if you contacted them?"

"Maybe," Roebuck replies. "The problem is reaching them right now, but I think they would help us if we asked. I could try."

"We don't know if Rossetti's team actually has three hours." Fynn's tone is harder, and she seems worried that I'm trying to gain access to a Hannarian ship for some other purpose. "Des Moines isn't far, but we're wasting time."

"All right." I shut my door and try to think. "What about borrowing one of your phones? Can I at least speak with the agent in charge there?"

"Yeah." Fynn brings up a number on her phone but sends the call to the car's speaker. The contact is only under the agent's first name—Jenna.

"Rossetti," the agent answers and then switches to a live video feed we can see on the car's console display. She doesn't appear to be much older than Roebuck. "I was worried I couldn't reach all of you. Let me see if I can zoom in on this thing."

It takes her a moment to steady her phone, but

the device and casing are similar to the one at the hospital—enough to be from the same person or group.

"Who removed the front cover panel?" I ask. "We were told no one had touched it yet."

"It looked like this when we arrived, but the timer wasn't running. It just started up on its own maybe ten minutes ago."

I recap everything I remember trying at the hospital as Roebuck drives. Agent Rossetti seems to understand even without us having access to 3-D feed.

"I'll go ahead and remove the receiver and reset the timer. The building has been cleared, so we hopefully won't have the issue of a gunman shooting the bomb this time. If the countdown resumes again, we can jam a secondary signal—only problem being we'll also lose contact with you and everyone else."

By the time we reach the IBI field office in Des Moines, the agents there have cleared us a path from the parking garage to their conference room. We pass a uniformed security guard, but he seems focused on something else ahead of him and ignores us. Once we're inside, we pass a second guard seated at a desk. He looks almost identical to the first—to the point I'm internally questioning if it's the same man. Roebuck notices my confusion but gives me an odd look.

"Twins?" I ask.

"Security androids." He shudders as we pass a

third guard but keeps walking. "They're not allowed to carry anything beyond rubber bullets and pepper spray, but the whole uncanny valley with this latest generation bugs me. I'd rather they just looked like robots, but idiots kept attacking them—scratching up the metal and stealing their parts to resell. Apparently these human-looking ones last about 15% longer—which translates into being more cost-effective than both the originals and the humans that those replaced. Somehow that doesn't give me a warm and fuzzy feeling about my own species."

"Hey—it's my species, too."

Fynn walks beside us but stays focused on her phone until we reach the conference room doors.

"Even with everything I've seen with this job, I still want to believe in the better part of people." She shows me a text message thread between her and Agent Rossetti from the past few minutes. Despite Rossetti's earlier confidence on the video feed, she's scared—worried about her husband and son. "I really hope we're right about you."

• • •

The conference room has been emptied—no chairs or table. I start searching the floor for some form of goggles when a scene projects itself around me. It's not perfect, but it's enough to make me feel surrounded by a group of five agents. Rossetti is the only one I recognize.

"Can you see me, too?" I ask. Two of the other agents give me personal space as if I'm actually in

Atlanta with them. "This is new to me."

"It's new to us, too—borrowed Hannarian tech, but they'll deny it if anyone asks," Agent Rossetti gestures for me to follow her, and I'm able to crouch down and look at the device. My hand goes through their outer wall, similar to a hologram, and I can feel the wall of the conference room just past it. "Thank you for your earlier help. If it comes down to it, we can continue studying and resetting this one. I'm just concerned that there are others nearby."

"Do you know what the original countdown would be right now?" I ask, looking at the current timer of over ninety-seven hours. "Probably closer to two hours, maybe?"

"That sounds about right. Why?"

"Assume that it hasn't actually changed—or that it could return to the original at any point. That happened to me even after I removed the receiver."

"I've been recording ever since we got here," another agent replies. "Give me a minute, and I can get the exact time for you." After he finds this, he shows us a timer program on his phone.

One hour and fifty-four minutes.

Another flash hits, and I can't force myself to snap out of it.

The warehouse is clean and doesn't look as if it needs to be demolished. There aren't any people like Ron said, but there are hundreds of stacked crates— each containing six-figure robots ready to ship to customers. I wonder how many hundreds of millions the company's owners will receive once they're destroyed. The majority of that would have to go back to the customers, though—refunds—unless this was some weird way to delay production...maybe to cover some other failure that would crash the company entirely. Either Ron didn't question anything he was told, or he lied to me. I don't like either possibility.

I have plenty of time—an hour and fifty-four minutes—and disarming it shouldn't be an issue since I designed—

"Anna!" Agent Fynn is in the conference room with me, shaking my shoulders. "Please, we don't have time for this."

I look past her. One of the security androids walks by the window and looks in at us. His—its— expression is neutral, but this one has scars on its skin-like material. They're similar to the gunman at the hospital.

"He wasn't human—the man I drew before," I whisper, unsure how well the androids can pick up sound. "There's an EIP connection to all of this, but it's not what you think. Look up everything about the warehouse attack where I nearly died—relay it to your other offices. You're all in danger, but I don't know how to stop them."

She nods, but the skepticism hasn't left her expression. "Focus on the bomb. We'll handle it."

She leaves, and I notice a portion of the agents in Atlanta have left. Only Rossetti and two others have stayed.

"Is any of the security there robotic?" I ask. Rossetti nods, and I can tell she overheard most of what I told Fynn. I hope that I haven't said too much and made things worse. "Be careful."

I hear gunfire, but it's not coming from the Atlanta feed. It's coming from the hallway.

• • •

My first instinct is to lock the conference room doors and move to a corner. Rossetti recalls her team, and I realize they're all staying to guard the bomb in Atlanta. I step out where they can see me again.

"I'm going to try to help the agents here. If a security android shows up there, it probably has the countdown transmitter somewhere inside it. Don't let it anywhere near the bomb. I'll be back as soon as I can."

When I leave the conference room, the hallway is empty. I can hear Roebuck and Fynn yelling—other voices I don't know—and the occasional shot and clang against metal. The androids are likely bullet-resistant, but they're not invulnerable. Kind of like me. I make myself go toward all the noise instead of away from it.

A hand grabs my shoulder—padded metallic fingers clamping down on me. My body reacts, and I slam the android to the floor. It twitches like an injured insect—metal limbs flailing—and I bend down and crush its skull. It still continues to move, and I realize the main control and power source are in its abdomen. It takes me a minute to get to them, but then all the mechanics stop.

My other senses kick in, and I'm able to distinguish the human agents from the androids by body temperature. Nearly all the agents are heading to a middle floor of the building—the androids following after them—and the agents are slightly out-numbered. I need to put myself between them.

There's a fire escape on the exterior of the building, and I open a window outside and begin to climb it. It's rusted, but the scratches on my hands heal within seconds.

I'm almost to the top when I see a hand extended to help me inside. It's Roebuck.

"How did you know I was—"

"We have a way of tracking Hannarians." He doesn't elaborate and leads the way down the hallway. "Nothing we've tried is shutting the androids down. Is the Atlanta team having the same issue?"

"If they're not, they will soon. The androids and bombs are connected somehow—same designer, maybe. I disabled one, and I can see some similarities."

We turn a corner, and three of the androids are trying to get inside the same room. They turn and rush toward us. Roebuck gets in one shot before the entire group knocks me to the floor. They're pulling at my arms and legs—digging into my skin and nearly snapping bone—but my fear causes my body to lock up. They're going to pull me apart if I can't snap out of this. Come on!

I finally roll and pitch one against a wall—nearly hitting Roebuck in the process—and start fighting off the other two. Roebuck recovers from being startled and finds a better angle, shooting the second one until it releases me and stops. I rip the chest plate from the third and pull out its power source, and it runs out its remaining energy. Roebuck approaches and offers to help me up, but I shake my head.

"I don't want to accidentally hurt you. Give me a minute and keep watch. There are still eight left in the building."

Seconds after I say this, I'm unable to sense the remaining androids. I worry that they've adapted until Fynn and another group of agents meet up with us.

"TWI customer service finally responded—claimed this was an isolated incident and that they're working on the problem." Her eyebrows furrow as she sees me. "What happened in Atlanta?"

"I thought all of you needed help." I stand up and start toward the closest stairwell. "I warned Rossetti about the androids—told everyone I'd be right back."

When I reach the conference room again, it's empty. The hologram generator is flickering, but there's no image.

Fynn tries calling Rossetti and then several other numbers. No one answers.

IT'S A BIRD! IT'S A PLANE!

• • •

The next half-hour becomes a waiting game. There's nothing major on the Atlanta news feeds—no detonation at the power station but no response from any of the IBI agents either. Fynn and I don't leave the conference room, hoping we'll reestablish contact.

"I'm not upset that you helped us," she finally says. "You could have left while we were all distracted, but you didn't. I'm just worried about Rossetti and her team."

"Me, too." I look at my wrist, and the blue light has returned to an occasional pulse. "Do you know what happened to my brother? All the time I spent in and out of hospitals is coming back, but it all blends together. Ron never visited me—even after the EIP got him out of prison. I always thought it was because he was angry I didn't listen to him...that I got him caught."

She brings up Ron's criminal profile on her phone, and I read through it. It's much worse than what I had imagined, and I realize why Fynn hasn't told Roebuck or anyone else my identity. Telling anyone could put me in danger, even within the IBI.

"Why are you protecting me?" I ask.

"Because my uncle would have..." She looks at the door. "I wish he was here."

Before I can say anything, the projection of the Atlanta power station returns. I can see the bomb—the countdown inactive again—and a few seconds

72

later Agent Rossetti walks into view.

"We're all right—had to use the jammer when we got cornered, and it took time to bring in new phones and cameras. All the security androids are shut down. TWI is calling it an isolated incident, but the other field offices are still taking precautions." She looks at me. "You probably saved our lives with the heads-up. Thank you. I know things were a little rushed earlier. Did Jernard send you to help us? I don't think I've met you before."

"Not exactly," I reply. Rossetti seems confused and looks at Fynn.

"Roebuck found her at the Chicago site," Fynn explains, but she hesitates when more of Rossetti's team comes into view. They seem more curious than anything else, but I'm not sure who I can trust. "She has amnesia, so she's staying with us until she recovers or Jernard contacts us."

"So when do we get our own alien superhero?" one of the other agents asks, grinning at me as Rossetti elbows him. "Welcome to the big team. I'm just glad you're on our side."

I look down at my arms. I'm covered in blood from the fight but have almost healed again. "Me, too."

Epilogue

Even with being over a million miles apart, I'm still nervous. The projection of a Hannarian ship's interior fills the conference room, and I'm face-to-face with Jernard. I know him as Hannaria's Ambassador from news broadcasts, and he hasn't aged since I was a child. His eyes flare bright blue when he sees me.

"Ronald Kressler did this to you?" He's speaking English without an interpreter, and his tone seems more horrified than angry.

I take a deep breath. "My more recent memories are still a bit hazy, but he came into my hospital room one night and injected me with something... some form of the bioweapon, I guess. I didn't know who he was at the time—just thought he was just one of the staff."

An alert on one of the ship's consoles distracts him for a second, and he turns his back to me to shut it off. "I had a friend send Agent Roebuck a dose of the cure. Did he give it to you?"

I take the syringe out of my jacket pocket and inject it, and the trails of light in my arms start to fade and then disappear. "I'm still going after TWI. They're behind the bombings, and someone there connected Ron Kressler to the very worst of the EIP. I'm not making any excuses for his actions, but the people who influenced him are still out there—could be doing the same to other children. I want to help Roebuck and Fynn rescue as many as possible."

He stares at me but then nods in agreement. "If you need anything else, tell Fynn and Roebuck to get word to us. We're being pulled in several different directions right now, but we'll help you any way we can."

"Thank you." I'm starting to feel nauseous, either from the cure or wanting the conversation to end before I slip up and say the wrong thing. "I hope this isn't rude, but I really could use some sleep. I'll probably be over sixty again by the time I wake up."

I start for the door.

"Anna," he says. I don't know how, but he knows who I am. I stop but don't turn around. "Your brother wanted me to kill him, but I saw what he was hiding beneath all the theatrics. It scared me."

"Evil?" I ask.

"Pain—very deep sadness and guilt," he replies. "I believed he was too far gone—that was right to allow him to end himself and not attempt to save him. Even with everything he did to my family and thousands of innocent humans, I still don't know how to feel about all of it. I know it's a lot easier to deal with mindless monsters than something you recognize. I'm sorry for whatever good in him you lost, and I want you to know you have nothing to fear from us."

"Thank you." I exit the conference room doors and take a deep breath in the hallway. Fynn and Roebuck are waiting.

"You all right?" Fynn asks.

"I'm fine," I reply, scratching my arm where it's itching. I'm wondering if the burn scars are about to return and push up my jacket sleeve.

The trails of light are back.

A Word from Patricia Gilliam

I began The Hannaria Series in 2006 as a set of short stories about a young alien ambassador named Jernard and his family. I had no idea at the time that I'd be working on my sixth novel a little over a decade later.

The majority of "Anna" takes place during events in *Book 2: Legacy*, and I have plans for more episode-style stories featuring Anna, Roebuck, and Fynn. The main novels contain the perspectives of at least two characters, and as a reader you're able to view the same events from different angles.

One of my favorite things about being a writer is getting to know people I wouldn't have encountered otherwise. I'm grateful to be a part of this anthology with an awesome group of fellow authors, and I want to thank Steve Beaulieu for the opportunity.

My husband Cory and I live in Knoxville, TN. We have a deceptively adorable cat named Butterscotch, who assists me with creating alien names by sitting on my laptop's keyboard.

You can find out more about me at my website: www.patriciagilliam.com. I'm also pretty accessible on Facebook and Twitter.

Thank you so much for reading! Have a great day!

THE ROACH

RISES

RHETT C. BRUNO

I STARED DOWN at the soiled water at the mouth of the Hudson River. I couldn't see my reflection—nobody had seen anything but brown in those waters since before the Dutch bought Manhattan for pennies—but I knew how I looked. Like a homeless, raving lunatic wandering the streets of New York begging for change. I spent a lifetime hiding in the shadows and now I could roam down the streets of the busiest city in the western hemisphere and go unnoticed.

As the river lapped at the concrete harbor beneath me in Red Hook, Brooklyn, I wondered what the tabloids would write when someone fished me out.

THE ROACH SURFACES ON THE HUDSON AFTER THREE YEARS.

MISSING VIGILANTE FOUND WASHED UP IN NEW YORK.

IT'S A BIRD! IT'S A PLANE!

Or maybe would I keep floating across the country until my body was bloated and mistaken by some farmer for driftwood, never to be found again. Forgotten.

I rolled my wheelchair an inch further until my legs were dangling over the ledge. How far is too far? I'd been asking myself that question every second of every day for three years. One last push and I could finally know for good. Some people called me a monster for killing. Some a hero for whom I killed. Not one of them didn't have it coming, that's for sure, and I was no different.

One last life to be taken.

I'd waited until sunset so that all the shipping workers helping to keep the city bustling had gone home to their wives. So I could be alone. A gentle breeze kissed my cheeks and rustled my scraggly beard. My fingers gripped the worn tires of my chair tighter.

I closed my eyes and pictured the tears running down the face of Laura, the last person I ever saved. I imagined the man who forced her into an alley lying bloody at my feet and that rookie cop in the wrong place at the wrong time who put a bullet in my spine when I didn't stand down.

My hands pushed slowly forward. I was inches from being free, and then I heard it. The familiar squeal of someone in trouble followed by the smack of skin on skin.

My eye-lids snapped open and I stopped. *Don't*

do it, Reese. I told myself. *Don't you dare turn around. You came this far.*

Another cry rang out, followed the thud of someone hitting concrete. My wheelchair whipped around before my brain could tell it not to. My wretch of a foster-dad did always rattle on about how you can't teach old dogs new tricks.

I raced across the small harbor toward the alley I heard it coming from, the shriveled husks I had for legs bouncing as I went over bumps. I rounded the corner of a work-shed on Ferris St. so fast I almost toppled.

Two kids were beating up on a scrawny runt who was probably famous in school for being bullied. He was no older than sixteen but the others had to be seniors. Legal Adults. Two future gang-bangers and wife-beaters in leather jackets and with their hair slicked back.

"Just fork it over, Chris!" One of the bullies shouted before kicking their cowering victim in the gut.

"Yeah, Chris," snickered the other. "Is it really worth getting your ass kicked over again?"

"Why don't you two head on home!" I shouted.

They glanced up at me, and even after three years it surprised me when someone regarded me without trepidation. New York's dark corners feared the Roach. Me. I did what had to be done. Someone stole a purse from an old lady, they lost some fingers. Someone murdered, they lost their life. Someone took a young woman into an alley and had their way with her...they lost the part of them they held most dear.

Instead, the two bullies looked like they'd just heard a good joke. They turned away from their groaning victim, nudging each other and grinning like two idiots.

"Go home old man," one said. He was obviously the leader. Taller, fitter, probably excelled at sports in school and little else.

"Yeah. This doesn't concern you," laughed the chubby one.

Of course, I rolled toward them. I knew how I looked wearing my old padded leather uniform. The red logo of the Roach on the chest used to instill fear, but it, like me, had seen better days. I looked like I'd been struck by a bus on my way home from a comic book convention. Like a joke.

"Back up old man," the leader said.

"Yeah," the other chimed in. "What do you think you're some sort of superhero wearing that?"

I stopped a few feet away. Close enough to smell the body odor of a couple of pubescent punks. "What happened to make you two like this?" I asked. "Parents didn't give you enough?" My gaze fell toward their nether regions. "Or maybe you inherited something too small from them."

"Old man's got a mouth on him, huh," the leader said. "What, you think I won't hit you because you're in a chair?"

"Trust me," I said. "This chair is the only thing keeping you from being sent home to your moms crying. Now leave the kid alone and beat it."

"Or you'll what?" He circled around behind me, cackling. "Run over my foot?" He shoved my wheelchair forward hard and his buddy caught it by the armrests.

"Yeah, what're you gonna run over our feet?"

"I just said that, moron."

"The next one of you who touches me is going to need a cast," I interrupted. *You were so close, I told myself. Now you're stuck here listening to nitwits.*

"Oh yeah?" the chubby one poked me in the side of the head. He beamed ear to ear afterward like he'd just accomplished some great feat. All I could muster was a sigh. I used to take down drug lords, pimps and murderers. I used to make front page news.

He went to poke me again. His finger never made contact. Before he knew what hit him I'd snapped his wrist and shoved him into the wall. Enough to give it a clean break. He wouldn't need surgery or anything, but he'd damn sure learn a lesson.

"You crazy bastard!" he howled.

That was usually when things de-escalated. It took a special kind of dirt bag to hit back at a cripple like me, but I'd apparently found them. The leader of the pack grabbed the push bars of my chair and tipped me over. His foot came screeching toward my gut. I caught it and flipped him, but he flailed like a wounded wildebeest and his steel-tipped boot caught me in the jaw.

My leg was caught on my wheelchair seat I couldn't get out of the way. Three years ago I was as familiar with getting hit in the head as drinking, but now the blow dazed me. The friend jumped in while I was dazed. I took a fist to the head. A foot in the ribs. I blocked as much as I could, but fighting isn't like hopping back on a bike. My muscles were weak. Untrained.

When they finally backed off the injured, chubby one said, "Dude, he's not getting back up."

"Good. Old prick." The leader spat on me, then they scurried off. They had something to say to the underclassman they'd beaten on their way by, but my ears were ringing and I couldn't hear.

I rolled onto my back. A bit of blood rolled over my gums and out of the corner of my mouth. That familiar tang of iron. My first instinct was to laugh. It made my sore ribs sting but I couldn't help it. How insane I must have looked.

"Thanks a lot, mister," the kid they'd beaten said. His voice still hadn't dropped. My head lolled over and I saw him kneeling beside me. Instead of clapping and bowing at my feet, he looked like he wanted to hit me.

"You just going to stand there?" I grumbled.

"They're gonna kick my ass even worse next time thanks to you. Why couldn't you just stay out of it?"

"I'm wondering the same thing."

He seemed fine in retrospect. A pair of dog tags hung crookedly from his neck. That was what the bullies were trying to take from him. A memory of a father or someone else who died back in Vietnam. They deserved worse than one broken hand between the two of them.

He put his hand on my arm to help me up and I slapped him away.

"Hands off, kid," I said.

"You're hurt."

"My pride maybe. I already got my ass kicked by two runts today, don't need a third helping me up like I'm a cripple."

"You are."

I glared at him and I could see the color drain from his cheeks. Now that was the look I expected when people came face to face with me. The one I longed for. He stayed quiet while I crawled across the pavement toward my chair. My head still rang, but I was able to flip it upright and position my body in front of it.

Then came the hard part. Lifting a body sculpted from wilting muscle and dangling legs. I got about halfway, arms shaking from the strain, before the kid helped me the rest of the way. I didn't notice until afterward because he'd grabbed my numb feet.

"I said not to touch me!" I snarled, giving him a shove. Even weak as I was, it sent him stumbling.

"Fine," he said. "Whatever. I just couldn't watch that anymore."

"Yeah? Do me a favor, kid, so I don't need to roll in and save you again. Next time those two idiots try to steal that thing around your neck, hit 'em in the nuts and run away. That's the beauty of having legs."

"My father told me never to back down."

I eyed the tags hanging from his neck. "And look where that got him." I started to roll away just as his eyes got watery and his cheeks flushed red. I wished I could take it back. Sometimes I snapped because I drank too much or was pissed at the world. The ungrateful kid didn't deserve it, but good advice is good advice.

Some people aren't meant to fight. Others, well, I'm still kicking... figuratively.

• • •

An empty bottle clinking along the floor woke me. My foggy eyes blinked open to see my empty palm where it had been. The next best thing to ending my life was getting lost in whiskey.

I rubbed my face and went to swing my legs off my cot. Only they didn't move. Three years and I still wasn't used to that. It was like having ghost-legs where they used to be. From time to time my brain would play tricks on me like I could still feel something. The human brain is cruel.

I rolled off the floor-cot, grabbed a hook hanging from the ceiling and used it to lift myself up onto my chair. I had no clue what time it was. My Roach suit was off and tossed haphazardly over the railing. Fresh, purple bruises covered my ribs, accompanying a smattering of age-old scars.

"Damn, kids," I grumbled.

I rolled along the grated catwalk wrapping an abandoned underground tunnel. The Roach's Lair, the press would've called it if they had any idea it existed. My control center. A wall of television screens and police radios rest in the center, unused for years. Covered in cobwebs. Behind them was a lit display case with a naked mannequin inside that was usually wearing my padded leather uniform when I didn't take it out for a suicidal spin. The flickering bulb inside was the only light in the entire space. Behind me, the seemingly endless tunnel offering access into the NYC underground remained black as the ace of spades.

I ran my fingers along the control station desk. A layer of filth so copious peeled away that it turned my pale flesh brown. I glanced up at the newspaper clippings arrayed on the wall behind it and chuckled. Here I was, the infamous Roach, living among the darkness and the grime like a real cockroach.

All those headlines. If the authors could only see me now. It was like the sad trophy case of a high school scholar athlete who never did anything else.

THE ROACH BREAKS UP MAFIA DRUG RING ON THE LOWER EAST SIDE.

IT'S A BIRD! IT'S A PLANE!

SUSPECTED PEDOPHILE MINISTER FOUND CRUCI-
FIED OUTSIDE SAINT PATRICK'S.

That one was a little too poetic. I always did have a romantic side.

MAYOR GARRITY'S DAUGHTER ATTACKED. VIGI-
LANTE ROACH SUSPECTED.

Of all the false reports, that last one was the only to ever bother me. That the sheep who I spent so long protecting could think that I would hurt a young woman made my blood boil. I knew the author wrote the piece just to get under my skin, but that didn't matter.

I swiped my hand across the page like I did every time I saw it. This time, the loose corner finally gave out and it folded over and tore across from the strip of tape in the bottom right corner. I'd posted every mention of the Roach in newspapers for as long as I can remember. The good and the bad. They weren't trophies, though it may have looked like that. They were reminders of how people really were... The good and the bad.

I rolled into the rickety lift off to the side of the room. The grated metal door was rusting. The pulleys in even worse shape. Every night I spent down in the Roach Lair we had an unofficial contest of what would fall apart quicker. My body, or the rumbling, squeaking lift that sounded like a rat being strangled. It wasn't easy to maintain a secret lift plunging illegally through NYC infrastructure without legs.

It stopped at the first floor of my townhouse with a moan. The grates folded open, and a switch signaled the hidden doorway built into a bookcase to slide open and reveal my study. I know. How original. But it isn't my fault that sometimes movies have great ideas that any real person would never think to check in a million years.

"There you are," a voice called from the kitchen. I recognized it instantly so I didn't panic—not that it would matter if I was found out at this point. The sizzle and smell of cooking bacon basically pulled my chair across the room like a fish on a lure. Laura Garrity knew me too well.

She was by the stove with a spatula, looking every bit as beautiful as the day I saved her. Her form-fitting pantsuit didn't fit the occasion, but she never was one to take a moment off. She may still have been the mayor's daughter, but she was no longer a kid. A burgeoning lawyer, a mother—the kind of person that made being a hero worth it.

"You're letting yourself in now?" I said to her, then coughed. My throat burned from liquor and cigarettes from the night before.

"I knew you were home," she answered.

I pulled up right next to her, accidentally ramming the counter. "I told you never to go down there."

"I didn't. *You* left the front door open. Again."

"I like the draft."

She rolled her eyes, then leaned down to observe my face. I hadn't passed by a mirror yet, but I'm sure it wasn't a pretty sight. "Did you get in another bar fight, old man?"

"Something like that. Where's Michelle?"

"In the living room watching TV on mute. She didn't want to wake you."

"Good. That's the smartest thing I've heard in weeks."

Laura rolled her eyes and returned her attention to the pan. The bacon was sizzling, probably already overcooked. Considering how busy she was, learning how to cook well wasn't in the cards no matter how hard she tried.

"And you wonder why she's scared of you," Laura remarked.

"I never wonder."

I spun and rolled into the dreary living room, curtains drawn over the front windows to keep the light and prying eyes out. As expected, tiny Michelle sat on my couch, which probably wasn't sanitary enough for a child. She pulled a pillow close as I appeared and didn't make a peep. I joined her in silence. I never was great with children, especially her. What could I say to her? *Hey, Michelle, I was there when you were conceived by some serial rapist in an alley having his way with your mother. Oh, and I sliced the bastard's favorite parts of himself off too, right before a cop took away mine.*

I checked what was on TV. *Good Morning America* covered in grain thanks to a bent antenna. Poor girl. I'm sure my grubby townhouse in Red Hook was the last place she wanted to stop before daycare.

"You know, you really don't have to keep dropping by," I said to Laura as I rolled back into the kitchen.

"Well then who would make sure you eat?" she replied.

I stopped by the low counter where I kept my booze. I was down to my last bottle of *Jack Daniels*. There wasn't much of a pension for retired Vigilantes, and the one for an NYC Sanitary Worker on permanent medical leave was barely enough to scrape by.

I opened the bottle and took a swig straight out of it.

"This early, Reese?" she scolded.

I drew my seat up to my corner table and clanked it down hard. "I'm nocturnal, remember? My whole body is out of whack."

She set a plate down in front of me. Overcooked bacon, scrambled eggs and whiskey. The breakfast of champions.

"You haven't been nocturnal for…. What is it… three years now?" she said, wearing a wicked grin.

"Rub it in why don't you."

"I'm just saying. You're going to kill yourself."

IT'S A BIRD! IT'S A PLANE!

I chuckled at the private joke inside my head as she carried breakfast to Michelle in the living room. We'd given up trying to get her to sit down for a meal without things getting uncomfortable. Children that age have a sixth sense, I think. Like she could see through my wrinkly shell and into my rotting core. It terrified her. I wondered every morning I saw her what that felt like. Feeling fear.

"Are you going to eat anything, or just stare at it?" Laura asked when she returned and sat across from me.

I lifted a piece of the blackened bacon and stuck out my tongue. "Now I really regret not going through with it."

"Through with what?"

"I tried to kill myself yesterday," I said nonchalantly. Like it was a daily routine when truthfully that was the closest I'd ever come. Laura was midway through a sip of water and nearly choked.

"What?" she asked.

"I rolled down the harbor. Right to the edge. It was perfect, Laura. The sun on my face. Gulls cawing. Hearing the waves call to me. It was the first time in so long I felt like I could breathe."

"Why would you do that?"

"Do you really need to ask that question?"

I watched a hundred different responses pass through her brain. Her pretty, brown eyes glinted from welling tears. "But you couldn't do it?"

"Apparently, I'm too good at playing hero."

"I... I don't know what to say, Reese."

I reached across the table and grasped her hand. Her fingers were soft like a women's should be. Not like mine, hardened from so many times wrapped around the throats of wicked men.

"You've never had to say anything. You've never had to take care of me or keep checking in. Your father took care of that a long time ago. You don't owe me anything. It's time to stop wasting your time."

She yanked her hand free and pushed away from the table. "You really think I'm wasting my time? I come every week because I care about you, Reese. I know who you are even if you've forgotten."

All I could manage was a feeble laugh.

"What?" she bristled.

"Still so stubborn."

"And you're not? You spend so much time in here wallowing that you've forgotten about all the people you saved. You may not be the Roach anymore, but he was you."

"So, you're telling me I shouldn't kill myself?"

She threw up her hands in exasperation. "You do whatever you think you need to, but I'm going to be here next Monday like I always am. I hope I see you."

"Was it something I said?"

She stormed out of the kitchen. I followed at a distance. Our visits ended this way more often than I'd probably care to admit. I really could be an insufferable bastard sometimes, but more than anything I wanted her to be mad at me. To not care when I returned to that pier and finished what I should have. She only got to hear about all the people I saved. About the kids being beaten by their step-fathers or sold smack by gangbangers. I saw the dark side.

Eventually, after you wipe enough filth from the streets but it keeps bubbling back like a sickness, it's all you can see in people. A roll down the street and I wonder which man in a prim suit struck his wife last night or is having an affair. Which harmless civilian doubled as a serial killer. The darkness of humanity clings to you like wet sand on the beach. And now all I could do was watch it fester and turn my city into a breeding ground for crime and villainy.

"Come on, Michelle," Laura said, mustering her calm tone. "It's time to go."

"Okay," Michelle replied with her tiny voice. She glanced over at me momentarily, hovering in the doorway with a bottle of Jack dangling from my grip. She immediately turned her gaze to the floor and grabbed her mother's hand.

They went for the door, but a hard knock stopped them in their tracks.

"Laura Garrity, I know you're in there!" someone shouted.

I raced over to my covered window and drew back the curtain just enough to peak outside. A skinny fellow wearing glasses and holding a notepad stood on my porch.

"Not this asshole again," I grumbled. "Laura, go to the back. I'll deal with him."

"He's harmless," she said.

"So am I. Now go."

She spent a long few seconds considering it before she finally listened and took her confused daughter with her. I rolled up to the door and stretched my fingers around the handle. That article in my basement about how the Roach might have attacked Laura Garrity? The man outside wrote it. Chuck Barnes. He used to write for the Times, but he had such a hard-on for revealing who the Roach was behind the mask that he destroyed his credibility. Stalking a young woman and her infant child will do that.

Now he was a pariah in the reporting industry, which meant he could bend rules and do whatever it took to try and prove what he'd pieced together without caring. In my prime, I would've broken into his house to get him to back off. But he lived in a walk-up across the city, and I couldn't very well get up that high in a wheelchair and manage to remain intimidating.

I tossed my bottle of whiskey onto the couch and then swung the door open. "I know she's in here Mr. Roberts," he said and immediately tried to peek his head in. I blocked him with my chair.

"How many times do I have to tell you to keep

off my damn property?" I said.

"Until you tell me why you're hanging around a much younger woman who happens to be the daughter of our illustrious mayor."

I gave him another nudge, this time pushing him down one step. "What can I tell you? We're in love." I stroked my ragged beard, straining out a few droplets of whiskey. "She can't resist me."

Footsteps echoed from my townhouse. "What was that?" He leaned over me again. I smacked the notepad out of his hand. It landed in a puddle and he quickly jumped down to retrieve it. Ink bled through the wet pages, rendering his mad scrawling illegible. He shook it off.

"Oh, real nice," he said. "You know how much work was in there?"

"I did ask nicely, didn't I?"

He stuck his finger out at me. "You know, one day the truth is going to come out! All the people you hurt. Taking the law into your own hands. I've looked into you, Reese Roberts. No hospital records of a paralysis case or anything. Sanitation says it's confidential."

"I'm self-healing." I rolled back and tried to close the door, but he bolted back up my stoop and impeded me with his foot.

"Who'd you bribe to keep everyone quiet? Anytime I try to bring anything to the city council they boot me out like it's all nonsense, but you'd have to be dense not to see all the pieces. The Roach used the sewers and subway lines to move around. You worked in them. I watched the last known person he saved step through your door earlier this morning. Every week."

I grabbed his wrist and squeezed. I was in the right mind to snap it like I'd done to that chubby bully in the alley, but I controlled my temper. He was lucky I'd only just started drinking that morning. "I suggest you walk away."

"I visited John Banks in prison, Roberts. You remember him?"

I bit my lip. "Can't say I have."

"He was the lowlife the Roach caught molesting Laura Garrity three years ago. Ring any bells? No? Well after the Roach made sure he could never rape a woman again, Banks said he saw him take a bullet in the back from a cop. The kind of shot that might leave a man's legs paralyzed."

In every comic, the superhero has an arch-enemy. Batman has the Joker, Superman has Lex Luthor. I had Chuck Barnes since all the other options were dead or behind bars for good. He was a man so hellbent on revealing the truth and redeeming his once-sterling reputation that he'd accept testimony from a piece of trash like John Banks. Except every part of what he'd said was true. The only reason my identity didn't come out was because of who I saved. Laura's dad got me the treatment I needed and kept everything quiet. From the Sanitation Department to the police chief in charge of the rookie who ended my vigilante career.

For about a year people asked what had happened to the Roach and why he disappeared. By the time her father was re-elected, nobody even cared. I was a memory. A name on some old newspaper clippings. Only Chuck Barnes kept searching, and I would've told him the truth just to shut him up if it weren't for Laura and Michelle. I didn't care if people knew. If old enemies came knocking on my door they could take as many swings as they wanted, but if they went knocking on Laura's? No.

"Walk away, Chuck," I whispered, squeezing his wrist tighter.

"Fine. Just tell me one thing first. Is that kid his, or yours?"

"I said walk away!" I burst through the door and shoved him with all of my might. He flew back off the stoop, sliced his hand on the rusty railing, and landed hard on the pavement.

"Well that's just great!" he shouted, glancing at his bloody hand. "So that's the kind of hero you are."

"Exactly the kind." I went to back into my house when a police cruiser turned the corner. They blurted their siren and flashed their lights once, then stopped in front of my townhouse. "You've got to be kidding me," I groaned.

"Is everything all right?" Laura yelled from the kitchen.

"Fine!"

The officers stepped out of their car, gazes set

on me. Chuck got to his feet.

"Did you see that?" he asked them. They walked right by him, and it took me all of two seconds to realize why. The chubby bully from the day before got out of the car too, arm in a sling.

"Is that him?" one of the officers asked the kid.

"Yeah," he replied. "That's the asshole who attacked me."

"Is that what the punk told you?" I laughed. "You've got to be kidding me."

The kid didn't say a word. All he did was stare at me while wearing a shit-eating grin.

"Oh, this is even better," Chuck said. He flipped to one of the dryer pages of his notepad and approached the kid. "I'm a reporter," he addressed him. "Would you mind telling me exactly what this man did to you?"

"Sir," the officer said to me. "I'm going to have to take you down to the precinct and ask you some questions." The way he regarded made me sick to my stomach. Like I was completely useless. If I had my legs I bet he would've arrested me right then and there, but who would believe that a flimsy old cripple could do anything to healthy a young man?

"What if I say no?" I replied.

"I'm afraid that isn't an option," the officer said. "Now please, let me help you down."

"You're going away for a long time, asshole!" the kid shouted at me. If he was a legal adult and their victim spoke the truth, I would get a slap on the wrist. But I hadn't taken the time to vet them like I used to when I was the Roach. If he was actually a minor and I broke his wrist. They'd hear the two bully's stories, and then the ungrateful prick I'd saved. Who knew whether or not he'd back me or be bullied into lying. By the time they got to my story it wouldn't matter what I said.

Is this really what I turned away from death for? I asked myself. *Is this the way the Roach goes down?*

The officer took my hand and guided my wheelchair down the narrow ramp tracks I'd built onto the stairs of my townhouse. He did it slowly like I was a delicate vase in an antique shop. The entire time I eyed the holstered pistol by his hip. I could grab it and finally end things. Quicker than drowning. It was less than I deserved, but there wasn't time to be picky about justice being done.

"What's going on, officer?" Laura asked.

My hand was halfway toward grabbing it when her voice made me freeze. I looked up at the door and saw her standing there, arms around her daughter.

"What's going on mommy?" Michelle asked.

"Forget about it, Laura," I said. Of course, she ignored me.

"Someone is making a mistake." Laura hopped down the stairs and stopped the officer. "Where are you taking him?"

"Ms. Garrity," the officer stammered. "He's wanted for questioning in the assault of that boy. I'm just doing my job."

"Well, I'm sure this is easily explainable. An accident."

"There they go," Chuck said. "Protecting this scumbag again. When are you two finally going to let him answer for his crimes?"

"When are you going to leave us alone and get back to your sorry life!"

The officer released my chair. "Look, Ms. Garrity. I don't know what's going on here, but I have to take him in. If the young man is lying we'll get to the bottom of it, but I have no choice now. Assault of a minor is a serious accusation."

"I'll tell you what's going on, officer," Chuck chimed in. The Garrity's have spent years protecting Reese Roberts to hide the fact that he's the Roach! Was the Roach."

"That's insane!" Laura shouted.

I missed the rest of the argument. While everyone got riled up, little Michelle slipped away from her mother and was headed toward a baseball that had rolled into the street. Three years old, no sense of the world's dangers, I saw it all happening it my head. A truck sped down the street, and when she stepped beyond the line of parked cars it would barrel right over her.

Michelle was the only person who saw me for what I really was anymore. Who saw the truth that Chuck Barnes so desperately wanted. That when you hunt monsters for so long, you become one yourself.

IT'S A BIRD! IT'S A PLANE!

But I wouldn't die a monster in a cage.

I grabbed hold of my wheels and launched my chair forward. The officer blurted something and tried to catch me but was too slow. Laura saw where I was going and screamed her daughter's name.

The wind blew through my hair as I raced across the sidewalk. I felt like I was leaping across rooftops again. My chair rumbled and had my legs bouncing as if I was running. Michelle didn't turn around when she heard her mother. The truck couldn't see her and wasn't stopping.

How far is too far? I've been asking myself that question every second of every day for three years and it was time to finally find out. I went just far enough, grabbed Michelle and threw her back onto the sidewalk. The truck driver hit the brakes when he saw me and tried to turn but it was too late.

In the second before it plowed into me, my whole life flashed. All the fights. All the monsters slain. I was the Roach, the bane of New York's criminal underworld, and at least I got to go out on my own terms...

A Word from Rhett C. Bruno

Thank you so much for taking the time to read "The Roach Rises." The story has been bouncing around in my head for years. First I wanted to try writing a TV Pilot script with the character, than a movie, and then Steve Beaulieu approached me with his idea for a superhero themed anthology. It was just the right push I needed to get the story of the Roach down in any format. Like with most of my work, I wanted to craft a story that was simultaneously heart-wrenching and up-lifting. While the title was a play on *Dark Knight Rises*, the word 'rise' holds a special meaning in this story. This will also be the first story of any length I've published that can't be classified as hard science fiction.

Beyond this anthology, I'm an amazon best-selling science fiction author and architect living in Stamford Connecticut. I'm represented by Mike Hoogland with Dystel & Goderich. My published works include the *Circuit* series (Published by Diversion Books) and the *Titanborn* series (Published by Random House Hydra). I'm also one of the founders of the popular science fiction platform Sci-Fi Bridge.

I've been writing since before I can remember, but didn't really start to take it seriously until my early 20's. While studying Architecture at Syracuse University, it was tough to find time to write while dealing with a brutal curriculum, but I persevered. I dedicated myself to reading the works of classic sci-fi authors like Frank Herbert, Heinlein, Phillip K. Dick and Timothy Zahn, and decided to start writing my first full length science fiction novel, *The Circuit: Executor Rising*.

It's been a long journey since! When I'm not working as an architect during the day, you can find me at home with my fiancee and dog trying to find time to write. You can find out more about my work at www.rhettbruno.com. If you'd like exclusive access to updates and the opportunity to receive limited content, ARCs and more, please subscribe to my newsletter. I hope to hear from you soon!

THE PALADIN

KEVIN G. SUMMERS

MY NAME IS JARED WEISS. I am the Paladin.

You may have read some newspaper stories last year about my war on crime. They're exaggerations... mostly. Apparently, a masked vigilante in a Washington, D.C. suburb isn't enough to sell newspapers. Well, let me set the record straight. I don't have super-powers; I can't fly or bend steel with my bare hands or move things with my mind. I'm not the bored son of a billionaire trying to make some excitement in my life, and I'm not doing this to try and market a new superhero concept to DC Comics.

Why am I doing this? Because somebody has to. Because gangs are moving into the suburbs, and kids are getting hooked on drugs every single day. Because what those kids really need is somebody to look up to. They need a hero, and that's exactly what I want to be.

I was twelve years old when my brother died; I was devastated. I worshipped Nick...wanted to be just like him. He did tae kwon do, so I did it too. When he was a freshman at Carmel High School, he went out for the wrestling team. All of a sudden, I wanted to be a wrestler. During his sophomore year, when he quit the team and started hanging around with the Drama Club, I discovered that what I really wanted was to be an actor. Then, near the end of that year, everything changed.

I thought it was me—that I'd done something to alienate my hero. I begged Nick to talk to me, to tell me what was going on. I didn't realize he was strung out on drugs until it was too late to save him. My mom was so busy trying to hold our little family unit together that she didn't even notice. My father? He abandoned us when I was nine. If he cared at all, he sure didn't do a good job of showing it.

School let out for the summer, and, for the first time in years, I felt totally alone in the world. I had just graduated from the sixth grade and was completely friendless. There's no way around the fact...I'm a geek. I'm short, dopey-looking, and hopelessly uncool. My English teacher, Mrs. Pearson, she'd say that I need to give my reader more information. Well, I don't know what else to say. I have a plain face and ordinary brown eyes. The only thing that's memorable about me is my hair, which is jet-black and totally unmanageable. I always look like I just got out of bed, and that's just one of the many things the other kids make fun of me about.

I try not to let it bother me, and, up until last year, it didn't matter what other people said. I had my comics and my hobbies and my big brother.

We live in the suburbs, in a little town in Northern Virginia called Carmel. It's the kind of place where a kid with a bike has access to everything he could want. I spent my days, and the money I earned mowing lawns, at the comic book store or the video rental place. I would have given up every single comic in my collection, including my copy of New Teen Titans #1, for Nick to start acting like himself again.

Unfortunately, things just got worse.

I got back from the comic store one afternoon and found the front door unlocked. Nick's Doc Martens were lying in the middle of the living room, and that meant he was home.

I rushed down the basement stairs to his room, but when I knocked on his door, there was no answer. I knocked again, and when there was still no answer, I decided it was okay for me to be the pesky little brother. I opened the door, and it was like I had stepped into a horror movie. The bag of comics slipped from my hands and slapped against my feet.

Nick was curled in the fetal position at the foot of his bed; blood pooled all around him, and his lifeless eyes stared at me in a perpetual apology that I will never forget. On the far wall, above the bed, were a skull and crossbones painted with my brother's blood.

God, there was so much blood.

I fell to my knees and puked all over the floor. Then I scrambled for the phone and called 911, but it was too late for them to do anything for Nick.

Our house became a crime scene, and my mom

and I had to live in a motel for a week while cops dusted every inch of the place. Of course, our fingerprints were everywhere, so the head detective, a man named Bill West, printed us to eliminate us from consideration. West said Nick probably knew whoever it was that had murdered him. He said that the skull and crossbones were the symbol of the Marauders, a big-city gang that had been spreading out into the suburbs, and that the prospect of catching whoever did it looked bleak.

The next eight months were the worst of my entire life. I couldn't understand how my brother could have gotten hooked up with the Marauders, but we found out soon enough. The toxicology report with Nick's autopsy said he had traces of marijuana, methamphetamine, and LSD in his system when he died. My mom was crushed. I know she wanted to be there for me, but the bills had to be paid and she was at work more often than not.

I threw myself into a fantasy world where Batman and Superman always got the bad guy in the end. I lived for Wednesdays, the day that new comics go on sale. I felt so helpless—Nick's murder was still unsolved, bullies picked on me at school, and the closest thing I had to a friend was the guy at the comic shop. I tried to act like I didn't care, but all I could think about was what had happened to Nick. I missed my big brother. I miss him still.

I turned thirteen on a frozen night in January. I

was home alone, hiding up in my room with a stack of comics beside me. Rain pattered against my window as an idea took shape in my mind. Some of my favorite superheroes—Nightwing, Green Arrow, The Question —they didn't have super powers or fight aliens trying to take over the world. They fought gangsters and thieves and murderers. They fought for vengeance, and for justice.

That was exactly what I decided to do.

My thoughts kept turning to one hero in particular: Robin. He was always my favorite. He didn't have super-strength; he couldn't fly; he wasn't faster than the speed of light. He was just a kid my own age with nothing but his brains, his muscles, and a handful of tricks in his utility belt. The more I thought about it, the more I could relate to him. I could don a mask and begin my own war on crime. I could make the Marauders pay for what they did to my brother.

On that dismal, winter night, the Paladin was born.

• • •

It was fall, nine months after Jared Weiss conceived of the Paladin, and for the past three days rain had drizzled over Carmel. Suburban houses seemed to shiver with cold as the leaves on the trees began to slowly die. Winter was quickly descending on the little town.

A teenage boy in a red hoodie leaned against a streetlight in front of the fitness center at Ruby Welton Park. He jabbed a cigarette between his lips, lit the end, and took a deep drag. Two girls dressed in workout clothes gave the boy a dirty look as they exited the building, and Tom Cole flung a menacing glare back at them.

The girls averted their eyes and stepped up their pace toward their car. Tom stared after them and took another drag on his cigarette. "Bitches," he mumbled under his breath. "Stupid sluts."

Greg Carter, Carmel High School's star basketball player, walked out of the fitness center a few seconds later. Tom gave Greg an almost imperceptible nod. They exchanged a few whispered words and a handshake, and then Greg was headed to his car with a tiny Zip-Lock bag in the palm of his hand. Tom watched him go as he slipped a wad of cash into the pocket of his hoodie. He took a final drag on his cigarette, flicked it into the parking lot, and began a long, meandering walk home.

At the side of the building, obscured by shadows, a figure stood watching.

• • •

I put in months of training and planning before making my first appearance as the Paladin. Every second that I was running or lifting weights, I kept thinking about how great it was going to be once Nick was avenged. I knew I was likely to be arrested, or even killed, but the thought of striking back against the Marauders kept me going.

I spent weeks trying to come up with a code-name, something that would scare the hell out of the bad guys, but everything I thought of sucked. *Kid Vengeance...Captain Retribution...*those are some of the better ones. Finally, I remembered playing Dungeons & Dragons with Nick. We made up characters and pretended to fight dragons and stuff. My character was a wizard, but Nick's was this special class of knight, sworn to battle evil at any cost, even his own life. He was a Paladin. The name gave me chills; it seemed the perfect tribute to my brother.

Once I had the name, I needed a costume. I dug out a black Halloween mask, a long-sleeved black tee shirt, and a pair of tae kwon do gloves, then rummaged through Nick's stuff. I found a pair of black cargo-pants and a dark gray hooded cloak that he'd worn in the Drama Department's production of *Robin Hood*. I took those, shoved some newspaper into the toes of his Doc Martens, and took them as well. Then I cut the shape of a chess piece—the knight—out of a white undershirt and sewed it onto the chest of my black tee shirt. The knight would be my symbol—like Superman's S-shield.

With my costume complete, I moved on to my arsenal. I bought a utility belt from the local army surplus store, and stuck everything I might need in my war on crime—flash bombs, throwing stars, a pair of metal handcuffs, a slingshot, and an old can of pepper spray—in its canvas pouches. Once I had everything together, I spray-painted Nick's red BMX a more suit-

able black. Now I finally felt ready to face the world as the Paladin.

• • •

The Paladin mounted his bike and followed Tom Cole. *I've heard all the rumors about him,* Jared's thoughts churned as he pedaled through one of the nicest neighborhoods in town. *Tom should be a freshman at Carmel High, but he's still in the 7th grade. He's the oldest kid at Carmel Middle School; he's always got the coolest clothes and the newest gadgets, and whenever he leaves the room, the other kids whisper that his money comes from selling drugs. I don't know how much of that I believe, but I know what I saw when we were changing clothes after gym three days ago—a red skull and crossbones tattooed on his shoulder.*

The Paladin kept to the shadows as he pursued his target to a run-down apartment complex called Carmel Commons. He ducked behind a dumpster and watched Tom enter one of the buildings. A minute later, a light flicked on inside a second-floor apartment.

"I've got you," the Paladin whispered.

• • •

I was crazy with excitement. In just a few hours I'd witnessed a drug transaction and found out where the dealer lived. I wondered if I might become a detective someday, or an FBI agent. I began to dream about the future, and after so many months of depression, it felt great. Then tragedy struck again.

114

Two days after I followed Tom to his apartment, a story spread through Carmel Middle School like a forest fire. Greg Carter was dead of a drug overdose.

I felt like I'd been hit by a truck; this was exactly the kind of thing I wanted to prevent. I should have done something that night, but I just crouched in the shadows and watched Greg throw his life away. My feelings of guilt were matched only by my furious anger. I wanted revenge for Nick, and for Greg. I wanted justice.

A plan was already forming in my mind.

• • •

It was a brisk Friday night in early November, and Jared was home alone; his mother was working late, as usual. Around ten o'clock, he donned his costume, slipped into the night, and pedaled toward Carmel Commons. When he arrived at the apartment complex, he parked his bike between two cars, took a quick look around, and crept toward the building.

"This is the end for you," he muttered as he closed in. "Tonight I'm going to make you wish you never heard of the Marauders." His cape rippled like a gray flag as he leapt onto the building's fire escape and climbed to Tom's apartment.

The Paladin peered through a dirty window and spotted Tom, dressed in a pair of gym shorts and a black Metallica tee shirt, walking toward the living room with a bag of microwave popcorn in his hands. The Paladin tapped on the living room window as Tom stuffed a handful of popcorn in his mouth and started to sit down.

Tom's eyes narrowed and he spun around. "Who's out there?"

The Paladin backed out of sight and waited.

A few seconds later, Tom opened the window, stuck his head outside, and glanced around. The Paladin drew back his fist and punched him right between the eyes. Tom's nose shattered, and he crumpled to the floor.

The Paladin climbed through the window, swept the apartment with his gaze, and then crouched over his fallen adversary. He grabbed Tom by the shirt collar and growled into his face. "Tell me where I can find the Marauders."

"Wh-who the hell are you?" Tom coughed.

The Paladin slapped him hard across the face. "Answer me!" Tom's body went limp as he passed out from the shock of his broken nose. The Paladin let go of his collar and straightened up. *I came here for information,* he thought, *and so far I've got zilch. I have to make Tom talk before someone comes home and finds me.*

He pulled the handcuffs from his utility belt, dragged Tom into the kitchen, and cuffed him to the handle of the refrigerator. Then he removed a dirty glass from the dishwasher, filled it with water, and dashed the liquid in Tom's face.

Tom's eyes fluttered open. "Wh-what the hell are you doing?"

The Paladin jammed his forearm into the older

boy's throat. "Tell me where I can find the leader of the Marauders, or I swear to God I'll..." Jared paused. There was one constant among all the comic book heroes that he admired—they never killed.

He took a deep breath and let it out slowly. *If I kill this guy, I'm no better than the people that murdered Nick. For all I know, Tom could be the very person that cut Nick's throat.* Rage overwhelmed him, and Jared glared at Tom with cold fury. "Tell me where they are," the Paladin's voice was a low, menacing growl, "or I'll kill you."

Tom groaned and ignored him.

The Paladin's expression twisted into a snarl and he increased the pressure on his prisoner's throat. "Th-the Majestic," Tom croaked as he tried to force Jared's arm away with his free hand.

The memory of an abandoned movie theatre on the outskirts of downtown Carmel sprang to Jared's mind; he nodded. He released his chokehold, rose to his feet, and dialed 911.

"Emergency assistance, how can I help you?"

"I've captured a drug dealer. He's a member of the Marauders."

"Is this your idea of a joke?"

"No, ma'am. This is my idea of community service." He set the receiver on the counter and headed for the window. The front door of the apartment opened before he could escape, and a dark-skinned man strode in. He caught sight of Jared; their eyes

117

locked, and time screeched to a halt.

The man lunged forward as the Paladin yanked a throwing star from his belt and threw. The star whirled through the air in a perfect arc and sank into the man's forearm. He screamed. The Paladin made a beeline for the window, but before he could make good his escape, the man ripped the star from his arm and rushed across the room. Sharp pain exploded through Jared's midsection as the man's fist connected with his ribs. He collapsed, gasping for breath.

"You ain't gettin' out of here alive, punk." The man reached for him, but Jared rolled onto his back and kicked him in the balls. The man's eyes widened and he crumpled to the floor, cradling himself and whimpering like a dog.

You never see them do that in the comics, Jared thought as he scrambled to his feet. The sound of a gun being cocked captured his attention, and he froze.

"Wh-who are you?" said a quavering, female voice.

The Paladin felt his muscles ripple as adrenaline rushed through his veins.

"Answer me, or I swear to God I'll shoot you."

Jared's cheeks flushed with embarrassment under his mask. "I'm...the Paladin."

"Turn around. Slowly."

Jared obeyed and found himself staring down the barrel of snub-nosed revolver. A small woman in a hot pink sweat-suit held the gun with two trembling hands. *God,* Jared thought, *Tom looks just like his mother.*

Ms. Cole's dark hair fell in strands around a face that was almost pretty. "You're just a kid." she squinted her terrified eyes. "How old are you?"

"Old enough to have seen my brother murdered by the Marauders!"

The strange man staggered to his feet. "Kill that little fu—"

Ms. Cole turned the gun on him. "Is he telling the truth? Did your gang murder his brother?"

The man stopped moving and his eyes fastened themselves to the gun. "H-how the hell sh-should I know?" Tears spilled from the woman's eyes and her aim wavered.

The Paladin kicked the gun from her hand. She shrieked as the weapon clattered to the floor and discharged into the sofa.

The Paladin dashed for the window, dove through it, and scrambled for the fire escape. As he started down the ladder, sirens sounded in the distance. He panicked. His foot slipped on a wet rung and he fell toward certain death, but his cape caught on something as he neared the ground and arrested his plummet. It tightened around his throat and began to strangle him. Jared kicked frantically, and the fabric ripped loose; he dropped the remaining five feet and landed in some thick bushes. Climbing from the scrub, Jared gritted his teeth and rushed through the shadows toward his waiting bike. He climbed onboard and shoved off, pedaling frantically into the night as blue police lights turned into the Carmel Commons parking lot.

• • •

When I got home, I stashed my bike and costume in our shed. I was climbing back through a window I'd left unlatched on the ground floor when my mother spoke from the darkness. "Jared? What on earth are you doing?"

My heart sank when I realized that she was sitting in the dark on the corner of Nick's bed, waiting for me. Her face was almost indistinguishable in the darkened room, but I could feel her anger. I stared at her and couldn't think of anything to say.

"Do you think I'm stupid? When I got home and you weren't here, the first thing I did was check all the doors and windows. Imagine my surprise to find that Nick's window was unlatched." She stood and drew in a deep breath, like a dragon about to spit fire. "You saw what happened to Nick! Now you're acting just like him!"

"Mom, I..."

She stormed over to me and grabbed my face. "Listen to me, Jared." Her voice was low and quavering. "I know I'm not around as much as I wish I could be, but I love you more than anything. I loved Nick too, and now he's gone. What he did, that wasn't my Nicky. It was the drugs. And now you...you're..."

120

She started crying and I reached out to her, but she shoved my hands away. "Jared, you need to tell me what's going on."

A thrill of fear shot up my spine. "What do you mean, Mom?"

She leaned over Nick's desk and flipped a switch on the wall. The lights came on, burning my eyes. Then she produced a crumpled piece of paper from her pocket and shoved it in my face. "You used to be a good student, but now your grades are terrible. This is your report card, Jared. You have C's and D's in every subject but gym. How in the world do you get a D in art?"

I bowed my head, ashamed.

Mom caressed my cheek with a trembling hand. "Jared, I'm worried about you. You don't have any friends, and ever since Nicky...you've been be so dark... so morbid. Now I catch you sneaking into the house..."

I could see tears welling in her eyes and I reached out to her again. This time she didn't shove me away. She hugged me tightly and started sobbing. I stood there in my dead brother's room and held her as she wept.

"Mom, I'm not on drugs," I whispered. "I hate that crap, and the people that push it."

A slight smile formed at the corners of her lips. "I'm glad to hear you say that."

"And I'll try to do better in school; it's just...I can't stop thinking about what happened to Nick."

"I know," she said. "I know."

IT'S A BIRD! IT'S A PLANE!

"About tonight. I was...I was hanging out with a kid from school. I'm sorry I didn't ask permission first."

"You better be." Some of the fire returned to her eyes. "You're grounded from the comic store for a month."

"But Mom..." She clenched her jaw and I knew she wasn't backing down. I bowed my head and accepted her punishment.

When I finally got to bed, I couldn't sleep. I kept thinking about the Paladin's next move. I nearly died at Tom's apartment, but at least I had the location of the Marauder's hideout. It was after three in the morning before I drifted off to sleep.

• • •

When *Carmel Today* came out the following Wednesday, Jared was horrified to read about his exploits in the local crime report. The article, labeled *Masked Intruder*, was listed between a drug arrest and the results of a police checkpoint.

"I can't believe this," Jared muttered as he read the newspaper over a lonely dinner of mac and cheese. "I wanted to be a hero, and now look at me." He shoved a forkful of noodles into his mouth and chewed without tasting his meal. "Whatever. Before this is all over, I'll show everyone."

An opportunity came several days later, when his mother had to work a double-shift. Jared slipped out of the house, a spare key in his pocket, and headed downtown.

The Paladin arrived at the Majestic a little after

7 p.m. Carmel was wrapped in a cloak of shadows, and the air was bitterly cold. The antique theatre, unable to compete with newer multiplexes in the outlying suburbs, was boarded up and surrounded by other dilapidated relics of a bygone era.

The Paladin pedaled down a narrow alley and stopped at a heavy wooden door that led into the theatre. He stashed his bike behind a rusty dumpster, eased the door open, and slipped inside. An ancient staircase rose into the darkness. He swallowed his fear and forced himself to climb the stairs.

A few minutes later, he stood in a small, dark room that had once held projection equipment. Voices drifted to his ears from the room below and he tensed.

"...can't believe that shit. He thinks he's Captain America or something?"

"All I know is that if I ever run into the little bastard, I'll show him a thing or two."

Light came on in the theatre and streamed into the room through the open projection window; the Paladin peered through the tiny opening. Dusty curtains colored with alternating streaks of black and red covered the walls, and most of the original seats were still in place. He watched as the first few rows of the theatre began to fill with Marauders. *Thirteen...fourteen...fifteen. Damn! They must be having some kind of meeting.* His thoughts were interrupted when a broad-shouldered man in a leather trench coat entered the auditorium. The man's face, framed by long blond hair, was dark and cruel. The rest of the Marauders rose to their feet and began chanting "Griffon! Griffon!"

Griffon strode to the front, his coat swinging around his legs, and faced his men. "Sit down."

The Marauders shut up and obeyed. Griffon stuck his hands in his coat pockets. "I spoke with our benefactor tonight. He promised he'd get the heat off our backs now that Bryant's in jail."

The name tugged at Jared's memory for a minute until he remembered the drug bust he'd read about in the newspaper.

"Hey, Griffon," someone said. "What about this Paladin character?"

"What about him?"

"Is he for real, Boss?"

Griffon turned his head and spat on the floor. "Yeah, he's real."

"What are we gonna do about him?" Tom Cole's voice rang out from the back row.

Griffon's face grew stern. "You see him, I want you to bring him to me. I'll make sure he ain't no more trouble...to anyone. Understood?"

As the Paladin watched, his thoughts tormented him. *Last night was a train wreck, and it's all my fault. I wanted to be Robin, but look at me. Assault... breaking and entering...I'm not Robin, I'm the Punisher. And I'm not sure that's so wrong. The cops aren't doing anything, and I'm the only person in the world that cares that Nick's murder is still unsolved. I know I shouldn't sink to their level, but how do I fight a group whose entire purpose for existence is to do evil?* Jared's eyes traveled around the fragile curtains lining the theatre, and a grim smile crossed his face. *This place is ready to fall down...no one would miss it if it burned to the ground.*

Still smiling, the Paladin reached into his utility belt and removed his slingshot and the road flare he had taken from the trunk of his mother's car. He slunk back down the long set of stairs and crept into the auditorium. "This one's for you, Nick," he whispered in the darkness. Orange flames burst from the end of the flare as he slipped it into his slingshot, took aim at the ancient curtains, and fired. The curtains ignited like flash paper.

The Paladin turned and raced toward the exit while pandemonium broke out behind him. He was almost free when the door burst open and a thug with a shaved head and a post through his eyebrow stepped into his path. The Paladin lowered his shoulder and rammed the guard. The man took a step back as the Paladin bounced off of him and sprawled backward onto the floor.

The guard reached for a switchblade, but before he could flick it open, the Paladin yanked the pepper spray from his utility belt. He took a deep gulp of air, held his breath, and fired. The thug bent over and began coughing violently. The Paladin sprang to his feet, shoved past him, and dove out of the door. By that time, the rest of the Marauders were right behind him. Sharp pain exploded across his lower back as someone punched him in the kidneys; he collapsed to his knees. Hands grasped Jared's arms and dragged him to his feet. He squinted up at Griffon through the haze of pain.

A thin smile spread over the gangster's features as he drew back his fist and punched Jared in the guts. The Paladin's vision blurred as Griffon drew a curved dagger from a sheath hidden underneath his coat.

I'm sorry, Nick. I've failed you. Jared clenched his jaw and awaited death.

A gunshot echoed down the alleyway, and Griffon clutched at his right shoulder. His dagger clattered against the concrete. The Marauders let go, and the Paladin sank heavily to his knees. Desperate to escape, he began to crawl through the thick smoke that was pouring into the alley from the theatre.

Jared collapsed behind the dumpster at the end of the alley, and sucked in huge, burning gulps of air. *I'm alive. I can't believe I'm still alive. Now, how do I get out of here? The cops have the alley blocked, and I can't go through the theatre.*

He scanned what he could see of the alley, and his eyes lit on a small door that led into an abandoned restaurant. Jared grinned, struggled to his feet, and headed for it. "Please, God," he whispered. "Please let this open." His hand closed on the handle and he tugged. The door creaked open and relief flooded through him as he stepped into the building.

Cardboard boxes and musty blankets littered the floor of the old restaurant. *Looks like some homeless person has been living in here,* Jared thought as he wheeled his bike through the empty building. Once again, dark thoughts festered in his mind. *What am I doing? I wanted to bring down the Marauders, but the way things are going, maybe I should apply for membership.*

The Paladin forced himself to keep walking until he reached the front door of the restaurant. He peeked through the filthy glass and saw firemen and police moving around outside. Frightened and exhausted, the Paladin opened the front door and slipped onto the street. He was halfway down the block, pedaling furiously, when police sirens screamed to life behind him. Flashing blue lights filled the street as he swerved around a parked fire truck and poured on the speed.

The cop sped around the truck in hot pursuit.

Jared fled down the street, skidded around the corner of a busy intersection, and narrowly avoided a collision with a small sports car. The driver slammed on his brakes and fishtailed into the cop car as it came around the corner. Echoes of the crash pursued Jared as he turned down a side street and escaped into the night.

• • •

In spite of everything that happened that night, I managed to make it back home before my mom. I thought I was free and clear, but I was in for a surprise.

127

IT'S A BIRD! IT'S A PLANE!

Everyone was talking about the fire at the Majestic and the capture of the Marauders while my mom and I were at the mall the next day. We were listening to the radio on the way home, and I heard on the news that no one was injured when the police car crashed. I was so relieved. Then the newscaster said how much property damage I caused, and that made me feel like a heel. I'm sorry about that. Really. I didn't go into this intending to wreck a police car or to set a building on fire...things just got out of control. The police had the guys that murdered my brother, but it didn't bring Nick back from the dead. By the time we got home, I felt pretty rotten.

Mom had just left for work that night when there was a knock at the door. I opened it and found myself staring at Detective West, the cop who investigated Nick's murder. He was in his mid 40s, with graying hair and slightly rounded features. He looked kind of like a short, overweight Jimmy Stewart.

He looked back at me and hitched his thumbs behind his belt. "Hello, Jared. Mind if I come in?"

"My mom's not here right now."

"Actually, son, I'd like to have a word with you."

My heart was pounding so hard that I thought it was going to burst. "You...you want to talk to me?"

"Yes. Can I come in?"

"I don't...sure, I guess." I let him in, and tried not to look guilty.

West sank into a leather chair in the living room while I perched on the edge of the sofa. The detective leaned forward and rested his elbows on his knees. "Jared, I know you're the Paladin."

I swallowed and shook my head. "Mr. West, I don't know what you're..."

"Don't play games with me, son." The detective reached into his coat pocket and removed a pencil rendering of the Paladin that had appeared in the newspaper. "Look familiar?"

"No." My stomach leapt into my throat.

He smirked. "All right. How about this?" He removed a throwing star from another pocket and held it up. "I was assigned to investigate a break-in at Carmel Commons a few weeks ago. I couldn't believe my luck when I found a fingerprint on this. Guess what? It matches a print found at the scene of your brother's murder...yours."

"What? I thought..."

"...that we wouldn't keep your prints on file after you and your mother were cleared of suspicion? Come on, kid, your brother's case is still open." West sat back in his chair and smiled. "I've got you, Jared."

I winced, then stared at the floor and tried to think of something to say.

"I should arrest you right now," the detective said. "You've committed a list of crimes as long as my arm: breaking and entering, assault with a deadly weapon, arson, destruction of property...not to mention taking the law into your own hands."

I felt tears welling in my eyes. What would my mother say if she saw me carted off to jail?

"That said, there are certain" —he paused, searching for the right word— "advantages to working outside the law."

I stared at Detective West. "What are you saying?"

"Jared, right now I'm the only person who knows you're the Paladin. Legally, it's my responsibility to place you under arrest. But I'm not going to do that." I stared at him, disbelieving. "Nobody got hurt who didn't deserve it. You damaged some property, but I'm willing to overlook all that if you'll do something for me."

"Something?"

West scratched behind his left ear. "The Marauders weren't working alone in Carmel," he said at last. "They had some help from someone on the inside."

"A benefactor," I said, recalling the little bit of the meeting I overheard. "I heard Griffon talking about a benefactor right before I..."

"Good. Then you know that it wasn't just some low-life hoods that murdered your brother. Oh, they did the actual killing, but it was to profit someone much higher up on the food chain."

"Who?" An edge of bitterness crept into my voice.

"Now, son, if you want to know that, you're going to have to agree to play the game...my way."

"What do you want from me?" I demanded.

"I want you to help me bring down the Marauders' benefactor." West's jaw clenched with fury. "Everything I have on him is circumstantial, but I know who he is, and I know what he's capable of. I can't just barge into his house and start looking for evidence, but if I get a 911 call because the Paladin is there..."

"You want me to set it up so that you can arrest this guy? Who is he?"

"Someone important." Detective West leaned forward, and I could see righteous anger burning in his eyes. "I'm sick of busting my ass every day for nothing because somebody with connections is getting their palms greased. I'm sick of it, and now that I've got you, I can finally do something about it."

"I almost died last night. Do you really think I want to risk my life again?" I was still aching from the beating I'd received, but that wasn't the reason I was holding back with Detective West. I wanted more than anything to destroy Griffon and anyone even remotely connected with that murdering son-of-a-bitch. What I was afraid of was that this was some kind of trap. Maybe West was lying about the fingerprint.

"Jared," he said. "I'm not giving you a choice here. I don't think it would be hard for me to make your life a living hell. Now, I need you to do what I ask, or I'm going to have to take you down to the station."

I stared at him in horror. "You're serious?"

"I don't know for certain, but I'd wager that you became the Paladin to exact revenge on the people who murdered your brother. Am I right?"

I nodded.

"I'm giving you the opportunity to do just that. Now all you have to do is take it. Otherwise, you can say hello to your new home at Juvenile Hall." Our eyes met, and I could see that he was serious.

"I'll do it," I said, realizing that I was out of options. "Now tell me who this benefactor is."

"That's a good boy," said West. He smiled a satisfied smile. "The rumors have been buzzing for years now, but there's never been any way to prove it. The man were going after is Ed Dixon, the Deputy-Mayor."

Everything turned black. "The Deputy-Mayor? He's involved with the Marauders?"

"Yes. I've been trying to bring him down forever, and now I'm finally going to do it. And, Jared, there's something else. I don't know if you've been paying attention to the news, but Griffon was released on bail about two hours ago."

My blood froze. "Released?"

"Wanna take a guess where the money came from?"

I shook my head, disbelieving. "That's crazy."

"It's not crazy," West snapped, "it's bullshit. This town was like Mayberry when I came here 15 years ago, and now look at it. Drugs...crooked politicians... I'm sick of standing by and watching my town go to hell. That's why I need you."

I was furious...I wanted to kill Griffon. The thought that he could get out of jail just like that while

Nick was lying cold in the ground made me crazy—if Griffon had walked into my house right then, I swear I would have cut his throat. "I hate this $#@!# town!" I balled my hand into a fist and punched the sofa's wooden armrest. Pain shot up my arm, but I didn't care.

Detective West ignored my outburst. He rose and walked over to the door. "I'll be in touch soon. Until then, I want you to get healthy, keep in shape, and stay out of trouble."

I stared at his back as he let himself out. After several minutes, I headed upstairs to my room, feeling as low and as lonely as I'd ever been in my life.

• • •

Thanksgiving came and went with hardly a whimper. As the weeks passed, as Jared's body healed and his thoughts simmered with revenge, he began to wonder when Detective West was going to call in the Paladin for his secret mission. "I hope it's soon," he muttered as he slammed his locker door and headed for his school bus. Carmel Middle School had just let out for Christmas break, and Jared was now facing the prospect of two lonely weeks at home.

I wish Nick were still here, he thought. Memories of his brother bombarded the teenager's mind. It's been over a year now...I wonder if I'll ever stop thinking about him. He climbed the steps into the bus and flopped into the first available seat. Pulling the latest issue of *Nightwing* from his book bag, he began to read. He was on page 3 when he registered a flurry of brown plaid from the corner of his eye. Looking up, his eyes fell on Shannon White, a pretty brunette who sat behind him in English, as she walked past. A minute later, she was standing over him, her green eyes sparkling behind a pair of glasses.

"Hi, Jared," she said pleasantly. "Can I sit here?"

"Sure." Jared moved his book bag out of the way.

"The bus is full today," she said as she sat down.

Jared stared at his comic, but he couldn't concentrate. Shannon was sitting right beside him—she was so close that he could feel it every time she took a breath. *I wish I had the courage to say something to her,* he thought. He stole a glance at her over the top of *Nightwing*. She was sitting with her hands folded in her lap, a pair of white earbud headphones plugged into her ears and a little pink iPod clipped to her skirt; he quickly turned back to his comic, not wanting to get caught staring.

The bus began to roll, heading into the sprawling suburbs surrounding the school. After several minutes, Jared heard Shannon stifle a sob. "Are you all right?" he asked before he realized what he was doing.

Shannon, who was clearly fighting back tears, smiled strangely. She pressed the pause button on her iPod and plucked one of the earbuds from her ear. "I'm fine," she said, with just a touch of amusement in her voice. "I'm listening to an audio book... *Bridge to Terabithia.* It's really sad."

"I read that book," said Jared. "It was sad."

Both Jared and Shannon stared at the seat in front of them, saying nothing. *At least she didn't tell me to drop dead,* he thought. "Well, sorry to bother you," he said after the silence grew uncomfortable.

"It's okay," said Shannon. She sounded nervous. "It was sweet of you to..." She looked away, her cheeks flushing pink.

Jared glanced out the window and noticed Carmel Baptist Church, which marked the halfway point of his ride home. *I wish this ride would last forever,* he thought as Shannon shifted beside him.

"What are you reading?" she asked.

"*Nightwing.*"

"I've never heard of him."

"He was the original Robin. When he grew up, he became his own man and..." Jared realized how geeky he sounded and stopped talking.

Shannon smiled, and Jared's heart leapt into his throat. "Go on. What were you saying?"

"He...he became his own man and took on a new identity. He and Batman had some father/son issues for a while, but they got over it."

Shannon nodded as if she understood. "Did you see *Batman Begins*?"

"Yeah."

IT'S A BIRD! IT'S A PLANE!

"I kept thinking about something after saw that movie. Here's a guy who saw his parents get murdered. A tragedy to say the least, but to Bruce Wayne, it becomes an obsession. He spends every waking moment with one image in his head—the dead bodies of his parents. When he becomes a man, what kind of man is he?" Shannon paused. "He's a monster. He can't have normal relationships with people because they might find out his secret. He doesn't even like other people; he can't relate to them, and they can't relate to him. Batman isn't the mask he wears; the mask is Bruce Wayne."

"You just described the plot of most of the Batman comics from the past 20 years." Jared smiled uncontrollably. *I can't believe I'm having this conversation with Shannon White. She's so hot!*

"Here's what I wonder," Shannon continued. "What do you think Bruce Wayne's parents would have wanted for their son? Do you think they'd be happy to know that their only child spent his life obsessed with the tragedy of their deaths?" She shook her head. "They would have wanted him to be happy, to meet a nice girl, and settle down."

"Like Spiderman?"

"Yeah. Spiderman has it together, and he's cute in a geeky kind of way."

The bus stopped and half a dozen kids stood up. "This is my stop," Jared said. "I...it was nice to...to talk with you."

"You, too," said Shannon. She was biting her lower lip.

"Hope you have a good Christmas." Jared shoved *Nightwing* back into his bag and rose to his feet.

"Merry Christmas," said Shannon. She slid out of the way, allowing Jared to pass.

As he climbed from the bus and began the short walk to his house, Jared felt the weight of the world had been lifted from his shoulders. Smiling for the first time in weeks, he turned into his driveway and headed to the front door.

Later that night, as Jared was checking his email, he saw a message from an address he didn't recognize. Normally, he would have just deleted the message, but he simple couldn't ignore the subject line: RE: The Paladin.

Jared opened the email and quickly read the cryptic message. *Thursday night. 8:30. Meet me in the tunnel under Seldon Island Road.*

• • •

Every kid in Carmel knows about the tunnel under Seldon Island Road. It's a huge, concrete monstrosity that allows some nameless little creek to pass under the road. The tunnel has been a refuge and a hideout to kids ever since it was built. It's the kind of place where middle-schoolers meet to have fights and high-schoolers meet to make out.

I was ready for a fight when I arrived at the tunnel. As happy as my conversation with Shannon had made me, it was nothing compared to how happy I thought I would be once I brought the people responsible for Nick's murder to justice.

Detective West was already in the tunnel, waiting for me. He wore a heavy wool overcoat and had a scarf tied around his neck. "Hey kid," he said. "Glad you could make it. Are you ready to beat the bad guys?"

I frowned at him, my muscles trembling beneath my Paladin costume. I pulled my cape tightly around my shoulders, but it was no replacement for a winter coat.

"According to my source, the Deputy-Mayor is having a business meeting in his house tomorrow night," West said, dispensing with any pleasantries. "You're going to crash the party. Are you with me so far?"

I nodded.

"He lives on King Street...number 52, the big white house. Here, I drew you a map." He handed me a folded piece of paper that I stuffed into a pocket of my cargo pants. "Dixon's bedroom is in back of the house, on the second floor—I think that's probably your best point of entry. The room will probably be empty during the meeting, and that should buy you a little bit of time to get yourself situated before you have to start fighting."

"Probably?"

West ignored my comment. "The house is rigged

with a state-of-the-art security system. As soon as you break the glass, the alarm company will call the house and hear all the commotion you're stirring up. Right after that, they'll place a 911 call and my officers will be dispatched to the scene."

"How long will I have before the cops arrive?"

"Five minutes. No more than ten."

I thought about it for a minute. "How the hell am I supposed to break through a window on the second floor?"

"There's a huge maple tree right next to the house," said West. "Just climb up the tree..."

"Then what? Jump across the gap like Superman? Are you trying to get me killed?"

The detective stared at me, frustration on his face. "You know that I'm not." He smiled. "I brought you Christmas presents. You should be able to put these to good use." He handed me a backpack.

"What's in here?" I asked.

"Check it out."

I opened the pack and found several items that even Robin would have envied. Detective West had provided a taser wand and a grapnel gun. "You want me to swing across the Deputy-Mayor's back yard like Batman?"

"You are wearing a mask and a cape."

"This plan sounds pretty stupid," I said. "It's been weeks. Couldn't you come up with something better?"

"These things are all about timing," West said. "I just got this tip yesterday. Besides, I don't think you're any stranger to dangerous situations. Here, let me show you how to use that stuff."

I removed both items from the bag and West instructed me on their basic operation. "What about Griffon?" I asked after a few minutes. "Any word?"

West turned to me, a look of deadly seriousness in his eyes. "I have every reason to believe that Griffon will be there tomorrow."

"What if he is there? Are the cops just going to let him walk away again?"

I'm sure Detective West could see the hatred in my face. Placing a hand on my shoulder, he leaned close to me. "I'm leaving his fate up to you," he said. "But I want you to think about it before you decide to sink to his level. You don't want to be a killer, Jared. Once you walk down that road, there's no coming back."

"Are you saying that you won't arrest me if I give that bastard what he deserves?"

West took a deep breath, letting it out slowly. "Just don't do anything stupid. You're a good kid. Maybe if this all works out, you can help me out again." He walked me to the end of the tunnel. "You've got all day tomorrow; why don't you come back down here and practice with your new toys?"

"Sure," I muttered. "I'll do that." I stepped from the tunnel and never looked back. As I raced home, my only thoughts were of vengeance.

• • •

The home of Edmund Dixon was one of the

most beautiful mansions in Carmel. Built in the 1920s, the house stood out in drastic contrast to the Victorian homes that lined the rest of King Street. Three stories tall with a flat roof and two chimneys, the structure was an ivory tower that symbolized the American Dream to most of the residents of the historic town.

To the Paladin, standing in a tree in the Deputy-Mayor's back yard, the house represented everything that was wrong with Carmel, with the United States, with the world.

Twenty feet above the ground, Jared closed his eyes and said a little prayer to his brother's ghost. "Help me get through this," he whispered into the night. "Help me make things right."

He opened his eyes. The time for praying and planning was done; now was the time for vengeance. Moving silently, the Paladin unzipped his backpack and removed the grapnel gun. He took aim, bracing his shaking right hand with his left, and fired at the roof of Dixon's house. The grapnel coiled around a pipe protruding from the roof. After several stiff tugs, Jared was sure that the line wasn't coming loose. "Now or never," he whispered. Then he wrapped the line twice around his wrists, drew his hood low over his face, and leapt out of the tree.

The Paladin's cape rippled behind him as he swung across the open expanse. Glass exploded into the room as he crashed, feet first, through the Deputy-Mayor's window. Jared was barely able to keep his balance, yet he somehow managed to land on his feet. He shook off hundreds of tiny shards of glass, thankful that his hood and long clothing had protected him from all but a handful of minor scratches. Jared looped his rope over the bedpost as he surveyed Dixon's bedroom. The room was opulent, with a king-sized bed, a huge flat-panel TV, and ornate furniture.

"What in the hell is going on up there?"

The Paladin drew the taser wand from his utility belt and flattened himself against the wall next to the door. Moments later, a gigantic man in an expensive suit flung the door open and entered the room. The Paladin pressed the button on the taser, twisted around, and jabbed the wand into the giant's chest. The man stiffened, his hair stood on end, and he collapsed to the ground, twitching.

Jared slipped into the hallway just as two more thugs came rushing up the stairs. Before they could react, the Paladin hit the closer of the two with his taser. The man collapsed backward into his partner; both men tumbled down the stairs and crashed through a railing into the main foyer. They lay unconscious on the ceramic tile floor.

Griffon rushed into view, his gun drawn, before Jared could duck out of sight. The gangster glared at him, and fired up the stairs. The Paladin rolled out of the way just as a bullet splintered the doorframe of one of the spare bedrooms.

Inside the darkened bedroom, the Paladin

waited as Griffon clomped up the stairs. He paused at the top, just a few inches away, on the other side of the wall. He was so close that Jared could hear his labored breathing. The Paladin fingered the button of the taser. A second later, both combatants spun into the open doorway. Griffon, his gun raised, fired into the bedroom, but the Paladin had ducked low, and the shot zipped over his head. Crouched at Griffon's waist, the Paladin saw his chance and took it. He jabbed his taser wand into the gangster's ribs and pressed the button. Electricity jolted through Griffon, who collapsed to his knees, his pistol clattering to the floor.

The Paladin rose, tucking the taser back into his utility belt. As he did, he noticed the dagger sheathed at Griffon's side. An image of Nick's mutilated body exploded in Jared's mind. All of the rage and hatred that had been building in him since his brother's death overflowed the banks of his self-control, and before Jared knew what he was doing, he grabbed Griffon's dagger. Lifting it high over his head with both hands, the Paladin stood over his fallen opponent. "Now you pay for what you did to my brother," he said. But before he could strike a killing blow, Shannon's sweet green eyes and pretty smile floated in the air before him.

He hesitated. *What am I doing? This bastard deserves death...deserves to die, to drown in his own blood...but if I do this, then what? I become the Punisher and spend the rest of my life creeping around in the shadows stalking thugs and gangsters. What would my mother think? The Marauders already turned one of her kids into a corpse; now they're about to turn the other into a murderer. And Shannon? She'll hate me once she finds out what a monster I've become.*

As the Paladin's mind teetered on the edge of a knife, Griffon began to regain control of his trembling muscles. While his opponent's attention was momentarily diverted, the Marauder drove his foot into Jared's crotch. The Paladin dropped the dagger and collapsed, holding himself in agony.

Rising, Griffon snatched up the dagger, grabbed Jared by the hair, and dragged him to his knees. In desperation, Jared grabbed Griffon's wrist with both hands and bit down as hard as he could. The gangster screamed and stepped backward, letting go of the Paladin's hair. Jared, operating on pure adrenaline, staggered to his feet and rushed Griffon. They collided at the top of the staircase, and before either could grab a handhold, they both went careening down the stairs. They landed in the foyer, right on top of the unconscious gangsters Jared had dispensed with earlier. There was a terrible crack as the back of Griffon's head smacked against the tile floor.

Bruised and battered but otherwise uninjured, the Paladin was the first to his feet. Fury still burning in his veins, he leapt on top of Griffon's prone form and began throwing wild punches at the man responsible for his brother's death. "I hate you," Jared screamed. "You son-of-a-bitch, I hate you."

Griffon held his arms over his face, attempting to block the assault, but finally the Paladin was able to land a solid blow to his enemy's face. Blood sprayed as Griffon's nose exploded. Jared, now almost feral with rage, couldn't stop himself—he kept punching until Griffon's eyes rolled back and he collapsed against the floor in a broken, bloodied heap.

Finally, panting with exhaustion, the Paladin ceased his attack. He checked Griffon's pulse; he was still alive. His bloodlust subsiding, Jared made his decision. "I'm not going to become like you," he said. "You murdered my brother, but I'm not going to let you destroy my life. You can rot in prison for all I care, but I'm never going to think about you again."

Jared stood, began to turn around, and froze. A small-framed man with thinning hair stood in the foyer, a pistol trained on the Paladin. Somewhere in the distance, Jared heard a wailing noise that might have been a police siren.

"Turn around, Batboy," said the Deputy-Mayor, "and don't try anything stupid. I don't want to shoot you, but I will if you make me." He cocked his pistol's hammer to emphasize his point.

The Paladin, who was desperately retrieving a flash bomb from his utility belt, had no choice but to comply. He closed his eyes, turned, and in one fluid motion released the flash bomb in his right hand.

The tiny ball exploded on impact, filling the room with blinding light.

"What the..."

Opening his eyes, Jared saw Edmund Dixon still standing before him, momentarily stunned. The flash bought the Paladin only a few seconds, but that was enough. He rushed at the Deputy-Mayor and knocked the pistol from his hand. Jared followed through with the attack, spinning around and delivering a solid elbow to Dixon's jaw.

The Deputy-Mayor went down hard, but Jared did not relent. He grabbed Dixon by the collar and dragged him into a sitting position. "You're about to pay for your crimes, asshole." The Paladin hocked and spat in the politician's face.

Edmund Dixon snorted bitterly, his eyes burning with hatred. He opened his mouth, revealing two rows of bloody teeth. "I'm going to walk away from this situation looking like the victim," he said. "And you're going to be the most wanted criminal in Carmel."

Jared tried not to show his emotions, but the words stung deeply. "You don't know what you're talking about. The people of this town need someone like me. They need someone with the balls to stand up against corrupt politicians..."

Dixon laughed. "You're so naive. There's someone like me in every town in the United States. Don't give me that holier-than-thou bullshit."

I should teach him a lesson, Jared thought. He

drew back a fist, ready to punch the Deputy-Mayor again, but he was struck with a sudden horrible revelation. *He's right. I don't prove anything by beating him up. Sure, it makes the pain of Nick's death go away for a few seconds, but what good has the Paladin done for Carmel? Because of me, the Majestic is in ruins, a couple of cars are in the body shop, and some of low-level crooks spent a few nights in jail. I would have done more good for my town by volunteering at the library.*

Edmund Dixon stared at the Paladin, his face a mask of disgust. "Real life isn't like the funny books, punk. If I weren't in the picture, it would just be someone else. That's how the real world works."

"Well, the real world sucks! It shouldn't..." Before he could finish speaking, the front door of the Deputy-Mayor's house shuttered with the force of a police officer's kick. Abandoning his sermon, the Paladin leapt over the prone bodies of the Marauders and raced up the stairs to the second floor. He heard the door cave in as he slipped through the darkness into Dixon's bedroom, stepping over the first man he had dispatched.

"He's upstairs!" Dixon shouted. "Get him!" Heavy footsteps started up the stairs.

His heart thundering, Jared grabbed his rope and climbed through the empty window into the night. He scurried down the line, letting go just a few feet from the ground. *Here I go again,* Jared though as he landed in Dixon's boxwoods.

IT'S A BIRD! IT'S A PLANE!

"Down there!" someone shouted from the window above. But the Paladin was already racing across the lawn, his hood blown back and his cape fluttering behind him. He was gone before the cops could converge on him.

• • •

Everything turned out differently than I expected. When the cops arrived, they found drugs and huge sums of money in the Deputy-Mayor's kitchen. Apparently Dixon and his cronies didn't have time to hide what they were doing because I kept everyone occupied until the police showed up. Everyone in the house was arrested, and now they're all awaiting trial.

Detective West showed up at my house the following day; he was smiling like he'd just taken a hit of Joker-gas.

"You did a good job last night," he said. "You know, there's a lot more good you could do for Carmel. Just because we got the bad guys this time doesn't mean there won't be others. What do you think, kid?"

"I don't know. I've been thinking about asking out this girl."

He winked at me, and I felt like punching him in the nose. "You've earned it, kid. But who knows, maybe I'll be in touch one of these days."

I hope not.

I wish I could tell you that everything has changed, but it hasn't. I still think about Nick every day. I thought revenge would make my pain go away, but I guess the only thing that can do that is time.

Now we've come to the end of the story, but I have one more thing to say before I go. When I got back to school, I asked Shannon White if she wanted to hang out sometime. I was about as nervous as I'd ever been in my life, and I was sure she was going to say no. To my amazement, however, she didn't.

She said yes!

We've been seeing each other for a couple of weeks now. I'm sure our middle school relationship looks ridiculous to just about everybody, but I really don't care. We may not end up getting married or anything like that, but what we have means a lot to me. When I'm with Shannon, I don't think about what happened to Nick, or the way it felt to hold my own mother when she was crying. Shannon makes all the bad things in the world go away for a little while, and that's why I like her so much.

I had my fourteenth birthday a few days ago. Shannon came over, and, instead of playing video games or studying, we decided to go for a walk. We started talking, and before I knew what I was doing, I admitted to Shannon that I was the Paladin. I don't think she believed me at first, but when I showed her the costume, as well as some yellowing bruises, she began to change her mind.

It was her idea for me to write this essay. She thought it would be good for me—that it would give me a sense of closure. I've been working on it for a few days, and now that I'm almost done, I guess she was *right.*

I've decided to retire from crime fighting, at least for the time being. I'll never forget what I was able to accomplish as the Paladin, but I don't want to live my life in the shadows. I hate what I was becoming. Putting on that mask gave me license to do things I never would have considered before. It scares me to think of what might happen if I ever did it again.

I was hoping that everything would be different when I returned to school after Christmas break. No more bullies; no more drugs—but nothing changed. I guess that's how it goes. It's like what Shannon was trying to tell me about Batman. The only person you can change is yourself. I'm turning my back on all the stuff that's making this world such a piece of crap. Popularity. Crime. Politics. Constant reinforcement of those things will only bring me down, and I don't want to wallow in my own misery any more. I'm choosing to live. That's what Nick would have wanted.

A Word from Kevin G. Summers

The story you just read, "The Paladin," has been around the block a few times and this isn't its first appearance in an anthology. It was originally featured in *Lords of Justice* anthology and then reprinted *A Thousand Faces, the Quarterly Journal of Superhuman Fiction*: Issue #13. I even released the story as a solo ebook and audiobook before Steve Beaulieu (pronounced Bowl-Your) asked me if he could reprint it in this anthology. Hopefully Jared Weiss has found some new fans as *It's A Bird! It's a Plane!* makes its way in the world. If you look closely, you'll find that "The Paladin" is full of references to comics and pop-culture... hopefully you enjoyed finding them as much as I did including them.

My first published fiction was the critically acclaimed short story "Isolation Ward 4", set in the Star Trek universe. After writing several other Star Trek stories for Pocket Books, I took the plunge into indie publishing with *Legendarium*, co-written with the well-known Michael Bunker. Rumor has it that there will be a Legendarium 2 someday, but I wouldn't hold your breath, unless you can hold it until maybe Fall 2017.

This anthology isn't my first foray with Steve Beaulieu (pronounced Bo-Lew), he was also my editor on *In Your Closet, In Your Head: A Monster Anthology*. When I'm not writing for Steve Beaulieu (pronounced Bee-awl-E-you), I've also written a number of other stories, including *The Bleak December*, a tale of supernatural horror set in the Great North Woods of New Hampshire, and *The Man Who Shot John Wilkes Booth*, a weird western about one of the strangest characters in American history.

I live on a working dairy farm, in a house built in 1910 by refugees from that time the federal government stole a bunch a land to make the Shenandoah National Park. I milk cows twice a day, every day, 366 days a year. When you're still asleep in your bed, there's a good chance that I'm out in the dark, milking cows and thinking about my next book, which in this case happens to be a space opera set on a starship called Gilead.

You can write to me c/o The Crowfoot Farm, Amissville, Rappahannock County, Virginia, United States of America, Continent of North America, Western Hemisphere, the Earth, the Solar System, the Universe, the Mind of God; or you can visit my website: www.kevingsummers.com.

CLEANVIEW

AARON HALL & STEVE BEAULIEU

EARNEST GROANED as he wheeled the cart down the hallway. Being a janitor wasn't the most physically demanding job in the world, but after doing it for three decades Ernest's body creaked and ached. His wife was always telling him to retire, that enough was enough. Ernest knew she didn't really care that much, she was just sick of him complaining every day. Besides, his wasn't a job you walked away from. He heard a story once about how all the secretaries and janitors at Google were millionaires. Ernest wasn't a millionaire, but his six-figure salary allowed him to live more comfortably than most janitors. It allowed him to put a daughter through college. Even if that daughter never called and always seemed to be busy working on all the major holidays when families normally got together.

Ernest paused as he passed a doorway, something on the floor catching his eye. He pulled a spray bottle and a rag off the cart and knelt. Something in his leg made a popping noise.

155

IT'S A BIRD! IT'S A PLANE!

He knew what the substance was right away, had cleaned up buckets of it in his time working here. As he sprayed and then wiped up the blood he was reminded that he didn't work for some tech company. The janitors at Google may have billionaires for bosses, but Ernest had some pretty powerful bosses himself. And they'd had themselves a rough night.

Satisfied that all traces of the blood were gone, Ernest stood, stifling another groan, and put the bottle back on the cart. He tossed the rag into a trash bag, then continued pushing the cart. He rounded a corner. Another massive hallway stretched out before him. The base was privately funded and shrouded in mystery. Everyone knew of it, but few had been in it. It stood as a beacon of hope and justice, located right on the outskirts of the San Fernando Valley, hundreds of miles south of Google. This was where the big boys took care of business.

Ernest entered the first room on his right—a medium-sized cafeteria. It was his favorite room in the entire base. It reminded him of the little cafeteria in his elementary school. When he'd been a little immigrant boy struggling to learn the language and the culture, he'd never struggled to understand lunch. Life had been simpler then. Before the world had met its first superhero.

So many people idolized the supers, but soon after the first heroes came the first villains. Ernest didn't blame the heroes—not in the least. He'd benefited from their presence far more than just the weekly paycheck. But much of the world hadn't experienced salvation at their hands, only destruction as the villains emerged. Nonetheless, although Ernest wasn't a man of notable intellect, he was smart enough to see what was right in front of him. The early heroes stopped bank robbers and put out fires and stopped cruise ships from sinking after they hit an iceberg. Twenty years later the heroes were fending off alien invasions, battling back reality-bending villains and trying to stop zombies from taking over South America. Something had changed in the world —intensified, exponentially. Ernest wasn't smart enough to know what it was, but he was smart enough to know *that* it was.

He remembered life without the superheroes. Tragedies happened from time to time back then too. Wildfires, serial killers, bad things. It all seemed sort of trivial now, though, compared to the sort of bad things that went on these days. Compared to the witch who just this morning had come back from the dead, put a death hex on an entire neighborhood, killing everyone who'd ever lived there instantaneously no matter where they lived now, before making her way into downtown and fusing together hundreds of cars on the highway, people inside and all, into a monstrous beast that had rampaged across the city, wiping out anyone and anything it came into contact with. The heroes killed it, eventually. It and everyone trapped inside the cars that made up its body.

A lot of people had died. But in spite of it all,

IT'S A BIRD! IT'S A PLANE!

Ernest was thankful for the supers.

Ernest reminded himself he was just the janitor and flicked on the light in the cafeteria. There were several pieces of trash on the floor near a trashcan. He bent down and scooped them up, then pulled the bag and replaced it with a fresh one. Turning to survey the state of the rest of the cafeteria, Ernest jumped as his eyes fell upon someone sitting at a nearby table.

His heart was pounding in his chest. Even though he'd been cleaning their base since they were established a decade ago, Ernest had never once run into one of the superheroes—it was his dream to meet one, and today his dream came true in the most incredible of ways. It was him.

Their identities, the sensitivity of what they discussed, the possible danger of just being around them, all of these had factored into the decision to restrict cleaning times to hours when the base was deserted. The security system wasn't supposed to even allow Ernest to unlock doors if a hero was in the base, alerting him immediately if one arrived while he was already inside. Yet sitting before him, until a moment ago all alone in the dark, was the leader of the team. A hulking mountain of a man, his physique so perfect that perfect felt like an inadequate way of describing it. Normally wearing an inspirational outfit of white and gold and a smile, the hero known as The Royal was shirtless, stripped down to a simple pair of exercise shorts. But there was no mistaking, it was him. He had a bloody gash across his chest, with smaller cuts crisscrossing it. Seeing that kind of damage on The Royal told Ernest just how serious the fight against the witch and her car monstrosity must have been. Most people believed The Royal to be invulnerable.

Realizing he needed to make a hasty exit, Ernest raised his hands and slowly started to back toward the door.

"I'm sorry to have disturbed you," Ernest said.

As The Royal made the slightest of movements, Ernest realized that the hero hadn't even been aware of his presence until this moment. His eyes had a faraway look in them as if he was still barely present in the moment. It looked as if the man hadn't moved in hours, a now-warm soda sitting before him, unopened.

"What?" The Royal asked.

He blinked several times, then spoke again, this time more forcefully.

"Who are you?"

For a moment, Ernest froze. Visions of getting fired and having to explain to his wife how it hadn't been his fault as she screamed at him, asking how he could've been so stupid, played in his mind. But his wife he could deal with later, right now there was a super man sitting before him that he needed to answer.

"Ernest Altamirano."

He let it hang in the air for a moment, then felt silly. The name alone wouldn't mean much to the most powerful man on the planet.

"I'm the janitor," he added, gesturing to his cart.

The Royal's head shifted slightly in the direction of the cart.

"We have a janitor?"

The same sentence out of the mouth of someone else might've been received as an insult, but Ernest just smiled politely. He pointed to multiple areas of the room that were dirty.

"You do," he said. "Normally the security system doesn't allow me inside if any of the...if any of you are here."

The Royal was unreadable, never truly looking at Ernest—but for the briefest of moments, a look of annoyance passed across his face.

"I disabled it. The thing kept—" He shook his head, almost dismissing the banality of what they were discussing. "It kept beeping so I blew it up with a mind pulse."

"Oh," Ernest said, looking around the room to see if he could spot the inevitable mess such a move would've created.

He didn't see anything, and it was likely best left for another time, anyway. No matter what had caused it, his run-in with The Royal needed to be kept as brief as possible if he hoped to keep his job.

"I'm going to come back and finish later. Once you've gone home," Ernest said.

He moved toward the exit, surprised when the hero's voice called after him.

"That's a stupid rule. You're here now, no reason not to do what you need to do."

Ernest paused. His bosses weren't going to be happy with him if he stayed in the base while one of the heroes were around, but saying no to The Royal didn't feel like a wise decision. Besides, it *was* a stupid rule, there was clearly no danger to be feared here or secrets to be discovered. Just a dirty room and a janitor with a job to do.

And a godlike being, staring at nothing, his mind a million miles away.

The elderly janitor turned back and nodded politely at The Royal.

"I'll be quick."

The hero was already lost in his own thoughts again. He didn't even seem to register that Ernest had spoken.

The janitor hastily cleaned, uncomfortable in his current situation. After a few minutes, the silence was broken.

"You know," The Royal said, "the world was close to ending today."

Ernest looked up from his dustpan. The Royal was still staring ahead, not in the janitor's direction.

"Yeah?" Ernest said with uncertainty.

"Not the first time either." He shook his head. "Salem used to be one of us. Now, she is a nasty blotch in human history."

Ernest was surprised by the amount of anger he could sense in The Royal's voice. Salem was one of the newer members of the team, and her usage of the dark arts had made her one of the most controversial superheroes around. After what she'd done tonight, it seemed people had been right in being wary of her.

"It never ceases to amaze me when a person can take the gift they've been blessed with and use it against their fellow man."

Since The Royal was still staring at nothing in particular, Ernest wasn't completely sure if the superhero was even talking to him. He figured the only way to find out was to ask.

"Are you...talking to me, sir?"

"Yes, yes. I'm sorry—there's something many people don't know about me," he said.

Was this super man really about to divulge secrets to the janitor? Ernest couldn't begin to answer that question, but he was suddenly very uneasy.

"I am blind." His head jerked toward the janitor and for the first time in their conversation, Ernest had enough wits about him to notice that The Royal wasn't wearing his patented headgear. Ernest had always assumed it was just another way to conceal his identity, but the hero always wore a half face mask and crown. The mask had no eye holes, but Ernest, like everyone else, figured it was made from a special fabric that had allowed him to see through it —or that The Royal had x-ray vision.

The revelation that the superhero was blind brought a new sense of wonder to the janitor. How had he done all the amazing feats without one of his senses? Much less, one as important as sight?

"Do you know what I am not blind to?"

Ernest realized after some silence that The Royal wasn't going to continue until he received a response.

"No, sir?"

"I am not blind to the injustice—the inequality of it all. Why should some of us be trusted with gifts that make us gods? Why should I be any different from any other blind man who's ever lived? Why should I be able to tap into a sixth sense? Be allowed to see without truly seeing? And why should Salem continue to be allowed to work her charms and spells when she is using them to bring destruction upon the world?"

Ernest sat down at the table closest to him—several tables away from The Royal. He wanted to listen, but he couldn't bring himself to sit at the same table as the hero. It wasn't that he felt less than—but different from.

"Thousands died tonight. We shed all that blood, and for what? In the end, it's meaningless."

The Royal's words were bleak. His voice seemed to defy logic, to drain some of the light from the room. The feeling of despair that settled on the cafeteria was simply too heavy, and Ernest felt as if he had to respond.

"But thousands more would have died had it not been for you," he said in a low voice.

"It is my fault Salem went evil," he said. "I pushed her. I drove her to this. It was me."

His fist slammed and sent a ripple through the hard plastic, cracking it in two.

"If I hadn't sent her after The Sister Sect they would never have manipulated her into believing

163

this was her divine right. It was my call. I believed her magic would be the best weapon against theirs. I could have called down fire from the heavens and rained *justice* upon them. But instead, I sent her and The Pentacle. One died, and the other should have."

Ernest stood and mustered the courage to go and sit at the broken table with the broken super-hero.

"Every event is seen from multiple viewpoints," Ernest said. "You see things from up above, but I've seen them from below."

He took a deep breath, almost losing his nerve. He now had the undivided attention of the most powerful person on the planet.

"Three years ago you changed my life," Ernest said. "I was shopping with my granddaughter. You know, my daughter, she's not around much. Tell you the truth, she ain't been too kind to my wife and me, but she did give me my precious Marie, my grand-daughter. That day I was carrying Marie through the grocery store parking lot when shrapnel of all kinds began to pelt the asphalt around us. I was hit in the leg by something blunt and I dropped her. She was only two years old. The cry she let out echoes in my mind to this day."

The hero's demeanor changed.

"I remember that day. Gorgatron."

"You don't remember it the way I do. I heard the ground rumbling—shaking violently. I looked up to see Gorgatron in the distance, his giant metal feet smashing everything in their path—just like Salem's monster today. He was kicking as he went, which accounted for the debris that threatened us with each step. The stuff must have traveled airborne for a mile. Even at that distance, he was huge."

"I was terrified. Petrified. I'm ashamed to admit that in that moment, I couldn't even make myself move enough to scoop up my granddaughter. Through blurred vision, I saw you, Salem and The Whistler. It wasn't Salem that stopped that semi from crashing down on top of us. It was you. It wasn't Salem that scooped me and my precious little baby girl up and flew us to safety. It was you. It wasn't Salem that stopped that maniac from destroying the city that day. It was you."

Ernest was standing now. His passion grew with each word.

"Tonight, it wasn't you that called the demon spawn from the depths of hell, it was Salem. Nor were you the one who built that monstrosity! Salem drew lines in the sand and she was the one responsible for all those deaths."

Ernest pointed a finger at The Royal. Knowing now that the man couldn't see him made the janitor feel like it was an awkward move to make.

"I don't know what all you're responsible for in this world, what darkness might have befallen this world in response to your light. But I do know this. You are responsible for all those who lived tonight. Maybe *some* of the dead are on you, but *all* of the living are. Every last one of them."

He was breathing heavily. His emotions always

got the best of him when he talked about his grand-daughter.

"You think your work is meaningless? My granddaughter thinks otherwise. I think otherwise."

A tear fell from the reddening eyes of the most powerful man on the planet.

"But what do I know?" the janitor said as he stooped down and began cleaning up broken pieces of the table, "In the end... I'm just the guy who picks up the trash."

A Word from Aaron Hall
& Steve Beaulieu

Thank you so much for reading our story. We hope you'll mention it when you review this book.

We met at church and decided to team up when we realized that each of us had strengths to compliment the other's weaknesses. You might say we complete each other! Please don't say that.

We love writing and we love Science Fiction. Really...we love anything that tells a good story. We are both huge movie buffs as well as complete nerds. Everything ranging from Aaron's Steam account boasting over 700 games to Steve's thousands of comic books, we just can't get enough of everything you do while living in your mother's basement. Unfortunately for both of us, Texas doesn't have basements and neither of us live with mom.

Aaron Hall was born in 1981 in Fort Worth, Texas. He has spent a majority of his life writing, finding a love of creating fiction at an early age. After spending a decade as community journalist, Aaron now works in communications for his hometown municipal government. He loves spending time with family and friends, watching TV and movies, and above all else, his savior and lord, Jesus Christ.

Steve Beaulieu was born in 1984 in East Hartford, CT. Having spent most of his life in Palm Beach County, Florida, he and his wife moved to Fort Worth, TX in 2012. He works as a Pastor and Graphic

Artist and loves comic books, fantasy and science fiction novels.

He married the love of his life in 2005 and he fathered his first child in 2014, Oliver Paul Beaulieu. His namesake, two of Steve's favorite fictional characters, Oliver Twist and The Green Arrow, Oliver Queen. His second child is due July 30, but Steve secretly hopes she will be born a day late so she can share her birthday with Harry Potter.

You should check out our story *Villain For A Day* in the sister anthology to this volume *World Domination: A Supervillain Anthology.* You might also like our full length novel *Brother Dust: The Resurgence.* We consider it a superhero story, even though Brother Dust wears a cloak instead of a cape. It started out as a comic book. You can see pictures of the original pages on our website: www.hallandbeaulieu.com

PHOTO OP

CHRISTOPHER J. VALIN

FALLING.

He felt like he was always falling.

For most people, this would be the most terrifying moment of their lives—being thrown off the top of a building and watching the street rush up at an incredible speed. It would probably also be the last thing they ever saw.

For Franklin Douglas III, it was just another day at his second job. His heart wasn't even racing as he shot his grappler at the building across the street. He knew better than to tighten up as the line went taut. He hated that part: the jolt as he went from falling straight down to swinging across the street hurt more than being hit with a crowbar (and, yes, he knew very well what *that* felt like). The only thing worse was slamming into the side of the building, even though his black body armor would absorb a lot of the impact. Which is why he aimed for a window that he might be able to reach at his current trajectory.

IT'S A BIRD! IT'S A PLANE!

But it wasn't quite right. He'd have to release his grip and time it perfectly. If not, he'd strike the brick wall so hard it might knock him unconscious, and then he'd finish his fall anyway and be just as dead.

He released the line and wrapped his cape around himself just as he dropped a few feet and crashed through the big plate window like a wrecking ball.

Ow. Why did that hurt so much? It never *used* to hurt so much.

He tucked into a roll, barely registering the screams of the office workers whose day had just become a thousand times more exciting. He couldn't help a small grin at the thought. Talk about terrifying moments.

Back on his feet in a second, he looked around to get his bearings. Yes, he recognized this building. In fact, he owned it. But it had been a while since he'd been inside.

And these were his employees. Not that it mattered. He would need to keep them safe either way. But there was something about the personal connection to the situation that made it more stressful for him.

"Everyone clear out." He felt his gravelly voice rumble in this throat. When the armor came on, the less-recognizable voice came out. And it was one of the few things that had actually become easier to pull off over the years. Probably because he'd fried out his vocal cords.

Nobody moved, far too shocked by and interested in what was happening at their normally-boring place of employment. All of them were wide-eyed, some of them slack-jawed, but none was the least bit interested in leaving.

Time for his extra-commanding tone. "Now!"

This time, they complied and started for the elevator. Most had never seen The Black Harrier in person, but they knew enough about him to understand you did what he said. As the office drones grabbed their cell phones, purses, and laptops, he kept his head down and turned away. The chances of one of them recognizing their billionaire boss in a mask and costume were slim, but not impossible. Plus, it only took one cell phone pic and instant internet facial recognition software to blow his secret identity.

That was definitely a headache he didn't need. He'd kept it a secret for two decades, and he wasn't about to ruin it now. Sometimes he wished for a simpler time. He bet the old WWII heroes like Eaglestar and the Bombardier never had to think about this stuff.

Harrier turned to make sure the last of the workers had left the room. Just then, a flash bounced off his mask. Someone was taking a photo. A young, blonde woman who had been sitting at the desk closest to the smashed window rushed out the door to the elevators.

He'd have to do something about that immediately. This was just one of the many reasons he rarely went out in daylight—too many civilians getting in the way. But it wasn't like the assassin he was dealing with, Deadeye, was going to wait until it was convenient for Harrier before attempting a hit on the mayor.

Maintaining his dual identity would be the least of his problems if Deadeye followed him in and started shooting up the place with all those civilians around. He scanned the building across the street to make sure, using the special equipment in his lenses. No sign of him. Could he have gotten lucky? Maybe Deadeye had—

SMASH! Of course he hadn't. The villain came through another window and fired two pistols at Harrier simultaneously while spinning through the air. He'd seen something like it done with special effects in movies, but this hitman was the only one he'd ever seen pull it off in real life.

Luckily, a move like that threw off even Deadeye's normally impeccable aim. A couple of bullets pinged off of Harrier's helmet, but if they had been direct hits, the type of projectiles the super-assassin used would have gone right through.

Dammit, he needed to get downstairs. The clock was ticking, and the young woman probably wouldn't wait long to post that photo.

Harrier calculated how long it would take for the elevator to get down to the parking garage. It was underground, so hopefully there wouldn't be a signal if she tried it from there.

BLAM! Another shot from Deadeye reminded him that he had other pressing matters to attend to as he dove behind the reception counter.

But what if she tried to post it from the elevator? There wasn't much he could do about that. He just had to hope she wouldn't be that quick and get down there as soon as possible.

The problems of the modern-day masked crimefighter.

He vaulted over the counter, jumped over a desk, and covered the distance to Deadeye in a couple of seconds. Not as fast as he would have in the old days, but not too shabby, either. Deadeye was an extraordinary hand-to-hand combatant, but Harrier's chance of surviving a melee fight with him far exceeded his chances of living with the assassin shooting at him.

The villain drew his sword and swung it so quickly that it was a blur, but Harrier was still able to block it with his bracer. The metal-on-metal sparked as they repeated the dance several more times before Harrier was finally able to knock the long blade from his hand. A decade ago, he would have had Deadeye unarmed and unconscious by now. Now he was having to work a lot harder.

The assassin's foot shot up at his face, but he was just able to avoid it with a back flip. Harrier felt a twinge in his lower back as he swung his body upward and back onto his feet. For a moment, all he could think about was the relief of sitting in the hot tub in his penthouse back at Douglas Tower.

Focus! What the hell was wrong with him? Harrier hoped his mind wasn't starting to go as well as his body. What do they call it? Early-onset...something. He'd certainly sustained enough concussions over the years to have something like that happen.

Maybe he wasn't going to be able to beat this guy hand-to-hand like he always had in the past. He reached around to the back of his belt under his cape and grabbed his second grappler. As Deadeye leapt for his fallen sword, Harrier aimed his grappler at him and shot. As soon as it connected with the killer's armor, he braced himself against the foot of a desk and hit the button to retract the super-strong cable. The super-villain was yanked toward him at lightning speed.

Just as Deadeye was about to collide with him, Harrier put all of his strength into a roundhouse kick and connected with his chin. The assassin went down hard, and Harrier wondered if maybe he had broken the man's neck.

Then he wondered if maybe that would be a good thing.

He should get the police and an ambulance over here immediately, but he had bigger fish to fry at the moment. He checked Deadeye's pulse to make sure he was still alive, then left him there, hoping he'd remain unconscious long enough for the cops to get him.

Harrier surveyed the glass-covered desk of the woman who had taken the photo and found a name: Danielle Taylor. He only hoped she was too busy running away from being potential collateral damage to start posting his face all over the internet immediately.

He disconnected the grappler from Deadeye and attached the line to a giant file cabinet. Taking one last look back at the assassin, he dove out the broken window and rappelled down the building as quickly as he could.

• • •

"Excuse me, but can you tell me what's going on?" Frank was sporting an expensive suit as he entered the parking garage from the street. Over the years, he had managed to turn the restroom stall quick-change into an art form. Another notch in the plus column of having years of experience on the job.

In the negative column, he wasn't able to slow down his heart rate and breathe normally when recovering from a battle as fast as he used to. He hoped she wouldn't notice how out of breath he was.

Danielle was running for her car, and seemed annoyed at the question until she turned and realized who was speaking to her. "Oh…uh…Mr. Douglas."

Frank smiled at her. Always helpful to be a wealthy celebrity in these situations. "It's just that it would be nice to know why my employees are all fleeing the premises in the middle of the workday." Of course, he had already received three calls from building security, but she didn't know that.

Danielle stared as if she had been asked a question by a famous movie star. "Sorry, I'm a little flustered. You won't believe what happened upstairs. We were just sitting there working, and—and then, there was this huge *crash*." Her eyes went wide as she described the scene. "And you wouldn't believe who fell through the window..."

Frank raised an eyebrow and waited, then realized he was actually expected to answer. "Who?"

"The Black Harrier himself!" She said it as if she expected Frank's head to explode when he heard the name.

He wasn't sure which was more difficult: trying to feign surprise or attempting to hide his annoyance. He summoned his years of practice at playing the shallow playboy. "Wow...that's—that's just crazy."

"I know! I was, like, what the fu—sorry! WTF? OMG!"

"Yes, I'm sure you were."

"*And*..." Danielle smiled and looked around like she was privy to the most exciting secret in history. "I even got a photo." She pulled her phone out of her purse, expertly tapping and swiping the screen with her thumb. "Check it out."

Danielle handed the phone to Frank and he looked at the picture that filled the screen. Yeah, it was his alter ego all right. He pulled his fingers apart on the screen and zoomed in. He hadn't had time to put his contacts in, and without the lenses in his mask, his eyes weren't so great any more.

Uh oh. The photo was nice and clear, too.

Between running a few companies, maintaining a playboy cover story, training a sidekick, practicing martial arts, staying in peak physical shape, and—oh, yeah—fighting bad guys as The Black Harrier, Frank wasn't exactly a smart phone expert. But he knew how to delete a picture, and he did it as quickly and covertly as possible.

"Oops." He had the airhead routine mastered from all those dates he had to cut short when duty called. "Not sure what I did there."

Danielle grabbed the phone back and her smile faded as she looked at the screen and started swiping around. "Oh, no. I think you deleted it."

"Really? Oh, geez, I'm so sorry. I'm no good with new technology." He flashed her his sparkling smile and tried to pour on the old Douglas charm to distract her. "I'm sure I can make it up to you someh —"

"Don't worry about it, Mr. Douglas. My dad does that kind of stuff all the time. But all my pics get uploaded to the cloud automatically, so I'll just download it when I get home."

Ouch. "Right. The cloud. Of course."

"Well, it was nice meeting you, sir." *Sir? Do I seem that old to her?*

"Uh... yeah. Nice meeting you as well." Frank clenched his fists as she hopped in her car and joined the parade of vehicles attempting to leave the parking garage all at the same time.

He pulled out his own phone and dialed. "Yeah. I'm going to need some help with something."

• • •

As he sped through the city streets, Harrier didn't think he'd have time to head back to his secret headquarters atop the city's tallest building, the Aerie. But he hoped his young sidekick was already working at the terminal to the giant supercomputer he had there, since that seemed to be his favorite pastime.

His sidekick was the opposite of him in so many ways. With his red body armor and shock of blonde hair sticking out from the top of his mask, the teenager stood in stark contrast to his mentor's black costume and dark demeanor. He was always surprised they weren't more alike, considering... well, he didn't like thinking about that. Suffice to say, they were much more different than similar.

He tapped the control on the side of his steering wheel that, for most people, would access a cell phone to make a call. With the upgraded tech in his vehicle, it immediately accessed a secure direct line to his lair.

"Harrier to Kite."

No answer. Was something wrong with the system? He tapped the control again.

"Red Kite. You there?"

After a long pause, he got a response. "Sorry, there's nobody here by that code name."

"What?" *Oh, right.* As if he didn't have enough to worry about already, he couldn't believe he was going to have to deal with this ridiculousness. It came with the territory of working with moody teenagers, he supposed. "*Raptor.* Red Raptor."

The teen's face appeared on the dashboard video screen. "At your service."

"Sorry. I keep forgetting." The truth was, he just couldn't accept the new code name. Not only did he hate it, it also no longer carried on the tradition of his two previous sidekicks. But he was tired of arguing about it. "Did you get my earlier message about —?"

"Already on it. I've been trying to hack into this woman's accounts, but I haven't had any luck so far. She's got DropFile, inCloud, and a couple of other backups going. I did eff up her cell service, though, so she won't be able to do jack on it. But as soon as she connects to Wi-Fi, whether it's at home or some coffee place, she's good to go."

"You think you'll be able to get into her account, Ki—er, Raptor?"

"For sure. But it's gonna take more time." He stopped typing for a moment as he turned to look at Harrier on the screen. "You think maybe you can stall her?"

Harrier gritted his teeth. He wasn't looking

forward to this. "What's her address?"

• • •

As Frank pulled up to Danielle's tiny condo in one of the city's less-affluent neighborhoods, he felt a twinge of guilt for not paying his employees enough to live someplace better. Especially considering the vast amounts of wealth he raked in for—truthfully—not really doing all that much work. But he also spent a great deal of that money on his extracurricular activities—saving the city—so it didn't bother him too much.

He parked down the street and made sure to set the alarm on his sports car. But he still felt like it might not be there when he got back, considering it probably cost more than the houses in the neighborhood. He thought about his plan as he headed up the block to her place. He would try to charm her, and then take her out to dinner at a fancy restaurant... one with no Wi-Fi. That should give Raptor plenty of time to delete his picture from all of her "clouds."

Suddenly, he found himself surrounded by several gang members. Normally, he would have noticed them before they even got close, but he was letting this situation monopolize his attention and get to him way too much.

The apparent leader of the group approached him first as the rest closed in on him slowly. "Whatta we have here, boys? Looks like this old rich guy got himself lost."

Old? C'mon. Sure, he was starting to get a little

gray around the temples, but—

"Maybe he needs some directions." The second guy smiled and showed off his gold teeth. "You need some directions, old man?"

Frank obviously wasn't scared, but he was concerned about one thing. How was he going to take on all these guys in broad daylight without everyone questioning how he did it?

The leader got right up in Frank's face. "I think maybe we can send him off in the right direction for a small donation. What do you think, mister? You wanna donate to our little club if we tell you where to go?"

Frank's eyes narrowed as he leaned in even closer to the leader's face. "How about I tell *you* were to go?"

The gang members all started whooping and hollering at this, thinking it was hilarious. The leader didn't think it was so funny. "Man, I was just gonna take your wallet and watch, but now you are *dead*."

The leader swung at Frank, who casually avoided the fist. Then he pulled out a knife and jabbed it at Frank's chest.

Frank reached out and grabbed the leader's wrist and twisted until it made a popping sound. Then he pulled him forward while he raised his knee so the gangster's face connected with it. Hard. The leader slumped to the sidewalk, where he would undoubtedly be spending the next several hours.

Frank looked down at his knee and brushed off

his pants. "I didn't get any blood on my new suit, did I?"

The rest of the gang members stood around silently, picking their proverbial jaws up off the ground. Frank straightened his tie and fixed his cuffs, addressing the young men without looking at them. "Is there something else I can do for you gentlemen?"

Gold-tooth backed away along with his friends. "Nah, nah, man, we're good."

"Then have yourselves a nice evening."

A few houses down, Frank climbed up a small set of steps and rang the doorbell to Danielle's duplex. He scanned the area to make sure the gangsters were really gone and weren't going to try something stupid, but there was no sign of them.

Danielle was lecturing somebody on the other side of the thin door, and it was obvious that she didn't realize people outside could hear her. "I'm pretty sure that was more than thirty minutes, don't you think? Should I try to get it free?"

She opened the door dressed in sweats and a t-shirt, and looked even more surprised than when she saw him earlier in the garage. "Mr. Douglas? Oh, wow. I was expecting a pizza."

"I'm sorry to just show up here. I felt bad about earlier, and I thought maybe I could take you out to dinner or something to make it up to you."

The door swung open wider, and a guy with an apparently ironic haircut and a beard like a bird's nest looked Frank up and down. "Who is this guy, babe? Why's he want to take you out to dinner?"

"Relax, Nate. It's just my boss."

Nate puffed out his chest and tried to look tough. "What is it you're trying to apologize for, old man?"

Again with the old man? Since when is 45 old?

"I just had a mishap with her phone earlier, and I felt bad about it. I can actually buy dinner for both of you if you'd like."

"Are you saying I can't pay for my own meals, or take care of my woman? What's your problem, dude?"

"I'm just trying to—" Nate tried to shove him off the steps, but Frank didn't budge. Nate looked like an idiot bouncing off of him. Frank tried to calm him down, but Nate was just getting angrier. "Look, I don't want—"

Nate took a swing at Frank's face, but Frank's hand came up like a blur. He easily caught Nate's fist in the palm of his hand.

Danielle panicked. "Nate, you're going to get me fired!"

Frank let go of Nate's hand as the man backed off, shocked.

"I'm gonna call my boys and we're gonna take this D-bag down." Nate grabbed a cell phone off a nearby table, and Frank immediately recognized it as Danielle's phone from earlier. Now was his chance.

Taking a step forward, Frank calmly grabbed Nate's hand with the phone in it and squeezed. Nate screamed as the phone fell to the floor and cracked open, then fell to his knees holding his hand.

Danielle knelt next to her boyfriend and stared at Frank. He recognized the combination of disbelief and fear in her eyes. He just wasn't used to seeing it while out of costume.

"Sorry, Ms. Taylor, but he seemed like he might be a bit out of control. I'm sure if you put some ice on his hand, it'll be fine. As for your phone…"

He picked the pieces up off the floor. He sensed someone else behind him and, thinking it was another attack, spun and almost kicked the pizza delivery guy in the chest. The guy threw the pizza in the air as he jumped back, and Frank managed to grab the box out of the air with the hand that wasn't holding the phone.

Frank put the pizza down carefully on a nearby chair and checked on the delivery man, trying to remember if it was this pizza chain he owned or a different one. "You okay?"

The guy seemed nervous, but he nodded his head. "You scared the crap out of me. I've been beat up three times in this neighborhood already."

"Here. Maybe this'll make you feel better." Frank pulled a couple of hundreds out of his wallet and handed them to the guy.

The pizza guy stood in shock and looked at the bills in his hand. Then his eyes widened as he realized something. "Hey! Aren't you—"

"No." Frank looked back to make sure Danielle

and Nate weren't looking at him, then quietly slipped the guy another Benjamin. "And you never saw me here, right?"

"Riiiiiiight." The pizza guy left with a huge grin on his face.

Frank turned back toward Danielle and held up the pieces of the broken phone. "I'm really sorry about all this. I feel like I keep causing more of a mess. I'll go down to the store right now and buy you the newest model, with all the bells and whistles."

Frank smiled, then turned around and headed out.

After he closed the door, he heard Nate's voice from inside as he walked away. "Bells and whistles? What the f—"

• • •

"Any luck?" Frank had called Raptor again from his car as soon as he got in.

"Yeah. It's wiped. At least the ones of you. There were also vids of her and some caveman getting sweaty if you ever need to blackmail her."

Frank grinned. "I don't think that'll be necessary."

"How'd it go? With the stalling?"

Frank thought about it for a moment. "It wasn't quite what I was anticipating, but it all worked out in the end. I guess I still have a few moves left for an old man."

A Word from Christopher J. Valin

I've been a comic book and superhero fan (especially Batman) as far back as I can remember. Some of my earliest memories are of watching repeats of the old Adam West TV series when I was growing up in the '70s and coloring in Batman coloring books. As I got older, I started writing and drawing my own comics and creating my own heroes while collecting comic books obsessively. I loved the covers of *Giant-Size X-Men #1* and *Amazing Spider-Man #129* so much that I tore them off and hung them on my wall (not the best financial decision I've ever made).

I was lucky enough to be able to get a job at, and eventually manage, a comic book and collectibles store while I was in college, and even got to work as a writer and inker for some small comic book publishers for several years as an adult. So I've been intimately connected to the industry my whole life. For a time, I was sidetracked by screenwriting, writing and teaching about history, and, later, short stories. But when I decided to write my first full novel on my own, there was no other choice but to go back to my first love, creating my own world full of superheroes and villains.

If you enjoyed my story, please check out *Sidekick: The Red Raptor Files – Part 1*, which takes place in the same universe, called the "Raptorverse" after its central character. You can also find my other books and short stories at my Amazon author's page and more about me at my website, Christopher-Valin.com. Finally, if you'd like to keep up with my new releases, as well as giveaways and other fun stuff, please subscribe to my newsletter. Thanks for reading!

MERCURIAL

ALEXIA PURDY

Cameron Ulrich
(Powerless Citizen—sort of...)

STINGER FLUNG HIS SHARP, thorn-like needles from his fingertips, an ability that made me cringe. Trying not to get in the way of the ricocheting projectiles, I focused on watching Mercurial Man give chase. The guy was massive, his bulky muscles flexing beneath his thin T-shirt and his well-worn jeans hugging his thighs. I could watch them all night, but from what I could see, they were unaware they had an audience.

I'd watched them for weeks. It wasn't too hard. Not when you knew their secret identities and had documented their quirks, habits, and powers down to what dental floss they used. Stalkerish much, right? Well... for me, it was a matter of life and death. Luckily, it just took some patience. I'd spent hours perched on rooftops and fire escapes near their haunts. Follow a superhero around long enough, you'll find where they live, eat, sleep... and pretty much everything else. Just as long as you didn't get

193

too close, they were mostly oblivious to the tiny woman watching them from afar. I guess they assumed I was just an overly obsessed fan.

But I was far from that. You could say I was obsessed, but I wasn't just stalking them. Ever since I'd discovered my own powers, I had watched the superheroes roam the city. One by one, I'd added them to my list until I had acquired quite a stack of names. It wouldn't be easy, but I already knew who I'd start with and who could help me complete my first mission.

Mercurial swung a loose, industrial-sized trashcan at Stinger, who dodged it easily. He was slender, quick, and agile. So was Mercurial, but his bulk did give him a slight half-second delay in catching up with Stinger. This fatal flaw was something he knew about. He had managed to avoid most of the thorns Stinger threw his way. Anyone else would've been pelted by these needles flinging through the air like tiny bullets. Not Mercurial. He'd managed to fend off the attack by holding up sheets of metal he'd torn from the dumpster's lid, like a shield.

It never failed to surprise me, the way these two fought. It was a visual dance that kept me glued to the action.

Stinger was inexperienced but gaining ground in street fighting. His main technique was slipping out of his opponent's hands, jumping from obstacle to obstacle, and climbing fire escapes like nothing. Mercurial's brute strength kept the guy grounded; he threw a flurry of objects into the air, catching Stinger before he could gain any height. It was a sight to behold, these two, and I knew I had chosen my first subjects.

An oversized stinger flung threw the air, and Mercurial released the trash bin, but he let out a yelp before he could dodge the projectile. I strained my neck to see if he'd been hurt, but I couldn't tell from this distance. I did notice, however, that Stinger ran right past me; a breeze shifted with his movements as he rounded the corner. I turned around, trying to see which direction he'd gone, when someone jerked my purse right out of my hands.

"Hey! Stop!" I hollered, taking chase after the robber who had my bag tucked beneath his arm and was bolting as though his life depended on it. I flew behind him, heading into the depths of Central Park, weaving through the paths without any thought to how dark it was getting. I had almost lost him when something large whooshed past me under the bridge and into the darkness.

I heard a yelp, then a string of curses and whines as I rounded the corner. Staring into the bushes, I narrowed my eyes and strained to find the source. Out there, the robber had my stuff, and I needed it for my next nursing class exam. Out there, someone had just smacked the doofus in the face, based on the sound of crunching bones I could hear echoing out toward me.

I bent over to catch my breath. I felt winded

and dizzy. I had to get into better shape if I was going to be chasing these guys around. Days of lying around watching superheroes and studying in night school to be a nurse had squeezed the endurance right out of me. First on the list to do was get back in shape. ASAP. Superheroes weren't out of shape. That was no way to behave if I wanted to be on their side.

From the continued yelps and cries emanating from the bushes, I suspected my robber had met an unfortunate end to his adventures. But by who's hand?

Warrick "Mercurial Man" Lorenson
aka: Merc

I FELT THE CRUNCH of bones beneath my fingers as I squeezed the guy's arm at an odd angle. He yelped in pain before he begged me to stop.

"You think robbing little girls and old ladies in the park is fun? This is fun. I think I can break both your arms and never break a sweat." I sucked in a breath, feeling the pull to my injured side. I'd have to deal with that later. "Now your robbing days are over, got it? I'll make sure to keep an eye on you, and if you do it again, I'll break a leg for each time you try to make a move to rob anyone. *Comprende*?"

"Yesss!" He screeched in pain, sobbing as he cradled his arm. "I won't do it again. I swear! Please, let me go."

I did as he asked, though being two feet above the ground, he had a short fall before he crumpled in a heap, his legs weak and dampened with his own urine. I wrinkled my nose as he scrambled away, whimpering into the night. Chuckling, I took another swig from my flask. The alcohol no longer burned down my throat but felt hot and tasted sweet as I let it infiltrate my head, leaving a heady and euphoric feeling behind.

"Your liver is waving the white flag, you know." A voice interrupted my wavering thoughts, and I spun around to find the girl who'd been chasing the hooligan down, screaming threats as though she had a leg to stand on.

"Go away. I got your stuff back." I grabbed her purse off the ground and tossed it in her general direction before downing another swallow. I stumbled and reached out to grab on to a tree trunk. The rough bark embedded itself into my palm. Staring out across Central Park, the lights danced in my vision as my eyelids grew heavier.

"Um, thanks? You could've just taken him to the police station. Breaking bones is a bit... malicious for a superhero, isn't it?"

"What's it to you? I handle things the way I handle 'em, and if you don't like it, why don't you try to do it yourself? Tired of saving you ingrates." I stumbled, falling right on my damn face.

Great.

"Oh, I can see you've got it all under control," the girl snickered.

I eyed her, throwing her a wry look, but instead had to squeeze my lids together to avoid the throbbing headache I'd just given myself. "What?"

She bent down and studied me, curiosity pasted across her shining eyes. This girl was far too close. "Are you all right?"

"Go away!" I snapped.

She turned up her nose and was about to stand and go away when her eyes widened in horror. "Hey, you're hurt! Oh, crap! There's blood all over your side there!" She turned to call for help, but I slapped my hand onto her arm, curling my fingers around her slender wrist and squeezing until she yelped.

"No cops. No hospitals. I'll be fine."

"The hell you will. You've got a hole the size of my fist in your side. Let me call an ambulance." She pulled her cellphone out and began dialing.

I swatted it out of her hands and groaned, the blood loss and alcohol winning the fight for consciousness. "No. No medics. I just need to heal. I heal fast, don't you know that? That's part of the magic of a superhero." I felt the world lurch and closed my eyes, concentrating on breathing in and out to keep my head from spinning. "The sky is falling."

"Hey, Mercurial Man." The girl's voice grew farther and farther away, and the lure of sleep beckoned. "Wake up! You can't pass out here."

"Watch me...."

Cameron

NO ONE EVER realizes the moment they pass out or

198

go under anesthesia or get knocked the hell out. You don't even know you're out until you rouse and find the godforsaken sun streaming through a crack in the curtains straight into your eyes like a laser beam.

"The hell?" I heard Merc as he flailed on my bed, attempting to block the sun with his hands. Just moving had no doubt sent sharp stabs of pain shooting from the wound, and a stream of swear words slipped from his mouth. Who knew the guy was a potty-mouth? "Where am I?" He managed to blink enough to adjust to the light.

"You're in my apartment. So, can I call you Merc for short?"

"What?" He pushed himself into a sitting position and gave me a bewildered look. "You—you're the girl from the park. I told you to get lost."

"And I told you that your injuries were far too great for me to walk away. You don't cooperate much, do you?"

He peered down at his side and frowned at the bandage. Some blood had seeped through the square patch. He touched the area, flinching.

"Dammit. It should've healed by now."

"I took the liberty of fishing a broken needle or thorn out of there. I thought you would've pulled it out yourself, but I could see why you weren't able to. It was hard with tweezers and a pair of pliers. It's really unsanitary to walk around like that."

He groaned, closing his eyes. "What's it to you? And why'd you bring me here?"

"Look, Merc—"

"It's Warrick. But you can call me Merc. I'll answer to either."

I lifted an eyebrow. "Just Warrick? Or Merc, I mean?"

He frowned, opening his eyes and focusing on me once more. "Yes."

"Okay, Merc, you were passing out in the middle of the park. You know... the place half the city's derelicts escape to at night? Leaving you there spread-eagled and bleeding to death wasn't in me. You refused to let me call the cops or an ambulance, so I had no choice. I helped you limp your way up here. It wasn't far from the park."

"I gotta go." Merc attempted to stand, but his healing had slowed to the point that his blood loss was severe enough to make him sway.

"Whoa there, Superman. I think you've found your kryptonite: severe blood loss. Takes a bit longer to heal from that, I reckon."

"This is taking too long. Why?" He wrinkled his forehead, tapping his temple.

"It might not help that you were drunker than a skunk."

"The alcohol was for the pain."

"Sure, it was. It also thins your blood. Probably didn't help."

He scoffed. "Are you a nurse or something?"

I shook my head. "Or something. I'm a nursing student. Not a nurse quite yet. It's taking me longer than usual since I have to work full time and attend classes. It's not easy."

He rolled his eyes. "Yep. I bet it isn't."

"Hey, this little nursing student saved your butt."

"Spare me the details. I need out of here." He tried to stand again but immediately sat right back down, clutching his head between his hands. "Got any water? My tank's empty."

"I'll say." I pointed to the glass sitting on the nightstand next to the bed. "Help yourself."

"Why are you helping me?"

"Because you were passed out behind enemy lines."

He shook his head, glaring at me. My breath hitched. That steely gaze was hard to ignore. His eyes were such a light grey-blue, they looked metallic. Dark eyelashes along with thick brows lined his eyes, which stood out stark against his pale skin. He watched me apprehensively noting my hesitation.

"What's the real reason I'm here?"

"Okay, look...." It was time to get real. "I have a favor to ask."

"What?" he groaned. Wow. Patience, anyone?

"I need to pick your brain. Do you remember a little boy named Tony Miller?"

His face darkened. "Don't know 'im."

"Yes, you do. Think hard."

He furrowed his brow, his eyes glazing over. "Doesn't ring a bell."

IT'S A BIRD! IT'S A PLANE!

"About six years ago. He was a kid. Aged twelve. You got to him too late before he caught a stray round from a bank robber on Fifth Street. You didn't get the shooter down on time and let him escape the scene. The kid almost bled out before paramedics got to him, and that was after his father was hit in the head by a ricocheting bullet."

He groaned. "Oh, yeah. That kid. What about him? I wasn't the only superhero there. It wasn't my fault."

"He called out to you when he realized his father had gone down. When you saw the guy was dead, you ignored the kid. Too upset to face him, maybe? The father, he was his only parent."

This made him inhale sharply, but I could see it wasn't going to get through to him.

"And your point is? This is boring me to death. That was a long time ago, and there was nothing that could've been done for that kid's father. What do you want me to say?"

"You left him when he needed you most. He was an orphan because you were too busy showing off how tough you were for the crowd while tossing the other bank robber about. Afterward, he publicly asked for you to come visit him in the hospital. That's all he wanted from you, but you failed to show up. He not only lost part of his leg because of an infection, he was all alone in the world. The least you could've done was visit him."

He shook his head, waving his hand in the air.

"It wasn't my problem."

I got in his face, risking getting shoved, but he didn't react. He just stared back at me, hard.

"Look. I don't want to do this, but a lot of stuff really *is* your problem. I want you to fix it because you've caused so much more harm than you'll ever realize. If you don't fix it, I'm going to blab every secret you've ever had to the media."

"You know nothing about me."

"I know you're an alcoholic. I know you drink to keep from remembering your failures. I know you gave up on humanity years ago and only help when there's a payment involved."

His eyes narrowed. "You know that's not true."

"Partly, it is. You'd give up on people if you could, wouldn't you? You've let people die because you weren't sure they were worth saving. I've written each one down, and I'll tell them all why you did it. You were too drunk to stumble your ass out of your apartment and help. Too stinking inebriated."

"You think this is an easy job?" His acidic glare dug into me as he stood and peered down at me. I hated to say it, but the guy was intimidating.

"No, I never said I thought it was easy."

"Then stay out of my life. And don't follow me."

He took a step and wavered for a moment, cursing as he swung his gaze around, looking for his shoes. Thankfully, his jeans were still on, but his tattered shirt was gone.

"Where are my shoes?" He demanded.

"They're by the end of the bed, but—"

He snatched them up and sank onto the bed again to pull them on, tightening the strings with a brisk movement.

"Wait... you can't leave yet," I pleaded.

"The hell I can't." He hopped to his feet, but I stood between him and the doorway. His frown deepened as he dared me to not move, but I stood my ground. "You need to get out of my way."

"Or what?"

He reached out, grasped me by my arms and proceeded to lift me up and place me down next to him before grabbing the handle of the door and swinging it open.

Desperate, I called out to him. "I know about Emilia."

He stopped dead in his tracks, facing the doorway. He slowly exhaled before he swung back around toward me. "Don't."

"She said you're better than this. That this person you've become, it's not you."

He stepped up to me, his face darkening as his skin flushed into his signature red coloring, lighting up his eyes like flames licking the surface of a pool. I'd been watching him from a distance, but I had never seen his hot and cold powers up close. With one hand, he could set the world afire. With the other, freeze it into an eternal winter. I dared not touch either.

"She's just a girl I used to know. You don't get

to speak of her like you know anything about us. You don't know anything."

I crossed my arms and jutted my chin out. "I know more than you think. I've been watching you a long time, Warrick. You're hurting, damaged. I know you'd never let a kid wait for you to come around. I know you didn't want his father to die. Your vanity proved you are not infallible. You just need to fix these mistakes. It'll get right if you do."

He didn't move, but his fists clenched and un-clenched as he stood there, willing his heated mood to pass. As his scarlet coloring began to fade, I re-laxed.

"What do you want with me, and who the hell are you anyway?"

"I'm Cameron Ulrich. I want to help fix the mis-takes superheroes have made along the way and make them truly super."

"You're barking up the wrong tree. Go ahead and tell my secrets. There's not very much to tell, so get out of my way."

He gave me a firm but effective shove to the side and kept walking straight to my door. I caught my bearings just in time and called out to him. "It's not just that," I said. "If you don't do this, you won't be a superhero anymore. You turn this down, and I'll take away your powers for good, and you'll never be extraordinary again."

Warrick was already at my door, one hand on the cool surface of the knob, before he stopped.

Pausing long enough to consider my words, he tilted his head to the side and firmly trained his eyes on me.

"Why would you do something like that? And how? You're nothing but a pathetic little nursing student." He frowned, studying me more thoroughly. My words had gotten him to stop and reconsider. Good. I smiled. Catching Mercurial Man off guard was a feat unto itself. He had done questionable things in his lifetime. Not only had he failed to save unworthy people and inadvertently harmed innocent ones, but he had also destroyed those who got in his way. It was part of his charm, I thought. He was unfathomable. Broken. Disturbed. It was why I had chosen him to be part of my first project.

"My powers are not as obvious as yours. They're subtle enough that no one can pin anything on me. I can take away powers and give them back whenever I want to. I can't use them once I take them, but neither can you. I simply hold them until I decide it's safe for you to have them back."

I knew this would infuriate him, but I still held my breath as I watched him process the words. It was Mercurial Man after all. Not only did his body light up as hot as fire, but it could also turn anything to ice. His mood matched his powers to a T. He could either be a raging bull or a frigid ice king. I prayed that he would find the strength to meet himself in the middle before I had to snatch away his powers. It would either break him or make him, and I wasn't sure which.

"Are you kidding me? You can't be serious." He laughed, a maniacal one that made my blood run cold.

"I'm as serious as a heart attack," I said, crossing my arms and standing my ground, hoping he couldn't see my hands shaking as I pressed them against my body. He was a large man, a good two to three feet taller than me. Any human in their right mind would wither under that stare, but I wasn't quite human, and it was time I accepted it. It was why I'd become a nursing student, so I could help those who couldn't help themselves. Finding some sort of atonement for those who'd had the unfortunate fate of crossing a rogue superhero's path, like Mercurial Man, was my first task. Maybe he would find it cathartic. Or maybe he'd choose to retire without powers.

Either way, it was a win-win for all those who were collateral damage when heroes thought themselves above the laws of humankind.

"Let's just say you're serious...." He dropped his hand from the doorknob and turned to face me fully, crossing his own arms and matching my stance. A sly smile played at the corners of his mouth as he eyed me from head to toe, taking me in. I could tell he wasn't impressed. "If you really can take away my powers and make me normal, maybe I'd want that. Did you ever consider I might choose that end, Nurse Ratched?"

IT'S A BIRD! IT'S A PLANE!

My mouth dropped open, staring at him in horror. The thought had never crossed my mind. Why would any superhero want to live without their powers? I pondered the situation and decided I would call his bluff.

"You really think I'm that stupid? You won't pick that kind of life. You'd wither and die so fast you wouldn't know what to do with yourself. Most super-heroes can't live a normal life without powers, or else I would be having people knocking down my door every other second."

I sucked in a breath, hoping my statement had jolted him out of his self-confidence. He didn't do anything, just eyed me up and down once more with determination forming in his gleaming eyes.

"Fine." He sighed, dropping his arms to his side, looking as exhausted as I thought he might feel. "How about I give you an answer in a day or so? You can at least give me that, right? It's kind of hard to decide on such a change of fate when I'm hung over and still healing. It's the least a nurse could do for a lowly superhero."

Internally, I groaned. He had me there. I had to be patient. He'd tricked me into lengthening the leash I needed to hold tight. Could I just force him to decide now? I guess I could, but the way he stared with his eagle eyes honed on me like I was prey—an unusually stable expression compared to the mercurial moods he was known for—I couldn't refuse.

"All right. Tomorrow. Five pm, latest. I better

have an answer by then or I'm coming for your powers."

"Oh, I'll give you a definite answer, all right. See you on the flip side, Nurse Ratched."

A moment later, before I could even blink, he was gone, the door still easing closed on its hinges.

Groaning, I sat down on my couch, shaking my head. Merc was more trouble than he was worth. Maybe, just maybe, he'd be worth it in the end. God, I hoped so.

Merc

"YOU SHOULD'VE SEEN THEM! He thought he really had me pinned, the crazy nut-job. He was begging for his mommy the moment I finished tying him up. He was practically wetting his pants!" Bolt cackled as he spun the story of his most recent conquest to the group. I leaned back in my chair, changing the bandage on my side and biting down a yelp as the tape ripped off my chest hair. The medical tape was no joke. Who needed waxing when you had a roll of this stuff stuck on you?

Our "hangout" was more of a small, musty basement than any kind of superhero digs. In what was probably one of the worst neighborhoods in town, it was the only haven for this ragtag team of superheroes. We were all washed up, worn-out rust buckets, but let me tell you, we had each other's backs. There was no one I trusted more than those shabby rejects.

IT'S A BIRD! IT'S A PLANE!

Listening to Bolt's stories was oddly comforting as I taped the new bandage onto the mostly healed wound. Sifting through a stash of clothes I kept there, I found a shirt and pulled it over my head. I had limped the whole way there avoiding being seen running across the rooftops and down abandoned stairwells in an old neighborhood which was part of one of the seediest areas of New York City. We all had our well-used undercover routes to get there when things got heated. It was our sanctuary from the chaotic world. Most of the time, we just killed time waiting for jobs.

"You could've gotten yourself killed." Bolt's girlfriend, Carly, pressed her lips together, refusing to look his way.

"Come on, Carly, don't be such a stiff. We stuck to the rulebook. Sometimes we need to think outside the box so we don't get turned around. What was I supposed to do? Let him go?"

Carly shook her head, her frown deepening as she shoved a brush through the tangles in her long strawberry-blonde hair. She had the ability to change into a little fox and sneak into almost any place she wanted. It was a useful trait, for sometimes we had to get into places which were locked up. She could get through all sorts of small passages and unlock the door for the rest of us. Or I could just crush through the front door, but most of the time, we needed to enter quietly. She was an asset to our team of five, as were each of its members.

We worked on various projects at any given time, whatever was thrown our way by local authorities. Or we kept to watching our pathetically outdated TV in the corner. As a washed-up team way beyond our prime, at least we could still work the local superhero circuits when we were called in. It was the only reason the cops left us alone for the most part. Otherwise, they'd probably arrest us for trespassing and all sorts of other misdemeanors and crimes.

The Superhero Sanctum Act kept us in the green each time we did get involved. As long as we either saved a life, kept a crime from happening, or saved somebody a load of money, we were immune to the law, which was how each one of us wanted to live.

But the older we got, the harder it was to stay under the radar, and the jobs got fewer and farther between. No one cared for slower, aging superheroes. Not on this side of town, at least. We were getting shafted on jobs, but none of us were willing to wave the white flag and call it quits.

"That's not the point, Bolt." Andy, who had the power to manipulate earth and rock, rolled his eyes at Bolt, whose lightning and rain powers came in handy on sunny days. "Your girlfriend doesn't want to scrape your innards off the asphalt. Your daredevil days are over, man. Get with it. Family first." He sighed, his eyes glazing over at the mention of family. His own waited for him at home every night. At least he had some place and someone to go to, which was more than I could say for myself.

The girl who claimed she could take away my powers drifted back into my thoughts. I had to meet up with that Cameron chick by five the next afternoon. In a way, I wasn't dreading it. How pathetic was that?

The fourth of the team was Kevin, but he snored away the days in front of the TV. His superpowers were subtler than the rest of us, meaning he was usually the getaway driver. He was a bottomless pit and could eat through anything, even metal. It came in handy when bombs were set to go off in the middle of town. He could literally swallow them, and the explosion within him would be minimal. Besides that, he was a big softy who preferred donuts over salads and siestas over working out.

I, the fifth member of the team, was on my own. Always the odd man out.

"You know, Carly's right. If you're not careful, you'll set fire to the whole town. Remember what happened at the bank on Fourth Avenue? You almost incinerated the staff in the back room. They're not going to trust us with any more jobs if you keep doing shit like that. I would like to pay my rent on time this month, what about you?" Andy rubbed the deep wrinkles between his brows. He was tired of working the odd jobs that were thrown our way.

The Superhero Sanctum Act also allowed for a fund for the superheroes of the city so they could have compensation for their services. More and more of that was being shunted away from us and to the younger heroes who responded faster and lived closer to the center of the city. If we didn't do a minimum of ten jobs a month, none of us would make our rents, let alone put food on the table.

I was the lucky one, the only one without kids or family. If you could call that lucky, I guess.

"Okay, okay," Bolt groaned. "I'll be more careful with the lightning bolts. You guys just need to pick up the slack next time. Every time it seems I need to resort to using my powers, a fire breaks out. We just need someone who can put out fires right away on our team. Know anybody like that?"

Everybody shook their heads, mumbling under their breaths. There were fewer and fewer superheroes popping up who would even consider working with us. I didn't know what it meant. Maybe it would be a good thing for all of us, or maybe it was a really bad thing because overall, our numbers were declining.

"Hey, Merc, you all right? You're awfully quiet." Carly threw me a suspicious glance, but I waved her away.

"Yep. Just got stabbed by one of Stinger's loose appendages last night. It broke off in the wound. Sucker was a pain to fish out."

"Ah, okay. Just let us know if you need backup. You haven't been drinking, again have you?" She wrinkled her nose. I shrunk in my chair. I hadn't taken a shower yet and probably reeked of alcohol.

"Nope." I could tell she didn't believe me. "I'm actually on my way home. You all good?" I hopped to my feet and turned toward the door before anyone could protest. They mumbled their goodbyes but didn't make a move from their spots. I headed back out into the night, the best time of the day for me. I could ignore any obsessed fans who still stalked me now and then and get home without cursing one out. Daylight brought recognition and loud city folk, both of which I loathed with a passion.

As I walked home through the darkened streets, passing derelicts calling out from alleyways for a buck or two, I thought over Cameron's demands. Maybe atoning for past mistakes wouldn't be a bad thing. Maybe it would help my own guilt over Emilia fade away. Maybe she was someone I could seek atonement with.

Or maybe it was a disaster waiting to happen.

Cameron

"YOU SCARED THE CRAP out of me." I held a hand to my chest, feeling my heart pumping madly beneath.

"You said you'd give me until today to give you an answer. Well, I have that answer for you." Merc threw me a sly grin, enjoying the fact that he'd surprised me.

I sighed, glaring at him as he sat nonchalantly on my fire escape. The guy didn't like using doors. Obviously. It was something I had failed to notice about him. I wondered what else I could've possibly missed about the guy.

"Okay, what's your answer?"

"I agree to your terms under one condition."

"What's that?"

"You come with me on every single one of these 'atonements' you want me to do."

"Why? You can do it all on your own." I scowled, lifting an eyebrow. "I'll know if you don't, trust me. Besides, it won't be safe for me. I am essentially powerless. I can't save anyone."

"True, but you never know. I just want to show you who I really am. You are under the impression that you know me. You know nothing about me and my life, but I'm willing to show you."

I chewed on my bottom lip. I knew a lot about him, his stories, his slight indiscretions, all from afar, all from the eyes of others, maybe, but he was wrong. I did know him... some.

"All right. If I agree to your condition, when do you want to start?"

He held out a hand, grinning mischievously enough it made my blood stop cold in my veins.

"Right now."

Merc

I APPROACHED TONY, who I had not seen since he was a scrawny, bleeding twelve-year-old. Now he was eighteen and far from the kid I'd watched screaming as his father lay in a bloody pile next to him. His leg had been shredded, but his only concern had been his father's life. Now his father was long dead, and he'd survived a string of foster homes filled with nothing but neglect and abuse. I wondered who I'd meet this time around. He didn't look like the same sweet kid.

Tony leaned on the street corner doling out whatever flavor-of-the-week drug he had stashed in his shirt and pants. Innocence was long gone from the piercing brown eyes as he flicked his used-up cigarette into the street and ran a hand through his unruly black locks.

This couldn't be the same kid I remembered tearing up as his father struggled to live. That kid with dirt streaking his cheeks was nowhere to be found. He leaned on his good leg, his prosthetic one hidden beneath baggy jeans which were held up by a worn-out black leather belt that had seen better days and probably a bigger waist.

"You Tony?"

The guy stopped biting down on a new cigarette and let it drop from his mouth, startled. "Who's asking?"

"I'm Mercurial Man."

His eyes traveled down my clothes. I'd long given up on my signature blue and orange, skintight outfit with a big yellow M across the chest. From the stunned, unbelieving look on his face, he wasn't the only one who had changed these past few years.

"You're not him. Get out of my face, freak." He

spat on the ground and snatched the cigarette from his boot, where it had landed. He snapped a Zippo lighter out of his pocket and clicked it, lighting up the end of his cigarette.

"Those things will kill you faster than I can."

"It's none of your business. I do what I like."

"Since your dad died?"

His eyes glazed over as he inhaled, then he proceeded to blow the smoke out into the atmosphere without looking at me. "My old man was good for nothing."

"He was your old man, nonetheless."

He snapped his eyes onto me, nothing but contempt swimming in them. "You buying or just going to take up space?"

"I heard you wanted to meet me once."

Tony took one confused look at me and burst out laughing. "You? Why would I want to meet you? You're a washed up old superhero not worth his signature on used toilet paper."

I folded my arms, letting his insults slide off me like oil. "You finished?"

"I got more where that came from, but I have money to make, so get off my corner. I've hurt a lot bigger guys than you for less, so get lost mercury dude."

"It's Mercurial Man." Cameron stepped from around the corner, clearly losing her patience with our conversation. "And you told your foster mom, Emilia, that you waited so long to meet him, and he never came when you were at the hospital. Remember?"

Tony's eyes narrowed onto her, and then he flicked his eyes away, his face reddening. "You know my Aunt Emmi?" I liked the term of endearment he'd given Emilia. If only I'd known she had fostered this kid at one point. She always did pick up the pieces I'd left behind. The woman was a saint.

"Yes. She told me a lot of things."

"She—she had no right to tell you anything. I'm dead to her, you know? Might as well be really dead for all she cares about me." Angry tears glistened at the edges of Tony's eyes, but he refused to let them fall as he inhaled another sharp lungful of smoke. The kid was on his way to COPD from what I could tell. Not good.

"But she does care, and you know it. I apologize for being so blunt, but she wanted you to realize that maybe you were wrong about Mercurial Man, about your dad. About all sorts of stuff. He wouldn't want this for you."

"This here is all I got." He tossed his half-smoked cigarette to the asphalt, smashed it with his heel, and waved his arms around. His clothes were pressed and clean. He took care of his things. I could tell he wasn't into being a junkie dealer. Maybe this was a detour for him, a stop on the way to bigger and better things.

I let the optimism slide off me.

"You have more than you know," I said. "I apologize for not coming to see you in the hospital when you were twelve and your father died. I wasn't in the right state of mind. Sometimes you can't save everyone the way you'd like, even as a superhero. It does things to our minds. It did to me. The disappointment, the madness that comes from failure, makes us do things we wouldn't otherwise do, like not visit a kid who desperately needed to meet me."

"Why do you even care?" Tony snapped. "You don't care about who you save. I know that now. You do it for the money, for the fame. There's no heart inside you. You're just a washed-up nothing who doesn't give a damn about anyone but yourself." Tony was yelling at him, not realizing the tears were dripping down his cheeks. He wiped at them madly, more from annoyance than anything. "You don't care. So why should anyone care about anyone in this world?"

My chest squeezed, and I found my own rage cracking. I was angry that I had failed this kid years ago, and that failure had manifested into this creature before me full of rage, resentment, and lacking any kind of warmth. Forgotten by everyone he believed in. And alone. So very alone.

"I'm sorry, Tony. I didn't realize at the time that my actions could cause so many ripples. I came here to make it right."

He shook his head and turned away, smacking a palm against the cement wall of the building. "The hell is this? This is crazy. Why'd you even come here?"

"I said I wanted to make it up to you."

He turned, his eyes dark red and glowing. He wasn't just a kid anymore, he was... something else. Realization bubbled inside me, and I felt my powers instinctively rise to attention.

"Liar. I make sure liars pay. I've done it since those days in the hospital. When the doctors lied about my leg, that it would be fine once they cut it off, they lied. I feel the pain there, every single day. My father lied. He said my mother left me because she didn't love me. She died. She died from cancer, and she left me a letter to tell me that she loved me, but my father hid it. He lied to me. Everyone is just a liar." He held out his hand and grabbed my arm. In an instant, I felt my flesh stinging like I'd been poked by a thousand bees.

"You—you're that Stinger guy I've been tracking... the one who's been leaving people to die on the street with thorns stuck through them. It was all you?"

He laughed. "You created me, Mercurial. Why are you so surprised?"

"Let him go!" Cameron screamed, but I shook my head to keep her from coming closer. If I could barely stand his powers, she'd certainly die from getting zapped. I doubted she'd be able to neutralize him before he poisoned her.

"Wait! Don't come any closer. He'll kill you."

She shook her head, yelling an answer I

couldn't hear. I fell to my knees, the pain overtaking my ability to heal and my arm searing where he touched me.

Tony was Stinger. That was who the kid had turned into, all because of me. All my fault. In my head, Tony was a kid again, calling out to me as his eyes widened in horror as a bullet slammed into his father, throwing him to the ground.

"No!" Tony the kid had run to his father, screaming for them to stop. The gunman took no notice that he was so young and continued to send bullets his way, hitting his left leg and sending him crumpling down next to his father. "Dad! Help! Mercurial Man, help my dad!"

I squeezed my eyes shut as these memories flashed across my eyes, shoving them to the side. "Tony, you don't want to do this. You can help people. You can do what I failed to do. Please. Stop."

"Tony, do what he says," Cameron pleaded from a few feet away. I peeked her way, barely able to keep my eyes open. It was then that I realized she hadn't stayed away from us. She was rolling up her sleeves and preparing to jump into the midst of it all. My eyes widened as I turned toward Tony.

She wasn't going to get hurt, Tony was.

Cameron

"LET HIM GO!" I demanded. Merc was on the brink of passing out if I didn't do something soon. "Killing him won't wipe the pain away. Nothing will. You must let him go, Tony. You can't go down that path. You don't want to face the consequences of killing Merc."

Tony's mouth tensed, a frown gracing the edges of it. He thought over my words, but as quickly as the doubt slid in, he shook his head and brushed it off. "Go away, woman. I don't even know why you're here."

"Emilia would be so disappointed."

"She's not here now, is she? No foul there."

"Tony... please. I don't want to hurt you." I sucked in a breath, curling my fingers into my palms.

He laughed, squeezing Warrick. He groaned, his eyes rolling back as he swayed. "You don't want to hurt me? You're nothing. You couldn't harm a fly. Don't come any closer." He flinched as I took a step forward. "He can withstand my powers, but one touch, and you'll die from my stingers."

"I won't die. I'll take your powers, and you'll be ordinary Tony once more. Is that what you want? Because that's what I do. I take the powers from those who abuse them. I'll do it to you if it kills me. Is that what you want?" I repeated my question, hoping he would believe me and stop hurting Merc.

Instead he turned toward me and smirked. "You're making a mistake, lady."

"No, you are." I reached out and grabbed his arm, feeling a sting on my palms like molten metal. It eased as my touch drained the power from him, and his eyes widened as his mouth dropped open.

"No!" He let go of Merc, who dropped to the ground in a heap. "Let go!" Tony screamed, but as the sting of his power biting into my skin cooled to a dull throb, he paled. I felt dizzy, sick, and let go just as the last thread of his power seeped into me. A violent nausea hit me as it absorbed into my core, my "haven" as I called it, for super powers.

Tony was on his knees, bent over and white as a sheet. "What did you do to me?"

"It's done." I heaved a breath out and flicked my eyes toward him. "You're powerless. You're just Tony now."

He stared at his hands in horror, realizing his powers were truly gone. Disbelieving, he reached out and grabbed my arm, squeezing enough to make me yelp. When nothing else happened, he let go, cursing. I cradled my arm as bright red marks blossomed on it, the outline of his fingers stark against my skin.

"I told you. Powerless." I pulled myself toward Merc to check his pulse. It was thready, but it was there. "Warrick, wake up!"

He mumbled, his eyes fluttering up at me. I let his pupils focus for a moment before helping him sit up. We threw one another a knowing look.

"What did you do? They're gone... my powers... Give them back!" Tony, who had dropped to his knees, crawled toward us, cursing his demands.

"I can't. You failed the test. I had to ask Merc to help me. I knew you were causing trouble and had to get to you before you hurt more people. I'm not strong enough to keep you down long enough to drain you, but Merc is."

Merc threw me a perturbed look before he got up to his knees, using the wall for support. When he was on his feet once more, he stared at Tony and held out his hand while his other pulled a pair of handcuffs from his back pocket.

"So, you're Stinger," he said in disbelief. "I'm sorry about your powers. I blame myself, but I'm prepared to make it up to not just the world, but to you too. And it starts by taking you in."

"My powers are gone. They won't believe you." Tony's loathing was hard to ignore, even as Merc snapped the cuffs around his wrists.

"I wouldn't be so sure about that." I motioned toward the small pin attached to my shirt which said "RN" on it. "I recorded it all with this tiny pin camera. I got it on sale at the You-Spy store. A nurse must always be prepared." I fished the attached video recorder from my shirt pocket and held it out, tapping the small screen on one side of the device. I ran the recording back and showed him using his powers on Merc. "You forgot to smile for the camera."

"No!" Tony bucked, but without his powers, he was too weak to break free.

"Let's go," Merc said. "I know just where to take you."

Merc

I SAT IN THE COMFORT of the familiar, run-down

basement, smiling at my pals as they played cards with Cameron. She was a huge asset to the team. After taking Tony in for rehabilitation, which included a six-month removal of his powers, he relented and began working with troubled youth. Turned out he had a knack for it and enjoyed talking about it when I visited him.

"Thanks, Warrick. I don't know why I did those things I did. My powers... they were dark, and they did something to me."

"Maybe if I had visited you, you could've known how much I felt like I had failed you when you and your dad got shot. I really was sorry."

"I don't know. But thanks for helping me clear my head. My powers were so strong, I felt like I was possessed when I used them. I didn't mean to hurt you or anyone else. Really. I just... it was so out of control."

"Well, when you get them back, we can work on that."

Tony's face brightened. "Really? You'll coach me?"

"You bet."

I shook the memory of the conversation away and returned to watching Cameron playing cards, laughing as she figured out the superhero game we'd made up as easily as if she'd been there the whole time. Now our team was complete. Bolt, Carly, Andy, and Kevin were all there too. Just the way I liked it. It was good to have fresh blood on our team, though we rarely had any down time now that we had Cameron. Her power-draining abilities had sent many super powered criminals to prison. Most didn't have the potential for rehabilitation like Tony, and I knew the consequences of bottling up their powers forever wore on Cameron's mind.

I watched her warily, but from the looks of it, she had accepted her fate as I had mine. She turned and sweetly smiled at me. It was a smile that now lit up my world like nothing had before. She leaned forward, touching my hand with hers and giving it a squeeze. One thing was for sure, things were looking a lot brighter for me.

"Your turn, Warrick. Don't worry, I'm still going to win. I'm totally slaying you all."

"You're just a quick study."

She winked. "Only when it matters."

"When you're involved, it always matters."

A Word from Alexia Purdy

Thank you for reading my short super hero story, "Mercurial." It was a blast to write it. I must admit, reading comics in my youth was a rare occurrence. Even so, I made a point to gather some *Archie* and *X-men* ones fascinated by the stories they told and awed by the artwork. How did they produce these mini works of art? It seemed so tedious to make a whole book full of mini frames telling a story in tiny words. So much happened inside them.

This only added to my fascination of telling stories and imagining worlds. I wanted to dive into those frames and watch these heroes and villains come to life. When Saturday morning cartoons dumped some of them into motion, I was hooked. These were the type of heroes I could write: strong, unafraid, loving, yet fierce. Darn if I wasn't going to try to do this my way, so there stemmed my love of writing. Unbeknownst to me, comics had fed into my already growing interest to write.

"Mercurial" was the type of story I would've made into a comic for I'd always wondered what would happen when superheroes were no longer in the main spotlight, somewhat aged, and worn out. Let me know what you think of "Mercurial". If you'd like to find out more about me or read more of my stuff, sign up for my monthly newsletter. It's full of awesome free stuff!

I'm known for my award-winning *Reign of*

IT'S A BIRD! IT'S A PLANE!

Blood series now titled *The Vampires of Vegas* series and my *Dark Faerie Tale* series. My third series, *The ArcKnight Chronicles*, propelled me to USA Today Bestselling author status in 2016. Paranormal urban fantasy and young adult fantasy are my loves, but I also write romantic suspense thrillers. I'm a jack of all trades but I hope you enjoy my takes on different niches, especially this superhero stuff!

ONE LAST TIME

ANDY PELOQUIN

GEORGE MADE the foolish mistake of checking his email before clocking out. He groaned at the unopened message waiting in his inbox.

For a moment, he considered leaving it unread. Mr. Henderson, his boss, loved to use the *"Urgent!!!!"* headline for anything he considered important. Given that the spreadsheet he wanted re-drafted wasn't due for another three weeks, his request didn't qualify as mildly necessary.

Stupid company email. George sighed. If he didn't deal with it now, Mr. Henderson would let him have it the moment he walked into the office tomorrow.

Sighing, George clicked on the email, downloaded the spreadsheet, and set to work. The colorful flyer beside his computer monitor drew his eye. *"Fight Crime!"* it declared in bold white letters on a red background that featured a yellow serpent dragon. *"Defend Yourself!"*

George winced as he shifted in his chair. The

231

radio on the janitor's cart droned in the background. "*...Bright City has grown dangerous since Mighty Man's last confrontation with Doctor Mastermind. The superhero barely managed to foil his arch-nemesis' evil plans to blow up City Hall, and the villain escaped to continue wreaking havoc on the innocents. Since then, Doctor Mastermind's goon squad has been working overtime, leading to an increase in street crime...*"

George tuned out the announcer's voice. The recent crime wave had included the mugging and beating of one George Peters two weeks earlier. His bruised ribs hadn't yet healed.

He checked the clock. *Crap.* At this rate, he'd leave work too late for the last class at the Gold Dragon Kung Fu Dojo.

His eyes strayed to the next cubicle, and his heart sank as he saw the lights switched off and the seat empty. He'd had a crush on her for the three years he'd worked here but never had the courage to say more than an awkward greeting. He'd finally resolved to talk to Doris Murcheson tonight; he'd spent the day practicing his nonchalance in front of the mirror. The coke-bottle glasses and freckled face staring back at him hadn't helped build confidence.

Removing his glasses and rubbing his tired eyes, George relaxed in his chair for a full minute—the longest break he could afford before Mr. Henderson texted him asking why he hadn't replied to the "*Urgent!!!!*" email more quickly. Then he sat up, replaced his spectacles, and reached for his thermos of room temperature coffee. He'd go over the stupid spreadsheet one last time before clocking out, and Mr. Henderson would just have to be happy with it.

• • •

The irritating voice of QKYZ 104.3's morning DJ broke into George's sleep around the same time his brain registered the pounding on his front door. His dreams of using his newfound Kung Fu skills to slam Mr. Henderson's face repeatedly into his cherry wood desk faded in the face of reality. George slipped on his slippers, shivered at the morning chill, and padded across his one-room apartment.

He pressed his eye to the peephole. "Hello?"

The well-dressed man looked sorely out of place against the faded, peeling wallpaper, moth-eaten carpet, and dingy lighting of the hall. He removed his sunglasses and gave the door a broad smile. "Does a George Peters reside at this address?"

"I...er..." George stammered. "W-Who wants to know?" He had no idea why someone with a decidedly "Big Brother" look would want to talk to him. He'd paid his taxes, voted in the last election, and had never come close to committing a crime.

The man drew out a leather wallet, flashing a badge. "Agent O'Malley, Department of Extra-Powered Affairs."

George's eyes widened. What could the DEPA want with him? Maybe the agent had come to ask more questions about the Mastermind henchman who had assaulted him. The BCPD detective who'd taken his statement hadn't even managed to be half-hearted.

Removing the chain, he unlocked the deadbolt and tugged the door open. "Have you found the man, Agent O'Malley? I'd be happy to give another—"

The well-dressed man shook his head. "I'm not here about your assault."

"Oh." George's shoulders drooped. "Then may I ask what this is regarding?"

"Just a moment." Agent O'Malley drew a palm-sized tablet from his breast pocket and frowned down at it. "To confirm, you *are* George Rehoboam Peters, born to James and Elizabeth Peters on June 1, 2450?"

George nodded, his curiosity returning. "That's me. But—"

"And you live *here?*" Agent O'Malley looked around, struggling to hide his displeasure at the linoleum floor, bland wallpaper, and walls devoid of any decoration save for the drab stock image George hadn't bothered to remove from its frame. "At 12986 Hunter Lane Apartment 13D, West Hawk, Bright City?"

"Yes."

"And your current place of employment is at The Grandiose Corporation's headquarters at 3452 Main Street?"

Again, George nodded. "Would you mind telling me—"

"Place your index finger on the screen for the

final confirmation of your identity." The DEPA agent extended his tablet.

George's face scrunched in confusion, but he complied. After a moment, the tablet gave a strident *beep* and a robotic voice proclaimed, "*Biometric match, identified. George Rehoboam Peters.*"

"What is this?" Panic gripped George in a vise. "Am I in some kind of trouble?"

"Congratulations, Mr. Peters." Agent O'Malley pocketed the tablet and extended a meaty hand to shake George's. "You've won the Mighty Man Lottery."

• • •

"Welcome to Power Broker Labs," a feminine voice proclaimed from the hologram behind the front desk. "We've been expecting you, Mr. Peters."

An hour and a ten-mile ride in Agent O'Malley's sleek D.E.P.A-issue car later, George still wasn't certain what was going on. He walked in stunned silence, barely conscious of the well-dressed man guiding him by the elbow toward an elevator.

The artificial voice continued speaking from the screen set into the elevator's control panel. "For twenty years, Power Broker Laboratories has provided extra-powered protection to Bright City. Weapons, protective exo-suits, and antidotes to defend the innocent citizens of our fair city against the predations of supervillains."

"But the threat of Dr. Mastermind demanded a new form of protection. Bright City needed a hero of their own. Thus, Mighty Man was born."

Everyone in Bright City would recognize the face that flashed across the screen. The chiseled jawline, pearly white smile, and perfect musculature could only belong to Mighty Man.

The elevator doors slid open, revealing a gaggle of men and women in white lab coats. They broke into a round of applause as George stepped into the polished marble floor of the lobby.

"Welcome, Mr. Peters!" A middle age man with a broad smile that stood out against his dark skin broke from the crowd. "I am Doctor Patel, and I must admit that I feel truly honored by your presence." He pumped George's hand.

George finally found his voice. "Er...thank you?"

"Come, come, we've much to do to prepare you for the procedure."

"P-Procedure?" George stiffened.

"Ah, yes, of course." Dr. Patel's wide grin returned. "I assume Agent O'Malley failed to properly explain to you what winning the Mighty Man Lottery entails. Allow me to rectify that. But first, if you'd be so kind..." He motioned down one hallway.

George fell into step beside the doctor.

"As you know, Mighty Man has protected our city for over twenty years. Power Broker Laboratories developed the serum that provided him with his powers—invulnerability, super strength, flight, X-ray vision, all the usual abilities. Unfortunately, the serum has its...limitations." Dr. Patel winced. "The exertions placed on Mighty Man's body by his abilities speeds up cellular aging exponentially. Despite all our research, we have failed to solve the problem, and thus have been forced to restrict the serum's effects to eleven months, two weeks, and three days."

That seems an oddly specific timeframe, George thought, but was too polite to say aloud.

"Do you remember the first encounter between Mighty Man and the evil Sea Lord Kahnar?"

George nodded. Everyone remembered the day the world believed Mighty Man dead. The city mourned his loss for a week before his triumphant return.

"The real Mighty Man *did* die. We were forced to find someone to replace him, but the transformation process takes time. When the second Mighty Man approached the end of the serum's viability, the DEPA helped us to find the next candidate. You."

"*What*?!" George's jaw dropped.

"I know it's a lot to process, but—"

"Why me?" George couldn't help asking. "What makes *me* the next Mighty Man?"

"The operant word is the Mighty Man *Lottery*, Mr. Peters. Certain genetic markers are required for the serum to take effect, but there must be an element of unpredictability to the selection process. Doctor Mastermind figured out our process years ago and killed off dozens of the most likely candidates for the procedure. The Department of Extra-Powered Affairs was forced to institute the Mighty Man Lottery, which is used to locate a substitute before the current Mighty Man's serum wears out. All at random so Doctor Mastermind cannot know who will be chosen beforehand. Agent O'Malley and his fellow DEPA agents are able to retrieve and protect the candidate, bringing them here for us to transform into Mighty Man."

George could scarcely believe his ears. It hardly seemed possible that *he* would become Bright City's greatest superhero, yet he saw no deceit in Dr. Patel's expression.

"I understand that it is overwhelming, Mr. Peters, but you will have a great deal of time to come to terms with the change *after* it is complete. Mighty Man has a week before his powers expire." He stopped at a door with a sign reading "Do Not Pass: Authorized Personnel Only" and lifted a clipboard from the hospital-blue wall. "I am legally obligated to ask if you understand what is about to happen, and that you agree to undertake this procedure of your own free will, of sound body and mind."

George glanced at the contract on the clipboard. The listed side effects included *prostate cancer, elbow warts, spinal shrinkage,* and *mononucleosis*, but he couldn't take his eyes off the words "super strength, flight, invulnerability, and X-ray vision." Excitement set his hand trembling as he reached for the pen and scratched his signature onto the form.

Dr. Patel grinned at him. "From this moment on, you are no longer George Peters. You are Mighty Man, Bright City's defender. You have no other identity—remember that, for Doctor Mastermind will seek to use your loved ones against you. The DEPA will be preparing a story to explain your disappearance, but…"

George stopped listening as Dr. Patel began explaining the plethora of complex medical procedures he would be put through. None of it mattered. He took off his spectacles and tucked them into a pocket, uncaring that he could see little more than the blurry shapes of Agent O'Malley and Dr. Patel. He was going to become Mighty Man, and nothing the doctor said could discourage him.

"Are you ready, Mr. Peters? Are you ready for your life to be changed?"

He took one last breath as George Peters, then nodded and stepped through the doors. "I am."

• • •

"Ladies and gentlemen, I give you the defender of Bright City, the one, the only, Mighty Man!"

The throng gathered before the stage broke into a deafening cheer as Mayor Hinton pumped George's hand. *Mighty Man's* hand, with a grip strong enough to pulverize concrete and crush steel.

The face displayed on a thousand T-shirts in the crowd and a million TV screens around the city belonged to him. He'd stared at the chiseled jawline, pearly white smile, and perfect musculature a hundred times in the last two days, and still it felt like something out of a dream.

Dr. Patel's team of plastic surgeons had worked magic while he lay comatose for three days, recovering from the grueling procedure to change him into Mighty Man. When he awoke, the power flowing through his veins had made him feel invincible. Which he was, thanks to Power Broker Labs' super serum. The days spent training with his newfound powers had passed in a blur.

He'd flown to the annual Mighty Man Ceremony, swooping through the city skyscrapers with a speed and coordination the old George hadn't come close to approximating on his video game console. Raw energy coursed through every muscle. He could run a thousand miles without fatiguing, fly twice that, and lift a thousand tons. Every shred of his limited self-control went into stifling the urge to turn his X-ray vision on the gaggle of Mighty Man fangirls clustered at the front of the crowd. Thanks to their strategically torn T-shirts and thigh-high skirts, he caught more than an eyeful without it.

Mayor Hinton stepped up to the podium. "Citizens of Bright City, today we celebrate the twentieth anniversary of Mighty Man's arrival to our fair metropolis. For 20 years, he has kept us safe from Doctor Mastermind, The Mad Genius, Captain Destruct-O, and others who would do our fair city harm." He turned to George. "Would you like to say a few words, Mighty Man?"

George blushed instinctively. He had no idea what to say. The thought of speaking in front of the crowd sent a tremor through him, and he fought the urge to retreat.

"Mighty Man!" one voice called.

The crowd took up the cheer. "Mighty Man! Mighty Man!"

They called for *him*.

He stepped forward and cleared his throat. "My friends, you honor me." Hearing the strong, commanding voice echoing from the speakers around the square felt surreal. "I am but one man, blessed with extraordinary abilities, but more blessed to live in a city of such strength and re-silience."

A roar swelled from the throng.

Excitement rushed through George. "Doctor Mastermind and his ilk may think you weak, helpless. They prey on you, steal from you, threaten your homes and lives. But they are wrong! You are not weak or helpless; you are strong. You stand firm in the face of their threats and hold your heads high." His grip on the podium tightened, crushing wood. "I live in a city of heroes: each and every one of you. And it is *I* who am honored to serve you."

A smile broadened George's face as the cries and cheers swelled to a deafening roar. They shout-ed his name again.

"Mighty Man! Mighty Man!"

He was no longer George Rehoboam Peters. He

was a hero—and not just any hero; he was Mighty Man, the greatest champion his city had ever known.

• • •

"Alert, alert!" The feminine voice of V.A.L.O.R., the artificial intelligence responsible for monitoring criminal activity in Bright City, echoed from the speakers built into Mighty Man's enormous bedroom.

Mighty Man leapt up from the super king-sized bed. "What is it, V.A.L.O.R.?"

"I've just received reports of seismic activity downtown." A hologram of a slim brunette outfitted in colorful, revealing latex appeared on his bedside screen.

He dashed to the console beside the window. "Could it be the Earth Master?"

"It appears to be concentrated beneath First Bright City Bank and Trust."

"The villain!" Mighty Man pounded his fist on the tabletop and winced at the *crack* of wood, steel, and electronic components. Even after a week, he had yet to master his superhuman strength.

"The BCPD have cordoned off the area, but they won't move in for fear the Earth Master will open a sinkhole again."

Mighty Man puffed up. "Tell them to stay back, V.A.L.O.R. Mighty Man's on the job!"

• • •

"Thank you, Mighty Man!" Police Commissioner Denton pumped his hand. "You've saved a lot of lives today."

Mighty Man grinned. "All in a day's work, Commissioner." He nodded toward Earth Master, who lay unconscious, surrounded by a squad of DEPA agents. Even as he spoke, Agent O'Malley slapped a pair of power-dampening cuffs on the prone villain, a pathetically dirty, balding, and paunchy man with skin ghost-white from living underground. "We'll take it from here. He won't be breaking out of the Stockade anytime soon."

"Woohoo, go Mighty Man!" A crowd of young men in uncomfortably deep-cut tank tops emblazoned with '*Alpha Sigma Tau, we do life our way!*' shouted from a nearby restaurant. The boisterous youths on their downtown bar hop had ruined many of George's nights, but Mighty Man basked in the praise.

With a crisp salute, he leapt into the air and sped away from the crime scene to the cheers of the people below.

• • •

"I must congratulate you, Mighty Man." Dr. Patel applauded. "In the last two months, you've apprehended Earth Master, The Yellow Whistler, and Captain Hammerhead. You seem to be taking to your abilities well."

Mighty Man grinned and raised his champagne flute. "It's all thanks to you at Power Broker Labs, Dr. Patel. Your serum is marvelous."

"Indeed." The doctor emptied his glass and set

it on the conference table. "How are you feeling? Any side effects?"

Mighty Man shook his head. "None." He didn't count insomnia as a side effect. He had so much energy to burn protecting the city; so far he hadn't noticed anything wrong with a few hours of sleep each night.

"Good." Dr. Patel checked something on his clipboard. "Any psychological changes since undergoing the procedure?" He raised an eyebrow. "Depression? Anxiety? Stress?"

"Are you kidding?" Mighty Man laughed. "I've never felt better!"

To demonstrate, he flew out the conference room window, circled the building, and landed on the carpeted floor with hardly a *thump.*

Dr. Patel chuckled. "Good. Well, it seems like the serum is working, and thanks to you Bright City has never been safer."

"Oh, I'm just getting started! I've got my eye set on taking them *all* down. First, Captain Destruct-O. After him, I've got a plan for finding Doctor Mastermind..."

• • •

Glass shards peppered the far wall as Mighty Man crashed through the window. Wiping a trickle of blood from his split lip, he leapt to his feet and flew at the colossal robot destroying the Business District. He had to stop Captain Destruct-O from unleashing his death ray on Bright City Stadium and killing the thousands of football fans gathered to cheer on the Capes.

Metallic laughter boomed from speakers set into the robot's head. "You won't stop me this time, Mighty Man! The upgrades to my Destruct-O-Bot render it impervious to your most powerful punches."

"I don't think so!" Mighty Man smiled as he caught sight of a familiar flaming red Porsche—Mr. Henderson's pride and joy. The vehicle had mocked him every time he drove past in the rattling Ford Fiesta junker he'd driven for fifteen years.

Swooping down, he gripped the car in one hand and slammed it into the robot's enormous knee joint. The metal monster staggered, arms flailing as Captain Destruct-O fought for balance. A huge hand crashed through the top four floors of the Grandiose Corp building. Mighty Man laughed; he had to hope Mr. Henderson had been working in his office. The red Porsche crumpled as he drove it into the robot's other knee.

"Noooooo!!!" Captain Destruct-O shouted as the metal giant toppled backward.

Mighty Man's heart stopped. Hundreds of people that had gathered on the street to watch the brawl were in danger of being crushed. He had a split second to act.

With every shred of speed, he dived toward the ground and surged up to catch the falling robot. He grunted beneath the impact. Metal groaned and twisted, the robotic limbs sparking as they crashed to the street.

Silence hung thick in the air. For a moment, it seemed Bright City held its breath. Then a roar broke from the gathered people. Mighty Man hovered a mere ten feet off the ground, the enormous robot resting on his broad shoulders.

"Mighty Man! Mighty Man!" The crowd cheered his name even as they rushed to clear the way.

Gritting his teeth against the strain, Mighty Man set his burden down. Air hissed from the robotic head; Captain Destruct-O was trying to flee!

"Oh, no, you don't!" Mighty Man snapped off one of the robotic arms and brought it down atop the escape capsule detaching from the fallen giant. "Justice may be blind, but *I'm* not." He thought that quite a clever line; he'd worked on it for the last few days.

Sirens blared and the BCPD officers scrambled over the wreckage of Captain Destruct-O's escape pod.

A police officer lifted his hat in salute. "We've got it from here, Mighty Man!"

With a nod, Mighty Man turned toward the crowd. "Is anyone hurt?"

"I might be!" A buxom blonde in a floral summer dress pushed through the crowd. "I think you need to check me for injuries."

Mighty Man raised an eyebrow in appreciation. The "*MM*" tattooed across her ample chest marked her as one of the Mighty Misses, his own personal fan group. His encounters with them had proven...interesting in the past. A smile broadened his lips. *Perks of the job, I guess.*

Something caught his eye. A red-haired woman in a purple dress stood near the back of the crowd. Mighty Man started. *Doris?* He hadn't thought of her once since the day he won the lottery. Before he could say anything, she turned and disappeared into the crowd.

He almost went after her. The blonde tugging on his bicep kept him rooted to the spot.

"Well?" She raised a suggestive eyebrow.

Mighty Man smiled. "If you'd like, I could give you a thorough examination somewhere more private."

"Mighty Tower, perhaps?" She leaned forward and whispered into his ear. "I've got something to make it a *real* party."

• • •

Mighty Man gasped as the white powder burned down his nose and throat. He'd never tried cocaine before—George Peters hadn't been able to afford it—but now he couldn't get enough of it. Though the effects only lingered a few minutes, he reveled in the sensation while it lasted.

This was a new sort of high. It reminded him of the first time he'd tested his power of flight. But instead of the rush of the wind through his hair, energy rushed through him in waves of fire. He felt as if he could defeat every villain in Bright City in one day!

"Don't tell me my superhero is *already* tired?" The blonde—Mandy or Mary, he couldn't remember—pulled off the sheet, giving him a generous eyeful of her curves.

Mighty Man smiled and took another bump. "I'm just getting warmed up!"

He'd taken a single step toward the bed when the alert on his computer monitor blared. "Warning, warning!" The feminine voice of V.A.L.O.R. echoed in the room. "Doctor Mastermind's goon squad has invaded City Hall and taken Mayor Hinton captive."

Mighty Man hesitated. He knew he should respond to the call and fly to the rescue, but he couldn't tear his eyes from the woman in his bed.

V.A.L.O.R. spoke again. "I have that data you requested, Mighty Man. You were right."

All thoughts of Malia or Mona —whatever her name was —flew from his head. He scanned the information V.A.L.O.R. displayed on the screen and pumped his fist in triumph. With a sigh and one last glance at the languid figure stretched out on the sheets, he flew from the room.

• • •

"You haven't heard the last of me, Mighty Man!" Doctor Mastermind's shrill voice cut through the crowd's cheers. "My master stroke will come when you least expect it!"

The door to the D.E.P.A. Superpowered Prisoner Transport vehicle slammed shut, cutting off the rest of the supervillain's ramblings.

"Mighty Man, over here!"

Mighty Man turned in time to have a camera and microphone shoved into his face.

"Connie Kim, Channel 18 News. All of us are eager to know: how do you find the time to do it all? In the last six months since you've captured Captain Hammerhead, you've put away nearly twenty other villains. Now, you track down and capture Doctor Mastermind himself. How did you do it?"

Mighty Man grinned. "A wise man once said, 'Follow the money,' Connie. So that's exactly what I did." He puffed up his chest; his accounting skills had come in handy. "Commissioner Denton and I worked together to trace where Doctor Mastermind's goon squad was getting their money. I won't bore you with the details, but they led us right to the bank accounts opened under Doctor Mastermind's secret identity: Judge Bill Reynard."

The reporter's face paled. "Doctor Mastermind, a judge?"

"A fearful thought, indeed, Connie." He turned his smile full into the cameras. "But have no fear, citizens of Bright City. You can rest easy knowing the supervillain is behind bars."

"There you have it, folks. Mighty Man has done the impossible and defeated his archnemesis. He's fast, he's strong, and he's super-intelligent—Bright City's own defender!"

The cameraman gave a thumbs up.

IT'S A BIRD! IT'S A PLANE!

"Thank you, Mighty Man." Connie smiled up at him. "Maybe one of these days I could get an *exclusive* with you?" She leaned forward, giving him a glimpse of the *"MM"* tattooed just beneath her shirt's neckline.

He winked. "I'm sure something could be arranged."

• • •

Mighty Man rolled over and placed a pillow over his head, but the pounding on his door persisted.

"Mighty Man, open the door!"

Groaning, Mighty Man climbed out of bed and took a quick snort of the powder piled on V.A.L.O.R.'s console. Fire burned the back of his throat and energy surged through him.

He pulled the door open. "What?"

Displeasure showed plain on Dr. Patel's face. "I've come for your monthly check-up. You've missed the last three."

"I don't need any stupid physical or psych exam." He tensed his enormous bicep. "See? Never felt better. Now go away before you wake up my guests."

Dr. Patel tried to peer into the room, but Mighty Man's bulk blocked the view of the three women tangled in his sheets.

"I must be certain the serum isn't having—"

"Forget about it, doc. I'm feeling great." The cocaine flowing through his bloodstream helped with that. "Bright City has never been safer, so I don't need your silly questions. I'm happy, no depression or anxiety, and I'm as strong as ever."

He closed the door in Dr. Patel's face before he could speak. The doctor's protests went unheard as Mighty Man filled his nostrils with more cocaine.

• • •

"Alert, alert!" V.A.L.O.R.'s artificial voice pierced the muddle in Mighty Man's head. "Mastermind alert."

Mighty Man swatted at the console. He'd captured Doctor Mastermind three months ago—V.A.L.O.R. had to be broken.

He ignored the blaring alarm, but it persisted.

"Shut up, V.A.L.O.R.!"

"Alert, alert!" V.A.L.O.R.'s tone grew more strident. "Explosions have gone off around the city, and the bombs register as containing Quintillium."

That caught Mighty Man's attention. He lifted his head, groaning at the pounding ache in his skull, and blinked at the bedside monitor. Four red blips showed on the screen.

"You sure it was Quintillium? Doctor Mastermind has been locked up for—"

"Three months, two weeks, and four days." V.A.L.O.R. spoke in a tone surprisingly snippy for a computer. "But my sensors don't lie. The bombs contain Quintillium, Doctor Mastermind's explosive of choice."

Mighty Man rolled from the bed onto unsteady

legs. He blinked to stop the world spinning and searched for a glass of water for his parched throat. His mouth felt as stuffed with wool as his head. No way he'd be able to save the city like this.

"Let the police handle it."

"BCPD is already on the scene of the explosions, as is BCFD. But they are requesting your aid in controlling the fires."

Mighty Man sighed. "Fine."

His eyes fell on the lines of green powder on the table. He'd take a hit of the new drug—a highly potent mixture of synthetic methamphetamine and cocaine one of the Mighty Misses had brought—one last time.

Why do I have to do everything *in Bright City?* One of these days, the pitiful people had to learn how to protect themselves.

• • •

Mighty Man hovered a hundred feet in the air, petrified. Screams of panic and fear filled the air as explosions rocked Bright City. He could do nothing but watch, horrified, as people leapt from crumbling skyscrapers.

"Mighty Man!" V.A.L.O.R. squawked in his earpiece. "You need to do something!"

His mind, befuddled by the lingering effects of the drugs, struggled to respond to the threats all around. Just as he dove to catch a falling woman, two more people tumbled from a collapsing building. He couldn't stop it! He couldn't save them all!

Carnage and chaos swept through Bright City, and he had no idea where to begin.

"Mighty Man!" the AI shouted. "Move, now. There are people trapped atop the Grandiose Corp Building. They need you."

The familiar name pierced his horror-numbed thoughts. *Doris!*

He shot through the city, dodging crumbling buildings, ignoring the cries for help. He wanted to save everyone but *had* to save Doris.

Grandiose Corp's shining tower rose in the distance, a massive hole ripped into its façade. Dozens of people stood on the rooftop. They screamed and waved as he zoomed toward them. He scanned the crowd—no Doris!

He couldn't leave them to die. He carried them to safety in groups of twos and threes, always returning for more. As he flew, he turned his X-ray vision on the enormous skyscraper, searching, desperate. He'd recognize the slight abnormal curvature of Doris' spine—the result of her scoliosis—anywhere.

But something was wrong! He squinted as his vision suddenly returned to normal. He tried again, concentrated harder, but his X-ray vision refused to work.

Damn it! He'd have to do it the old-fashioned way.

He swooped through the collapsing high-rise, catching falling debris, saving those he could see with his normal human vision.

A woman screamed, pinned beneath an enormous metal beam. Mighty Man darted toward her and seized the beam in his powerful grip.

"Don't worry, ma'am. You'll be out of here in no —"

The beam refused to budge. He heaved, his enormous muscles bunching. Slowly, with the groan of twisting metal and shifting concrete, he lifted it enough for her to squirm out from beneath.

What's wrong with me? The ache in his head had to come from the drugs. So why were his powers failing him?

The skyscraper collapsed atop him, burying him in ten floors' worth of rubble. He hurled himself upward and poured all his strength and power of flight into it. The debris shifted slightly.

"Migh...Man...you need...out...there!" V.A.L.O.R. crackled in his earpiece.

"I can't hear you," he shouted, a hint of panic in his voice. With his powers, he should have no problem escaping.

He drove his shoulder into the rubble. Concrete clattered aside and a pinprick of light pierced the darkness.

"You need to get out of there, Mighty Man!" the AI shouted. "The serum's effects will be gone any minute."

Horror frozen Mighty Man in place. *No!*

"Did you hear me? I said —"

"I—I heard you, V.A.L.O.R." His voice sounded so weak—like George's voice.

Desperation surging within him, he scrabbled at the obstructing debris, widening the gap until he could crawl out. He emerged, gasping fresh air, and coughed the dust from his lungs. Blood trickled from dozens of cuts—shredded concrete, shards of glass, and twisted rebar had pierced his once-invulnerable skin.

Fear buried an icy knife in his gut. He stood on the 35th floor; the street seemed a *long* way down. For a moment, he felt something he hadn't in months: helplessness. Without his Mighty Man powers, he was as trapped as the ordinary people. And no one would come to rescue him.

• • •

George sat on the ratty, food-stained couch in his old apartment, his eyes never leaving the blank TV screen before him. The face that stared back at him bore no resemblance to the George Peters he remembered. Folds of skin formed jowls that drooped beyond his chin, and bags hung thick and dark under his bleary eyes.

"I've never seen this before," Dr. Patel had said. "The cosmetic surgeries were intended to be temporary, and your facial structure should have reverted back to normal. It's possible that you ingested something—a strong amphetamine, perhaps—that interacted negatively with the serum." George had stopped listening after the words "There's nothing

255

we can do."

The first rays of sunlight filtered through the dingy glass. The curtains that usually covered the apartment's single window were slightly open. The irritating voice on QKYZ 104.3 echoed from George's bedroom.

"This is Crazy Mike and the Fox, reporting from QKYZ radio room. We like to start the morning with something upbeat, but after the events of two days ago, I don't think *anyone* is in a happy mood. Our thoughts and prayers go out to the families of the four thousand victims of Doctor Mastermind's attack. This was a sad day for Bright City, folks. The city skyline is forever changed, but worse than that, my belief in Mighty Man has been shaken to the core. Did anyone else see him flitting around like a drunken bug? Where was the *old* Mighty Man, the one who put away Doctor Mastermind and Captain Destruct-O? When is that guy coming back? The city needs him more than ever."

• • •

"This is Connie Kim, reporting live from the site of Bright City's greatest tragedy in more than a decade. Behind me, the clean-up crews are valiantly attempting to restore order to the city, but I've heard reports that it will take *months* to clear away the debris and rubble and find all the bodies. The repairs are estimated to cost the city over two billion dollars. My sources in City Hall are saying Mayor Hinton was killed in the attack along with his entire cabinet.

Many are calling Mighty Man's efforts to help 'too little, too late,' asking 'Where were you, Mighty Man, when the city needed you?' Some believe an investigation into Mighty Man's —"

George switched off the TV and reached for another beer. The swill made his head ache and his stomach churn, but he didn't give a damn. He just needed to close his eyes and shut everything out.

He tipped the can to his lips. Empty. Hands that had once pulverized metal struggled to crush a single aluminum can.

George stopped trying. The can clattered to the floor, adding to the growing pile. He hadn't moved from the sofa in days except to use the bathroom and accept takeout and beer deliveries. With the settlement he received from the city for his service as Mighty Man, he could spend the next year on his couch. He had no reason to get up, nor any desire. Everything he was had gone. Only the weak, pathetic George Peters remained.

He'd begged Dr. Patel in vain to give him another hit of the serum. So what if the transformation killed him? His old life would kill him just the same. It would all be worth it to feel the rush of power, the strength of Mighty Man one last time.

• • •

George drifted in a haze of fire and misery. The heroin had begun to kick in, flooding his veins with a rush of heat that fought to push back his stupor. He lay back on the filthy, moldering couch and closed his eyes. Slowly, the stink of garbage and urine filling the alleyway faded beneath the first threads of euphoria clawing through his brain.

Nothing else mattered but this. He'd never fly over the city, never feel the surge of adrenaline as he battled the Earth Master, Captain Hammerhead, or Doctor Mastermind. The Mighty Man serum had given him everything he ever wanted. Its absence left him with nothing.

He was George again. *Just* George.

He couldn't have his superpowers back, so he had only one other way to feel that way again. Paltry and pathetic by comparison, but he'd take it however he could get it.

Snatches of conversation from a nearby radio filtered through his euphoria. "Mighty Man failed Bright City once...something's changed in him, like he's a new man...learned from the disaster three weeks ago...integral to the reconstruction efforts... renewed vigilance. The streets have never been safer since..."

The heroin's euphoria dimmed. George had failed as a superhero and someone *else* had to clean up his mess. Groaning, he climbed to leaden feet and stumbled away from the ratty couch. He had to get away from the voice that reminded him of everything he *hadn't* done for Bright City.

The world spun around him, the wind rushing through his hair. Once again, he flew through the air above Bright City, the power of Mighty Man coursing through his veins.

A scream echoed from the mouth of the alley. Two men wrestled with a woman. Something about the simple floral print of her dress and the bright headscarf wrapping her scarlet curls seemed so familiar.

Doris! Hadn't she died in the Grandiose Corp building collapse?

"Help!" Doris screamed.

"Shut up, lady!" A thug wearing the purple and green of Doctor Mastermind's goon squad drew a gun. "Don't make us hurt you."

As he had so many times in the last year, George charged toward danger. He threw himself at the goon and wrapped him into a powerful embrace. He'd show these thugs what it meant to face a real superhero. He was Mighty Man, defender of—

His face slammed into the huge man's chest, twisting his neck at a painful angle. He rebounded and sagged to the mud of the alley.

"Who's this fool?" the second thug asked. "Thinks he's some sort of hero?"

George's mind struggled through the numbness of the heroin. Why weren't his powers working? Why wasn't he—?

The gun barked twice. Twin impacts slammed into George's back. Pain raced up and down his spine, tearing through his side.

"Please!" Doris begged. "Don't hurt me."

George struggled upright.

"Stay down, hero." Another bullet punched into his back.

George grunted and sagged back to the muck. He couldn't move; an icy numbness seeped into his legs, pushing back the soothing fire of the heroin.

"Hey!" A man's voice sounded from the far end of the alley. "BCPD, stop right there!"

"Dammit, cops!" The pounding of booted feet grew fainter.

"You alright, lady?"

"Yes, but he's hurt!"

"Officer Atman to Main, I need you to roll an ambo to the alley between Alamo and Third. Victim with three GSWs to the back, and he's not..."

The officer's voice faded from earshot.

A shadow fell over George's face. "Can you hear me?" Doris asked.

George tried to respond but couldn't summon the strength to speak. The heroin's fire grew fainter, and every panicking beat of his heart pumped more blood onto the muddy street.

"Wh-Whoever you are, thank you! You saved me." Her hand gripped his. "Hang on just a little longer. An ambulance is on the way!"

George closed his eyes, a smile playing on his lips. He didn't care whether he lived or not. Only one thing mattered: he'd been a hero one last time.

A Word from Andy Peloquin

I hope you enjoyed reading "One Last Time," even if it was a tad darker than your usual superhero fare!

I've been a hardcore comic book reader for over a decade now, falling in love with the more anti-heroic characters like Deadpool, The Punisher, and Spawn. To be able to write a superhero story like this—even one so cynical and dark—is a true thrill. It is still my lifelong dream to write for Marvel Comics and have my cruel way with the comic book characters I fell in love with so long ago.

"One Last Time" is a look at what happens when you give an "average mortal" amazing abilities. Not everyone turns out to be a shining hero or a dastardly villain. Some are just normal people who let the power and fame go to their head.

If you'd like to let me know what you think of "One Last Time" or you just want to say hello, feel free to email me (at andy.peloquin@gmail.com). If you'd like to find out more about me or read more of my stuff, sign up for my bi-weekly reader's list. You get a free book (the first in my fantasy half-demon assassin series) plus updates on my writing and lots of goodies.

To see more of my writing, check out my Amazon Author Page. Thank you for reading!

HERO WORSHIP

JOSH HAYES

One: Now

"THAT'LL BE $5.87, SIR"

Harold Givens looked up from his phone, not bothering to hide his dissatisfaction. "$5.87? Are you kidding me? It's just coffee."

The barista held the paper cup up with a grin. "This is HeroBucks coffee, sir. You won't find a better brew this side of Liberty City."

Harold swiped his debit card through the terminal, shaking his head. He took the cup, careful to keep his grip light as to not burn his fingers. The "sidekick" size was barely taller than his hand.

"Thanks," he said, then headed for the door.

He took a sip as he stepped outside, and winced, the overpriced contents singeing his lips. He glared back through the glass door at the barista, who was busy serving the next customer, and wondered how much money this store made standing on the shoulders of some trumped up hero.

The sign above the door featured a stylized cut

out of a hero wearing a red and blue uniform, her hands on her hips, hair blowing in the wind. "Furious Grounds" was written in large block letters across the heroine's waist.

"Your coffee's not that great, Fury," Harold told the sign.

Harold stopped short as a boy ran by, pulling his father by the hand. He muttered a curse under his breath, holding his coffee out to keep it from spilling on his shirt. That's all he needed today, a coffee stained shirt for what could be the most important job interview of his life.

"Damn kids," Harold said, watching the boy pull the man down the side walk.

"Look, Dad, look!" the boy shouted, pointing. "I told you he was here."

The man laughed, allowing himself to be pulled along. "I know, son. I believe you, I see him too."

Harold followed the boys finger down the street to a row of tall buildings. He snorted when he saw the cause of the boy's excitement. *Of course*, Harold thought.

On the corner of the tallest building, Blaze stood, arms crossed, looking over the city. His green cape whipped in the wind behind him, giving the whole sight a dramatic flair.

On the street, others were stopping, pointing out and swapping stories about the iconic hero

"Did you hear about the time he took on the entire Columbian Army by himself?"

"I was there when he defeated Chaos."

"How about that time he took on the entire Giglio Gang?"

"He's probably the most powerful Hero ever," a boy said, tugging on his father's hand, trying to get a closer look. "Do you think I can get a signature?"

The father finally managed to stop the boy's advance, then lifted him up above the crowd for a better view. "Let's not bother him, son. He looks busy."

The boy continued to pull, face pleading. "Pleeease."

Laughing, the father said, "Okay, son, we can ask."

Harold rolled his eyes. "What a bunch of crap."

A woman next to him frowned. "What?"

Harold pointed at the hero with his coffee cup. "Them. The whole world sings their praises, putting them up on pedestals like they're gods or something."

"I don't think they're gods," the woman replied, "but look at how much they do for us."

"People forget, we used to help ourselves."

"Seriously? If it hadn't been for Blaze, Chaos would have destroyed this city and everyone in it."

"And how much did that victory cost the tax payers? 200 million dollars, last I heard. They say it will take ten years to rebuild everything they destroyed."

The woman crossed her arms. "You make it

sound like you blame Blaze for everything."

"I don't blame him for everything, but I think they all need to be held accountable."

"You're crazy," the woman said, turning away from him.

"Accountable?" a man standing beside her said. "And who's going to do that? You?"

Harold scoffed when he saw the pin on the man's shirt. A closed fist emblazoned on a tradition shield. Harold shook his head. There would be no point arguing with this man. Trying to convince hero worshippers that heroes were not infallible was like playing chess with a pigeon, no matter how good you are, the bird is going to crap on the board and strut around like it won anyway. In their eyes, the heroes could do no wrong.

Harold knew better.

Two: Then

A horn blared, pulling the boy's attention from his copy of *Contact* by Carl Sagan. He looked over the seat-back in front of him as the bus driver laid on the horn, cursing loudly. The boy had enough time to frown, wondering why the man was waving his hands like a crazy person, before he was thrown forward, smashing into the seat.

Groaning metal and terrified screams echoed around him as he landed on the floor, knocking the air from his lungs. He tried to cry out, but his scream caught in his throat.

He reached up, using the seat to pull himself off the floor. The bus bounced, tossing him back into the wall. Pain shot through his skull as his head bounced off the window. Stars danced in his blurred vision.

"Bec—"

He caught a blurred glimpse of the world outside the bus just before it shifted. His body became weightless and he watched as backpacks, books, and his classmates all rose into the air. The world outside turned upside down, and a second later, everyone and everything came crashing down and began bouncing down the street.

For a moment, the roof of the bus was the floor and the boy scrambled to find something to hold on to. Several kids near the front were sliding around, slamming into each other. A book flew past the boy's head as the bus continued to roll. Another bounce tossed him into the air and the sense of weightlessness returned.

Papers, books, pens, and people all seemed to float in the air around him. For a long moment, an eerie silence came over the chaotic interior as the world outside turned again. He could see cars, the street, and the grass along the road. The sky appeared, the sun blinding him for half a second before it vanished.

In that eternal moment in time, a single thought resonated through the boy's mind: *Becky.* He looked over the faces of this classmates. Where had she been sitting? He had to find her. Had to—

He caught a glimpse of something flying through the air, then everything went black.

Three: Now

Harold gave the Hero Worshipper a half-hearted smile, then made for the street. With everyone's attention focused on the hero, maybe he could make it to his interview early.

He hailed a cab and a minute later, one pulled up to the curb. As Harold opened the door to climb in, shouts of excitement and awe echoed through the gathered crowd. He looked up as Blaze lifted into the air, slowly at first, then twisted and shot out over the city.

Good riddance, Harold thought, and slipped into the cab.

"117th and Washington."

The driver tapped the address into a small computer and smiled. "Absolutely, sir."

Harold held his coffee in front of him as they pulled out into traffic. He looked outside and saw the boy giving his father a high-five.

"Just wait kid," Harold said. "They'll disappoint you someday."

The driver looked over his shoulder. "What's that?"

"Oh, nothing." Harold jerked a thumb outside. "Just a whole bunch of misguided people. I wish people would realize all these heroes," Harold held up air quotes, "aren't gods. They're just people who can do some pretty weird stuff."

"Maybe so," the driver said. "But weird or not, most of them do more good than any of us. And they don't ask for much in return."

"No, only our compliance and mindless devotion."

The radio music cut off abruptly, replaced by a female voice. "We interrupt our regularly scheduled program to bring you this breaking news bulletin."

The driver turned up the volume.

"We are receiving reports that a passenger train has derailed on the mid-town line. Preliminary reports estimate twenty-two cars have left the track. Emergency response crews are on scene and encouraging everyone not directly related to the rescue effort to stay away from the area."

Harold leaned back in his seat. "Guess that explains where Blaze went off to. Hey man, can you hurry it up, I really need to make it to this appointment before the world ends."

The driver turned. "I can only go as fast as the traffic, sir. I'm not a magic carpet or anything."

They drove several blocks, listening to the news updates on the derailed train. Two hundred and forty-two people injured so far, and the numbers we're still coming in.

"...This could be the worst disaster the city's ever faced," the reporter said.

Harold felt the cab slow just as he heard sirens coming up behind them. An ambulance sped past, lights flashing.

"I bet you they call in everyone for this," the driver said. "Last time, something like this happened, Chaos blew up that airplane. You remember that? It landed in the Bay and Blaze lifted the entire thing out of the water. Man, I remember seeing it on the news that night, what a crazy day, right?"

Of course, he'd heard about that. Everyone at the office had talked non-stop about it for weeks. What everyone failed to mention, even the news, was that Chaos bombed that plane in retaliation for Blaze destroying one of his factories down south. Blaze wasn't blameless. His hands were just as bloody as Chaos's.

But no one cared about—

A horn blared. Something big plowed into the driver's side of the cab, crushing metal, shattering glass. The impact slammed Harold into the door as the car spun. His head smacked against the window and his world became a blur.

He slid back across the seat, fingers grasping for anything to grab hold of. The car hit something else, violently reversing its spin. Metal popped and the clear plastic partition snapped loose and folded back on itself.

Pain shot through Harold's arm as the partition pinned him against the door.

Four: Then

Screaming brought the boy back to consciousness. He opened his eyes, his vision blurred, head throbbing. He was laying on his chest, his entire body hurt. Something warm was running down his face, he touched it and brought away bloody fingers. He tried to move and lightning—pain like he'd never felt before—shot up his leg.

He cried out, looking back and seeing his leg was twisted badly between one of the seat-legs and the wall of the bus. His jeans were twisted around his leg so tight, the fabric pinched his skin. Every time he moved, another wave of agony pulsed through him.

Tears mixed with the blood trickled down his face, dripping on the window he lay on. Instead of blue sky, trees and the city, the boy only saw dark grey concrete, two solid yellow lines painted across it.

The street?

The bus was on its side. Over the top of the seat, he saw several other kids crawling on the side, which was now the floor, of the bus. Some pulled themselves up to stand between the seats, others just sat and cried. Several didn't move at all. At the far end of the bus, the bus driver was slumped over in his seat, held up only by his seatbelt. His arms dangled limply in the air.

Terrified cries and wailing filled the air around him. The boy gritted his teeth against his pain, making every effort to lay perfectly still so he wouldn't aggravate his injury.

IT'S A BIRD! IT'S A PLANE!

Smoke seeped inside through the shattered windshield, curling along the top, the now-side, of the bus. Something was on fire.

"Becky!" the boy called out, his voice broken and hoarse. He swallowed, trying to work up more saliva. "Becky, where are you?"

He adjusted his position to get a better look, but stopped short as another burst of white-hot pain shot through his leg. He gritted his teeth against the pain, blinking away tears.

"Help!" he called, twisting his body, trying to see more of the bus. "Becky, are you okay?"

"Becky!"

A face appeared from behind the seat in front of him. Long, brown hair hung in a tangled mess over a face smeared with dirt, grime, and tears. Her confused, terrified expression turned to relief at the sight of her brother, then she burst out into sobs.

"I didn't mean to throw that spit wad at Steve," his sister said, sobbing, her entire body shaking.

"Becky," the boy said, reaching for her. "Becky, it's okay. It's going to be okay."

She moved around the seat separating them, and wrapped her arms around him. He groaned, his face twisting in pain as she squeezed. She realized that he was in pain and quickly let go, scooting back.

"I'm sorry, I'm sorry!" she cried. "I didn't mean to hurt you. Are you okay?"

The boy swallowed hard, trying not to vomit. "It's my leg, I think it's broken."

274

She craned her head to look as his injury and grimaced.

"It's okay," the boy reassured her. "Someone is going to come for us."

Despite the chaos around her, Becky's face lit up. "You mean a hero is coming?"

Through his pain, the boy smiled back at his sister, knowing that she would believe anything he said. "Yeah, sis, a hero will save us."

Five: Now

Harold's world came back into focus to the sound of honking horns and panicked shouts. His head throbbed, his vision still slightly blurry. He tried to sit up and a pain pulsed in his arm.

He cried out, trying to pry at the partition with his free hand. He tried to jam his fingers around its metal frame, but it wouldn't budge. Everytime he moved, the electric-like pain coursed through the length of his pinned arm.

He looked forward. The driver was slumped over the small computer mounted to the center console. Blood streamed out of a deep cut on his head.

"Hey," Harold pounded on the partition just behind the driver. "Hey, man, wake up!"

The driver didn't move.

"Help!" he yelled, looking around. He could see several vehicles stopped in the street. People appeared around the cab, all looking over the damaged car, their expressions a mixture of shock and concern.

"Help me!" Harold shouted.

Two men came up to the passenger door and began trying to pull it open.

"Hold tight, friend," one said. He wore a Liberty City Fireballs ball cap, its solid white front decorated with a fiery baseball. "We're going to get you out of there."

"It's jammed," the other said, grunting as he pulled on the handle.

They looked over the door for a second, then the man in the ball cap said, "Look, the frame's bent. No way we're getting that door open."

"Come on," the other man said. "Let's try the other side."

Two more people reached the front passenger doors and encountered the same problem. Harold looked over his shoulder at the driver's side of the car and knew they wouldn't have any better luck there. Both front and back doors were caved in from the impact. Crushed like a beer can.

"Cover your face!" someone yelled.

A second later, Harold heard a *thwack* and looked back in time to see a pole bounce off the window just behind his head. The man cursed then swung again. The pipe connected with another *thwack*, but bounced off without so much as cracking the glass.

Harold held up his free hand. "No, stop, don't..."

The man swung a third time. This time the glass shattered, showering Harold with hundreds of tiny shards. He cursed, raising his free hand to shield his face.

"For Pete's sake, watch it!" Harold shouted.

"Hold on, man, we'll just..."

Harold felt hands reaching under his armpits. Panic shot through him. "No, wait!"

The man grunted. "...pull you out."

"No!"

The man pulled and Harold cried out in agony. Stabbing pain tore through his arm as muscle pinched and skin pulled. He screamed until his breath ran out.

"Stop! Let go you son of a bitch!"

The hands released him and the pressure on his arm subsided, though the dull pain remained. He took long pained breaths, willing the pain to lessen. Memories from his childhood flooded his mind. Memories of that damn school bus and how it had ruined his life.

Memories of his sister.

Six: Then

Something popped and metal groaned as more smoke began to stream into the bus. The screams of his classmates died away, replaced by cries of pain and fear. Several of the kids pounded on the windows above, trying to break them, but none were strong enough.

IT'S A BIRD! IT'S A PLANE!

The boy could hear voices outside on the street, adults by the sound of them, discussing the best way to get the children out of the bus. One asked about the police, another asked where the firemen were, the boy just wanted someone to help him and his sister.

"No one's coming to help us." His sister said, wiping away tears from her cheeks. "Where are they? Why don't they help?"

"I don't know. But they'll be here. They'll come."

"Oh, shit look at that!" someone outside the bus yelled.

Becky gave her brother a surprised look. They'd heard cussing before, but that kind of language was strictly forbidden in their house.

A loud *thunk* as something hit the top—side—denting the body, shook the entire bus. The impact knocked several kids off their feet, and the chorus of terrified screaming returned.

Then, through the cacophony of voices, a loud metallic ripping sound drowned out the screams and light shone in from above as a whole section of the bus was ripped away.

Children scrambled away from the impossible sight, rolling over seats and falling over each other in an effort to get away.

Becky looked, her eyes wide with wonder. "It's a hero!"

The boy watched as a lone figure descended

278

into the interior of the bus, his green cape flapping. His red and green uniform was spotless and formfitting. The image of a golden shield bearing a closed fist was emblazoned on his chest. He touched down and held up two red-gloved hands. When he spoke, his voice was calm and reassuring.

"It's okay everyone, there's no need to be afraid. We're all going to get out of here, okay? I need you all to be brave for a couple more minutes and I'll get you all to safety. Everyone got that?"

Becky nodded emphatically.

Blaze motioned for two of the closest kids to come to him. They wrapped their arms around him and stepped on his feet, then he ascended slowly upward, out of the bus.

"See," the boy said. "A hero's here, everything is going to be all right."

Then the engine exploded.

Seven: Now

The memory of his sister flooded Harold's mind, pushing everything else happening around him to a distant, unimportant section of his awareness.

He could still feel her fingers in his. She wouldn't let him go, refused to give up. She held his gaze, her eyes filled with determination as he cried.

"I can't feel my legs," she said.

Harold remembered the panic. "What does that mean? That's bad. What are we going to do?"

"We're going to be okay," she told him. "A hero will come for us."

During those horrifying moments, Harold watched, helpless as the color slowly faded from her face and her eyes started to droop, almost like she was falling asleep. To this day, he never understood how she'd been so confident someone would save them. But as she lay there, her body crushed under twisted metal, she was still trying to reassure him.

"A hero will come," she said, her voice barely more than a whisper.

Then her fingers loosened around his and her head collapsed to the seat.

Someone pounded on the door behind him, bringing Harold back from his terrible memories.

"Hey," a woman's voice said. "Hang in there, stay awake. The fire department is almost here,"

Harold swallowed hard and tried to turn and see. A wave of nausea came over him as pain assaulted him. He concentrated hard, forcing himself to hold back vomit.

"Easy, man," a man's voice said, pointing at Harold's arm. "Hold still, you don't want to make that worse."

Then Harold heard the sirens and the crowd around him began waving and shouting.

"Over here!"

"He's trapped!"

"I think the driver's dead."

Harold couldn't tell who was talking, everything seemed like it was all a bad dream. He could feel himself on the brink of passing out again, his body slumped against the seat.

A man in a suit bent down, looking through the broken window. "You're going to be okay, guy. The fire department's here, they'll get you out of there no time."

The searing pain in Harold's arm had become a dull throb. His fingers tingled but he was having a hard time moving them, they were beginning to go numb.

The thought of losing his hand sent the first real pangs of fear through his mind. *They aren't going to get here fast enough*, he thought. The memory of his sister's eyes closing for the last time flashed before him and panic returned.

Desperately, he began trying to free his arm, pulling hard despite the terrible pain. He jerked back hard screaming against the pain. His stomach turned, then he twisted and vomited on to the cab's floorboards.

He heard concerned voices, muted like they were underwater, but couldn't understand the words. Tears blurred his vision. He gritted his teeth against the constant throbbing of pain.

Please, he thought, slumping down against his seat.

Someone pounded on the cab's door behind him. "Hey, you're okay. We're going to get you out. Just sit tight."

IT'S A BIRD! IT'S A PLANE!

Harold craned his head around. Two firefighters worked furiously on the doors.

Harold opened his mouth to speak, but no words came out.

One of the firefighters kicked the door, then turned and shouted, "Gary, bring the jaws." He turned back to Harold and smiled. "It's okay, bud. "I'm not going anywhere."

Harold blinked away the tears, wiping his face with his free hand. "Thank you, I—" He stopped. A small pin gleamed on the lapel of the firefighters jacket. A closed fist on a golden shield. He couldn't stop one side of his mouth from curling into a sneer.

The words left Harold's mouth before he even realized he was going to speak them. "Damn, you people are everywhere."

The firefighter paused slightly, his expression confused.

Harold grunted. "Guess your god had better things to do, huh?"

The firefighter frowned and opened his mouth to speak but his partner returned, carrying the large jaws of life.

"We ready to open this bad boy up?"

The Hero Worshiper, took the heavy machine from his partner. "Let's get this guy outta there."

Eight: Then

Flames roared to the chorus of groaning metal and screaming children. The explosion had tossed them both, along with several other children, to the very back of the bus. They were a mass of emotion, climbing over each other to get away from the flames creeping through the bus.

The boy shoved one of his classmates—Derick, he thought. It was hard to tell, the smoke stung his eyes. Panic had seemed to grip everyone around him as a singular thought repeated in the boy's mind: *Help Becky.* But help her how?

The boy poked his head around the seat back, quickly counting the remaining students. Six left. Three more trips until the hero would get to them. *If he got to them at all.*

Blaze appeared again, grabbing two children around their waists then disappearing again out of the top of the overturned bus.

He's not going to reach us in time, the boy thought, pulling his sister close. They'd curled up in the last seat, and remembering his many fire drills from school, stayed as close to the floor as he could. Even then, he coughed hard, breathing in wafts of black smoke.

Blaze appeared again, grabbing another two, taking them to safety.

"What's taking so long?" his sister asked, refusing to lift her face from the floor as she sobbed.

"It's going to be okay," the boy said through a coughing fit. He stroked her hair, trying to reassure her and finding that it reassured him too.

The flame engulfed another row of seats and

more black smoke rolled into the air. Most of it curled out of the hole Blaze had made in the bus's metal skin, but some of it crept back in. As the boy watched, the trail of smoke crept along like some formless monster reaching out to grab him.

The sound of metal tearing echoed around him and a split-second later another section of steel and glass was ripped clear, then hurled into the air. It vanished in the billowing smoke and almost immediately, a wide stream of water broke through the smoke, raining down into the bus. It splashed off seats and the floor, soaking the boy almost immediately. Becky screamed and tried to scramble away from the stream.

"It's okay!" the boy shouted over the roar of water. He sat up, bracing himself against the water.

Blaze dropped through the spray, grabbed two more, and lifted them out through the water and smoke.

The boy felt a smile form at the edges of his mouth as the flames retreated against the onslaught of water. The smoke dissipated, but the boy could still feel it in his lungs, making it painful to breathe. The roar of the water drowned everything else out, even Becky's sobs. The boy didn't even hear when the Hero touched down in front of them, only looking up when the he spoke.

"It's okay kids. We're getting out of here." Blaze smiled down at them, arm outstretched, hand open. Relief spread through the boy like a wildfire and despite the pain it caused, he laughed as he took the Hero's hand.

The boy wrapped his arms around Blaze's waist, feeling the strength in his arms. Becky scrambled off the floor, half crying, half laughing as she too grabbed onto Blaze. He told them to hold on tight, then lifted into the air. They rose through the stream of water, through patches of smoke, and finally in to clean, fresh air. He laughed again. He was flying. The sensation was like nothing he'd ever experienced before.

A line of cars was stacked up three wide down the length of the street, and a large crowd had gathered, all watching as the fire department set up more hoses and police ushered people away. The on-lookers clapped as Blaze set the boy and his sister down on the sidewalk, making sure they had their footing before letting go.

"You're going to be okay," the Hero said. "You're safe."

The boy looked up at the Hero, his eyes still blurred and stinging from the smoke. "Thank you, Blaze. That was awesome"

Blaze smiled, kneeling down. "What's your name?"

The boy sniffed. "Chris."

"Well, Chris, you were very brave today."

Pride swelled in the boy's chest. He opened his mouth to thank the hero again and an urgent shout interrupted him.

"Hey, someone give me a hand over here!"

Blaze turned and the boy leaned to the side as a firefighter waved to him near the front of the bus. Blaze shot away, a gust of wind from his sudden movement pushed the boy back a step.

The Hero reached the car, looked in through the crushed back window, then quickly pulled the back passenger door free of its hinges. He tossed it aside without looking, and reached inside the car. A second later he pulled a boy from the wreckage, handing him off to a waiting firefighter. Immediately, he reached back into the car, crawling halfway inside it, then slowly, carefully, backed out, carrying what looked like a little girl.

Chris felt his stomach turn. The girl wasn't moving.

Blaze called for the medics as he set her down on the pavement. An anguished scream cut across the street as the boy Blaze had just saved fought against the Hero, trying to get to his sister, her little body surrounded by the medics and firefighters.

They were still working on her when Chris's parents arrived to take him and his sister home. They never gave up, some doubling over from exhaustion as they worked to save her, but it was no use.

A week later, the boy read in the paper that the seven-year-old girl, Bethany Givens, had passed away despite the fire department's valiant efforts to save her. That same week, he learned his teacher was going to have a Future Jobs day in class and Chris knew exactly what he wanted to be.

Nine: Now

The firefighter draped his heavy coat around Harold's shoulders as a paramedic wrapped a cuff around his uninjured arm, slipping a sensor on his finger. Another paramedic inspected his injured arm, taking care not to move it too much.

"Can you move your fingers for me?" the paramedic asked.

Harold gritted his teeth and wiggled his fingers. The dull pain had been replaced by the sensation of a thousand needles, all poking his skin. His arm was turning a light shade of purple where the plastic partition had pinned it to the seat.

The Hero Worshipper appeared behind the kneeling paramedic. He leaned over her, looking down at Harold's arm. "Hey looks like you're going to be okay. Glad we got here in time."

The paramedic finished taking his vitals and pulled the blood pressure cuff off his arm. "Blood pressure is good. Heart rate's a little elevated, but considering what he's been through, I'm not too worried about it. Are you wanting to go to the hospital today?"

Harold shook his head. "I'll be fine."

The paramedics moved away, leaving Harold alone with the firefighter.

"Thanks for getting me out of there," Harold

said.

"Hey, no worries, bud. All part of the job. Hell, it's not very often I get to use those things." The firefighter motioned to the street behind him.

Harold looked past him to where the Jaws of Life lay on the ground next to the wrecked cab. He grunted. "Probably not a whole lot of opportunities with all those damn heroes flying around. Fat load of good they did today."

The firefighter shrugged. "They can't be everywhere all the time. You were lucky we were just down the street."

"I guess he had better things to do than help little ol' me." Harold stood, pulling off the fireman's jacket with his good hand. "Here."

"Thanks."

"Tell me something," Harold said, probing his injured arm.

The firefighter pulled on his coat, adjusting it so it hung correctly. "What's up?"

"Why do you wear that?"

The firefighter looked down at the silver pin on his jacket's lapel. "The pin?"

"Yeah."

"A long time ago I needed a hero. Blaze was there, he saved my life."

Harold sniffed, trying to think of something to say. Finally, he held out his hand. "Well, I'm glad he did."

The firefighter pumped Harold's hand, hard.

"Me too. That's kinda why I do this, you know? Try and repay that debt."

He let the jacket fall back into place and Harold read the name stenciled across the chest pocket, C. THURMAN. "Thank you, Mr. Thurman."

The firefighter laughed. "Ha, that's my father's name, call me Chris."

Harold smiled, then a thought struck him and he looked down at his watch. He grunted. "Well, I guess I'm not making my interview."

"What interview?"

"Council position for the city," Harold said. "My interview started 10 minutes ago."

"I'm sure they'll reschedule, considering," Chris said, motioning to the wreck. "Hell, if they do, you'd kinda be my boss. Hey, if you make it on to the Council, remember me when salary talks start up again, would ya? We've been kinda overlooked for the last few years."

Harold chuckled. "Well, I'm not sure about that, but I'll do what I can. Heroes like you deserve better."

A Word from Josh Hayes

Hi, there! I hope you liked my little story "Hero Worship." It's my first foray into the super hero genre and I wanted to do a little something different. I wanted to write a story about the people that sometimes we forget about when others seem to be doing extraordinary things. I believe there are heroes around us all the time, but most of the time we either don't see them or don't relate what they are doing as heroic.

I have four other short stories published in three anthologies and one I've published on its own. I have two other books published, *Breaking Through* and *The Forgotten Prince* the first two books in my *Second Star* series, a sci-fi reimagining of *Peter Pan and Neverland*. The third book *Shadows of Neverland* will hopefully be out the summer of 2017.

In addition to writing and having a full-time job, I also run a live interview show and podcast with fellow authors Scott Moon and Ralph Kern, *Keystroke Medium*. We talk with authors of all sorts, finding out what makes them tick, what excites them about their stories and connecting them with new readers. Please check us out at www.keystrokemedium.com.

I live in Kansas, with my beautiful wife Jamie, who supports my crazy ideas and ridiculous ambitions. When I'm not driving her crazy, I'm chasing my four children around the house. Check out my website for more at: www.joshhayeswriter.com.

AN ORDINARY HERO

A PANTHEON SHORT

C.C. EKEKE

THE QUESTION PULLED Raylan Oakmont's attention away from the grocery store's television screen to his far right. He turned and frowned. "Sorry?"

The woman before him in the check-out line was dumpy in build, a little shorter than Raylan in height, several years older than him by the streaks of grey in her mop of curly coal black hair. "The fancy wine," she pointed, her round face highlighted by beady light grey eyes and a big smile. "What's the occasion?"

Raylan followed the direction of her finger down to his grocery bag and the neck of the Pinot Grigio bottle peeking out. "Oh...right. It's the four-year marriage anniversary with my better half, Robbie."

The woman's eyebrows rose so high they near-ly hit the store ceiling. "Oh really?" Her voice hit a hilariously high tenor, smile frozen on her face. "Congratulations!"

Raylan rolled his eyes, but bit down on the

caustic remark forming in his brain. "Thanks," was his terse reply instead.

"Is that the extent of the special night?" she continued in some semblance of her normal tenor.

"Nah," Raylan shook his head. "A home cooked meal and some random bad films. Work for both us is so crazy that we keep it simple." Actually it was more Robbie's job that had the crazy schedule, involving lots of travel. Raylan's job as a technical writer for load Hunter-Varese Manufacturing was a 9-5 job without too many late nights. The promise was for next year's anniversary to deviate toward something more extravagant, no matter what.

"Ah," the woman asked after a long lull in their conversation. Whether she expected more details, Raylan had no clue or concern. "Well, good luck tonight." The woman's turn in line to get rung up came and she stepped forward.

"Thanks," Raylan returned his focus on the grocery store TV. Before the woman had interrupted, he'd been zoned out on a local San Diego news broadcast. With the TV screen so far away, he only saw images, which was the typical broadcast news collage of chaos. A school bus lay flipped on its side with flames shooting out of its engine area. A swarm of preteens scrambled about, some bloodied and screaming, a few bloodied and motionless on the ground. A familiar winged figure swept down for the school bus.

Seeing this type of wreckage was nothing new

for Raylan. But still, he remained bizarrely fascinated by the disaster. "What happened there?" he asked a Latino gentleman behind him who looked no older than twenty.

"Some dumbass in a BMW blew a red light at 54th and University and struck a school bus full of middle school kids," the young man spat, his dark eyes alight with vitriol. "Thank God that Red Sparrow swooped in," the young man's face brightened at the irony in his words. "Ha! Red Sparrow 'swooped in.' Get it?"

Wish I didn't. Right then, Raylan's turn came up and with that came a merciful end to the young man's bad jokes. After paying for his wine, vegetables, and turkey, Raylan lingered near the grocery store exit to keep watching the news broadcast. The footage finally switched away from the accident porn to show San Diego's patron superhero in all her glory —the Red Sparrow.

Raylan's breath caught at the sight of her slender physique as she pulled yet another kid from the soon to be flame-engulfed bus. Her outfit was head-to-toe, blood red spandex, flame retardant and flexible Kevlar covered all but her face. For that she wore massive opaque orange flight goggles to cover her eyes from identification and high wind shear. The sharp-looking silver wings protruding from the underside of each arm were part of the uniform, put in place to deflect gunfire and projectiles. Red Sparrow's supersonic flight was an ability derived from her being 'homo superior.'

Red Sparrow had just landed well away from the school bus with her passenger, a frightened young girl who seemed to be the last of kids on the bus.

With that, Red Sparrow shooed all the kids away from the bus with over-exaggerated arm movements as the bright hungry flames consumed it entirely.

Only then did Raylan exit the grocery store, secretly pleased. The time was 3:30PM, meaning he had about three hours to cook dinner and get cleaned up.

On the way to get tonight's dessert, Raylan's thoughts wandered back to six years ago when San Diego finally got involved in the American Superhero Initiative that placed at least one patron superhero with a select number of the country's largest metropolises.

Washington, D.C. had One-Man-Militia when he wasn't on Freedom Watch duties.

Atlanta had gotten rocky powerhouse Rushmore.

San Miguel, the so-called 'City of Wonder' had the cream of the crop; Lady Liberty, Titan sometimes, that psycho vigilante, Geist—unofficially —and the Extreme Teens every now and then.

San Diego got Red Sparrow, a superhero that barely stood 5'4 and had no 'cool' powers like shooting laser beams from her eyes. All she could do was fly really fast.

The majority of the city had been outraged, believing that they'd been cheated out of a real superhero. Red Sparrow might not have been as powerful as Titan or as statuesque and 'pinup worthy' as Lady Liberty. But she was spirited in personality, had courage enough for five, resourceful with her flight abilities, and effective in beating back San Diego's gang problem. In short, she proved everyone wrong and won the whole city over.

Those other cities could keep their overexposed, overpowered heroes. San Diego was lucky to have Red Sparrow, in Raylan's opinion.

Later after he'd returned home, boiled the pasta and cooked up goulash-style stew, Raylan showered. He looked at the ruddy, freckled face in the mirror with the green eyes cropped ginger red hair. He'd shaved and then threw on a black button down with dark blue jeans. A spritz of *Davidoff Good Life*, Robbie's favorite cologne on him, and Rayland was ready to go. The first floor of their spacious three-bedroom condo was low lit. Candles for the table were lit. Balloons with 'Happy Anniversary' printed on them in bold pink lettering were tethered to a spare chair on the dinner table. Raylan had Robbie's present covered in Christmas wrapping paper, which was sure to draw a laugh.

Dessert was red velvet cake with French vanilla ice cream, waiting in the fridge and freezer respectively. The crap movie for the evening was 'Street

Fighter,' which had garnered a glorious 12% on Rotten Tomatoes.

6:30PM came and went, but Raylan knew better than to serve the food yet.

7:00PM came and went. No Robbie.

7:30PM came and went. No Robbie. Raylan doused more cool water on the pasta to keep it from sticking and reheated the goulash stew before it completely cooled.

Soon 8:00PM began to approach. But Raylan was not even slightly perturbed. He expected his partner in at closer to 9:00PM. Robbie's job was fulfilling yet excruciatingly demanding, and over the course of their marriage both of them had learned to accept that.

Rayland plopped down on the L-shaped black leather couch in the living room and flipped on the 51" plasma TV. Instead of that banal lamestream entertainment show usually on at this time, Raylan saw a special news report—and the news ticker stamped on the screen's lower third.

He jumped out his seat. "Whoa!"

SUPERHERO TITAN DEAD.

CBS News 8 anchors, Marcella Lee and Carlos Cecchetto, appeared on the screen in all their perfectly coiffed glory wearing genuinely saddened expressions. "...was found dead in the Liberty

Heights neighborhood of the Central Coast city, San Miguel," said Michelle minus her usual camera-ready smile. "Understandably this is a shock felt round the world, as Titan was globally renowned not only for his never-ending battle against crime but his charitable acts."

Raylan's brain didn't compute. Titan, dead? Super strong and nigh-invulnerable Titan, dead?

The same Titan who had saved the Statue of Liberty when Dr. Magnos had tried toppling it into the Atlantic—Dead?

News anchor Carlos shook his head more sincerely. "Indeed, Marcella. Titan was, in many people's eyes, the forefather of America's superhero revolution. Now at this time, San Miguel police are calling this a homicide, based on the evidence fund at the crime scene. But given the high profile of this case, we will not get official word until the FBI gets involved."

Raylan slumped back onto the couch, jaw hanging open as the news broadcast continued. His mind reeled. Titan wasn't just dead, he had been murdered.

Of course the obligatory video package of Titan at his best rolled with an unnecessary voice discussing his legacy. The brawny 6'4 superhero soared across Raylan's screen. The silvery white Caesar haircut, his bronzed complexion, that steely unwavering expression in the face of world-ending disaster, the instantly recognizable baby blue body suit with the silvery 'T' running across his arms and down his torso. Titan was ageless in appearance, relentless against evildoers, yet eternally optimistic and caring to those he protected.

Raylan felt like he'd been shot. Who could have killed Titan? Dr. Magnos? Tom-Da-Bomb? Demolition? And why?

Suddenly his eyes were watering. He, like most, had grown up watching Titan. Raylan started flipping through the major broadcast channels, then all the major cable channels. The death of the world's greatest superhero dominated every single one.

Titan, while a bit vanilla in personality, had been one of the legitimately good superheroes.

Titan was a constant in the face of these new, corporately-backed 9 to 5 superhacks with costumes that were more and more a gross collage of sponsors.

Titan...was Robbie's inspiration to even become a superhero.

"Oh my god..."The realization struck Raylan harder in the gut. His tears flowed freely and steadily now. Somehow a hand had found itself over his still-open mouth.

The front door slammed shut. "Happy anniversary...almost two hours late!" a high and clear voice announced.

Raylan whirled about in his seat. "Robbie!" He dove for the TV remote. His hands shook so badly it took a few frantic clicks to do switch to the blank AV screen and then turn the damn thing off.

No doubt Robbie already knew. No wonder she was late for their anniversary dinner tonight.

The anniversary can wait, Raylan told himself as he wiped the tears from his face. *She'll need you now to be a rock.*

"I know! I suck so BAD!" Roberta 'Robbie' Corales-Oakmont swept out of the foyer and into the common room. She was a petite little thing, five-foot-three-and-a-half with a heart-shaped face and smooth olive skin courtesy of her Filipino heritage. Robbie, with her black pixie-cut hair curled and textured, wore a burgundy blouse and taupe pencil skirt that flattered her amazing figure. That face, those large dark eyes, those lips, was all so lovely, especially when she smiled. "I remembered the flowers!" she held up a bouquet of white roses, the only part of tonight that Raylan allowed her to take part in.

"Thanks," Raylan turned away to wipe his face and then approached his wife. Robbie was probably putting on her best façade for his benefit. Best to make no mention of the anniversary.

Raylan took the flowers and placed them on the dining table so gently one might think they were motion-sensitive bombs. "How are you?" he asked after a long, full kiss on the lips.

The kiss left Robbie flushed and giggly, like always. She was putting a good show for his benefit. "Fine. Got your gift this morning. I'll bring it out after dinner. I would have called to tell you I was running late but I've had my cell phones off, like we promised —" Robbie's adorable rambling trailed off when she got a good look at her husband's face. "Raylan what's wrong?!" she cried, any signs of cheeriness evaporating.

Raylan gaped. *She doesn't know about Titan.* He wiped his face with the back of his hand and put on his most nonchalant tone. "Naw its nothing. Just the onions from cooking. The phones?" Raylan held out his hand expectantly, somehow holding it together.

With an over-the-top sigh, his wife handed her phones over, an iPhone 5 for work and a Nexus 4 for personal calls. Robbie worked so hard during the day and a lot of times at night. She deserved a night off, even from news about Titan.

"How was your day?" he asked, heading for the kitchen.

"Great!" she was beaming again. Good. "Just one major accident, other than that it was kinda boring." Raylan spied her walking gingerly toward their couch, favoring her right side.

She must have re-aggravated her knee strain, Raylan realized. "Saw your save on TV."

Robbie gazed back at him with the happiest look. "Did you?!"

"Of course," Raylan replied. No matter how shocked and numb Titan's death had left him, the memory of his wife in action filled with unshakeable warmth, joy and pride. "I was in the grocery store and I almost shouted out, 'That's my wife' to the whole world." He poured them both a glass of the Pinot.

"God," Robbie laughed, easing herself onto the couch. "I'm just glad none of those kids were seriously hurt or anything."

"How's your knee?" Raylan strode for his wife with the two wine glasses, placing them on the common room table.

Robbie grimaced at the fact that he'd noticed. "A bit sore, but not as stiff as earlier," she admitted sheepishly, stretching out her left leg with experiential caution.

Raylan fished around in his wife's purse for the Ibuprofen bottle. "Here," he dropped two round white tablets in her hand.

"Aww, is that my favorite pinot!" Robbie popped two tablets in her mouth like candy then chased them down with a long swig of wine. "Hey," she tilted Raylan's chin up so that their eyes met. "Sure you're alright, hun?"

God, she was so beautiful. For a second, Raylan wavered. He hated lying to her. But tonight was just about them, for once. Let the world come knocking with all its demands and sorrows tomorrow.

"I'm fine Robs," he lied with his sweetest smile. "To us." They clinked glasses and drained them.

Raylan headed back to the kitchen, but not before snatching up the TV remote. "The food is almost ready. The crappy movie is set in the Blu-Ray player," he began serving their food in earnest. "The anniversary is about to begin."

"Ray-Ray?" Robbie called from her comfortable perch on the couch.

Raylan, in the middle of serving out the goulash stew, froze. "Yeah, babe."

Robbie looked back at him with a megawatt smile, melting his heart. "I hit the jackpot with you didn't I?"

"Yeah, maybe a little," Raylan teased. With two steaming hot plates of goulash-styled stew on curly pasta noodles, he put on his happiest façade and headed for the common room. "Alright, honey. Here I come."

A Word from C.C. Ekeke

I spent most of my childhood on a steady diet of science fiction movies, television shows and super-hero comic books. I discovered my desire to write books in college when studying for a degree in advertising. An international trip or two provided further inspiration for the aliens and worlds in my writing. After a couple years and a full rewrite of the first book in my *Star Brigade* space opera series, I took the plunge into book writing as a serious secondary career. I'm currently working on the four book in the *Star Brigade* series. Feel free to drop by ccekeke.com if you'd like to download a free novella and find out about my next release or talk about all things sci-fi and fantasy!

Find me on Facebook, Twitter, Instagram, Amazon.

THE SPOTLIGHT

JEFFREY BEESLER

UNLIKE OTHER HEROES, Sally "Myna Byrd" Cates didn't have a sixth sense. Not that she needed one. Her drama teacher, Mr. Seymour Rauch, blew through two packs of cigarettes during the class's final dress rehearsal of "A Pair of Lunatics." No need for special mind powers when she kept stepping on discarded butts right outside the side door to the auditorium.

Had it really been that awful of a dress rehearsal? As an assistant to the lighting technical manager, Sally hadn't thought so. But with the way Mr. Rauch kept sneaking out that side door for a cigarette break every five minutes or so it seemed, she could've been wrong.

"All right, everyone," Mr. Rauch said, gathering them in the auditorium for what Sally expected to be his final prep speech before performance time. "Tonight's the night. Let's go out there and put on a phenomenal show. I still think we can pull off a fine performance of 'A Pair of Lunatics.'"

IT'S A BIRD! IT'S A PLANE!

Everyone rallied around each other, chirping their excitement amongst themselves. Sally smiled politely, making sure not to stare too long at Mr. Rauch. Had no one else noticed his voice growing raspier with every puff of smoke he inhaled? She had to talk to him.

"Who's up for pizza?" the male lead, Caleb Milton, asked. Originally the junior year captain of the football team, he'd joined the Ruby Hills High School production only because his girlfriend, Natalie Van Sykes, played the female lead.

"Sorry. I've got other things to do," Sally said, shaking her head while the others salivated over the prospect of pepperoni goodness.

"Well, you're no fun," Natalie teased, hanging onto Caleb's arm. The pair looked like a modern-day Bonnie and Clyde. Or maybe that was how Sally wanted to see them, given the air of superiority those two always seemed to carry about themselves.

At least those two can't leap tall buildings like me, Sally thought, smirking.

She left the class gathering to check on other things. As she wandered up to the control booth, something seemed off. She'd been inside the booth many times before, so it took her a moment to figure out why things looked so weird. An unfamiliar green light flickered somewhere inside the room. The abrupt sound of footsteps behind her halted her advancement.

"What are you doing?" Mr. Rauch asked.

"I couldn't find my keys," she said, pulling out her keychain a second later. "Oh, wow, look at that. There they are."

Mr. Rauch raised an eyebrow. "You were snooping."

"No, I wasn't." she asked, trying to cast doubt upon what she was doing.

"I hope that's true," he said, the rasp in his voice edgier than before.

Sally looked at him with great concern. "Are you okay, Mr. Rauch?"

"I'm fine," he said, moving past her to slam the control booth door shut. He took his own set of keys and locked the door, a resounding click ensuring his success.

"If you say so."

He spun back around at her, his eyes bloodshot. "What's that supposed to mean?"

Sally struggled not to let the smell of tobacco on the guy choke her nostrils. A cough quickly betrayed her attempt.

"I'm worried about you."

The words seemed to calm him. He drew a sigh, wheezing as if his lungs were offended by the non-smoker's air of the auditorium.

"I'll be fine. Once we get through the production's run, I'll be able to call it quits on the whole drama class thing," he said, his lips twisting into a frown that seemed tempered with sadness rather than rage.

"You don't want to do this anymore?"

"I do, but..."

As he trailed off, Sally caught a round of applause coming from the other side of the auditorium. She watched Mr. Rauch glance over in that direction, and then allowed herself the same luxury. Some of the cast members, including Caleb and Natalie, were still hanging out, their need for pizza not yet met. Sally listened intently to their group.

"You guys are gonna kill it tonight!" a boy said.

"I wish I was as talented as you, Natalie," a girl remarked.

"Oh, please," Natalie told them with a wave of her hand, although it appeared she rather welcomed the high praise.

"Thanks, guys," Caleb said.

Sally immediately looked to Mr. Rauch. She saw the hurt in his eyes as the cast praised one another. The way his eyes narrowed at this made Sally's heart almost freeze.

"Mr. Rauch?" she asked.

Mr. Rauch blinked but held his head up high, offering her a smile that didn't seem genuine. "I *told* you I'm fine!"

He marched off, whistling like only the devil may have cared about anything. Sally thought to go after him, but the way he slammed the door behind him convinced her otherwise.

• • •

With Mr. Rauch gone, Sally approached the

cast.

"You guys got a second?" she asked.

"Sure," Caleb said, grinning as someone high-fived him. "What's up?"

"Has anyone else noticed the way Mr. Rauch's been acting?"

"This is the drama club," Natalie remarked with a snort. "Everyone here is always acting."

Sally sighed, realizing her mistake. "No. What I mean is, does anyone else think he's upset?"

The group exchanged glances among themselves.

"Not really, Sally," Caleb said. "If he's stressed, it's only because tonight's opening night."

"Did you see how many cigarettes Mr. Rauch went through during the dress rehearsal? He probably smoked a pack or two."

"What makes you say that?" Natalie asked.

"Just the pile of cigarette butts outside that side door," Sally said, pointing in the right direction.

Caleb waved his hand as if to dismiss the notion. "That's the door where all the smokers go to smoke. Everyone knows that."

Sally shook her head. "There's more to it, though. I'm sure of it."

Caleb grunted a laugh. "Come on, Sally. Mr. Rauch is a professional. He's doing his job just fine."

"I wish I could believe that," Sally said with a sigh.

"He'll be fine, Sally," Caleb said. "See you later."

IT'S A BIRD! IT'S A PLANE!

Sally gazed over at the control booth, the footsteps behind her growing softer. A small voice inside her head compelled her to go back there again and check things out despite Mr. Rauch's demand to stay out.

Something didn't seem right.

• • •

With the curtains rising at 7:30, Sally hadn't left the school. Her mind was on Mr. Rauch. What was he trying to hide from everyone? She didn't have much time to act as everyone would soon return. At the entrance to the control booth, she tried once more to twist the door knob, her access still denied without the key.

Time to get ready. Glad I don't have to strip down in a phone booth like in those old Superman *movies.*

She sauntered off toward the dressing room and made the change into her costume, a pair of dark shades and a matching one-piece suit. As Myna Byrd, she had only once ever had to use her powers to stop someone, although it really hadn't been the megavillain she'd hoped for. Rather, someone had climbed to the auditorium rooftop and teetered on the ledge, threatening suicide in a reckless, playing around sort of way. Fortunately, her ability to fly enabled her to catch the young man before he died.

If I could save that kid, then I can stop Mr. Rauch from doing whatever the hell he's planning on doing.

She left the dressing room and headed down

the hall without being seen. Only an hour or so re-mained until the auditorium filled, hopefully to ca-pacity. They'd all worked so hard on this production.

Then again, if Mr. Rauch tries to do something, we might be better off if no one shows up at all!

She made it to the auditorium's backstage area and peeped through the crack in the curtains to see if anyone was out in the audience yet. Her powers activated by way of song, she hummed a random melody. Her body began to rise and a breeze carried her up into the air, propelling her forward toward the stage. She hoped to use the cover of shade back-stage to stay out of sight. She found a perch big enough for her to sit, the curtain sufficient cover. She waited.

Footsteps caught her attention five minutes into her watch. She tried to get a better peek of the action unnoticed. A flash of lighting nearly caught her in the act of movement. It swept past her without incident.

"Anyone seen Mr. Rauch or Sally?" someone asked from the audience sitting area. It sounded like Caleb.

"Sally's missing, too?" a girl who wasn't Natalie asked.

"I haven't seen her in hours."

"She better get back soon," Natalie said.

"Let's get into costume, guys," Caleb said, lead-ing the group away.

Ten minutes later, Sally drifted from her hiding

spot. She edged toward the front curtain, looking out toward the seating area and the control booth just beyond. A couple of people moved up and down the aisles, sweeping up garbage left over from the dress rehearsal. Mr. Rauch threw the side door open, marching towards the crew cleaning up whatever trash came their way.

"Get out of here!" he barked at them, pointing a finger at the main door. The crew members scurried out of there, Mr. Rauch right behind them.

Sally swooped down from her hiding position and flew toward the control booth. The level of fury in his voice just now made her wonder if she was already too late.

I have to stop him.

She stepped in front of the control room door and waited for him to return from chasing the others out. He showed up a second later.

"Pathetic outfit," he murmured, not breaking his stride.

"Mr. Rauch, wait," Sally insisted.

The drama teacher scanned her with a deadly glint in his eyes.

"Be quick. I have work to do."

Sally resisted the urge to remove her shades. In the dim lighting of the auditorium, the shades kept Mr. Rauch from seeing her eyes. She knew her green eyes would betray her, if not her red hair. She was one of a handful of redheaded girls in attendance at Ruby Hills, but at least that meant there was more than one. Maybe Mr. Rauch wouldn't figure her identity out.

"Mr. Rauch, go home and get some rest You don't look good."

The man grunted. "I'm fine. Now go away."

Sally didn't budge. She didn't need to. All it took was for one thought for her abnormal strength to keep her rooted to the floor.

"I'm not leaving until you do."

"I don't have time for this," he growled. "Get out of my way."

Sally shook her head. "No way."

"People are about to arrive," he said, fuming.

"Don't do this," she urged.

Mr. Rauch clenched his fists. "Get lost now."

Sally crossed her arms. "Make me."

The drama teacher's palms flew into Sally's chest, forcing her back before she could summon the bulk of her strength to block the effort. She tripped over her own feet but steadied herself a second later. Then she glanced up and saw Mr. Rauch was gone. She dashed into the control room in time to see him press a green button that must have been the source of that strange light earlier.

"What are you doing?" she asked, catching her breath.

Mr. Rauch let out a nasty cackle. "Ending it. I'm so sick and tired of it all."

"Sick and tired of what, exactly?" Sally glanced around quickly for something that might detain him until the cops showed up. Anything of actual value lay backstage.

"This production." He pointed towards the stage. "I'm surrounded by idiots who wouldn't know talent if it bit them in their backside."

"Weren't you the one who selected the cast?"

"Whatever. You're just some heroic fool wearing an outlandish costume."

"I'm not backing down, Mr. Rauch."

Mr. Rauch kicked her in the leg. As he reeled from the pain he unwittingly inflicted upon his toes, she reached out for his arm and twisted it, taking care not to break any bones. He yowled in pain and hurled his fist into her jaw, only to cause himself a second round of agony. The momentum of the blow nudged her backwards by about one step, but didn't cause her any physical harm. As she caught herself again, Mr. Rauch hobbled for the door, cradling his injured hand in his good one. Two crew members responsible for ticket sales suddenly opened the main door, blocking his escape.

"What's going on here?" one asked.

"Go call the police!" Sally told the ticket sales crew. "Mr. Rauch has done something to the lighting system. There may be a bomb attached to it."

"Wait. What?"

Mr. Rauch spun back toward Sally, grinning. "My dear, it seems you may have a credibility problem."

Sally took in the confused expressions on their

faces. Had it even occurred to her that maybe other production staff members had already seen the green button and asked Mr. Rauch about it?

"He's out to hurt people," Sally tried to explain.

"Why would Mr. Rauch want to do that though?"

At that moment, Caleb and Natalie appeared in their costumes on stage, along with half the rest of the cast. Everyone murmured and glanced in Sally and Mr. Rauch's direction.

"We heard the commotion out here," Caleb said. "What's up?"

Smugness stretched the drama instructor's smile to as far as his lips could reach.

"I'm fine now that you're all here. This costumed vigilante just attacked me for no good reason."

Sally saw everyone looking at her as if she were the villain. She tried to say something, but no words emerged from her lips. How had she not thought things through? She was trying to save them all from a distraught, overworked drama instructor hell-bent on paying everyone back for their naivete. How had she handled things so wrong?

"I'm sorry, but the show can't go on. There's a gas leak."

"Didn't you say there was a bomb?" the first ticket sales crew member said, nudging his glasses closer to his eyes.

Sally shook her head, again struggling to justify

her position. "Something bad will happen to anyone standing right where you two are standing," she said, pointing at Caleb and Natalie.

"This has to be some stupid prank you got from YouTube or something," Natalie said.

"It's not a prank. Mr. Rauch did something to the lighting because this production has him stressed out."

"She's lying," Mr. Rauch said, his voice wavering. The arrogance melted off his face the longer her words lingered in the air.

"Is she?" Natalie asked.

"Yes," Mr. Rauch said, dismissing the accusation with a wave of his hand.

Sally wouldn't let him deny the truth any longer. "Stop lying, Mr. Rauch."

"Fine. You want to know the truth? I've had it with this production. None of you has an ounce of this thing called talent. Your performances are comical at best, robotic at worst."

Everyone but Sally gawked at Mr. Rauch, shock plastered to their faces.

"Oh wow, Mr. Rauch," Natalie said, chafing her arms as if a draft permeated the air onstage. "No need to act like a jerk."

"A jerk, am I?" Mr. Rauch pulled out a gun and grabbed one of the ticket sales students. Pushing the barrel of the gun into the kid's back, he nudged him towards the stage. "Idiots, all of you. Back off, or I'll shoot him, God help me, I will."

"Let him go, Mr. Rauch," Sally said. "This is between you and me."

Mr. Rauch's hand shook, his nerves unsteady, as he pushed the kid towards the stage. The cast on stage started to run towards the exit. Mr. Rauch fired a bullet into the air.

"Leave the stage and he dies, simple as that."

Sally fought back against her pounding heart, trying to think fast. Only problem was, she hadn't gotten super speed as part of the hero package. Without that element, she didn't know if she could reach the stage in time to stop him.

Mr. Rauch kept his gun raised as he faced Sally again. "You're the hero who saved that kid from jumping that one time, aren't you?"

Ice spread across Sally's heart. Why was Mr. Rauch bringing that up now of all times?

"You think you're such a hero. You're not. You're just an actress in a costume, pretending to be something you aren't," Mr. Rauch said, staring up at the lighting. "There's nothing you can do to stop this. I set a timer which is about to go off any minute now."

Before Sally could do anything, a green light spread out from the ceiling stage lights. The strange glow filled her with dread. When Mr. Rauch grinned, she realized his deadly intent.

"You can't save everyone, Myna Byrd. Not this time." Mr. Rauch then looked at Caleb, who held onto Natalie with one arm. "Don't be mad, Caleb. You wanted to die from jumping off the auditorium roof, Caleb. Remember? I'm just helping you out now."

"I don't want to die," Caleb said with a whimper.

"That's a lie and you know it," Mr. Rauch shot back. "Not that anyone can stop the light. Here it comes!"

He pointed up at the stage lighting, now flickering that same green glow from before.

"Mr. Rauch, no!" Sally protested.

She flew towards the stage, pushing herself to get there as fast as she could without super speed. An intense heat struck her in the back as she flew into the direct path of the lighting. She tumbled downward out of the air, the pain frying the nerves in her back. If not for her strength, the pain would've been much worse.

Then screams pierced the air. Propping herself on her arms so she could look up, she watched the energy from the stage lighting flash. It vaporized Mr. Rauch, Caleb, Natalie, the other five or six cast members, and the ticket sales student right where they all stood, their bodies fading into the abyss. A second later, the light itself blew out with a resounding snap.

For a moment, no one said anything, a cloud of disbelief lingering in the room. Sally eyed the technical crew off to her right. As they fell into one another's arms, offering themselves hysterical solace, she buried her face in the cold auditorium floor.

• • •

Two hours later, Sally left the Ruby Hills police station after the cops got done talking to her about what happened. Numbness washed over her heart. She chafed her arms as she wandered the streets, taking only enough care to watch for traffic at crosswalks. She heaved a sigh, thoughts of Mr. Rauch still on her mind. How could she have handled things differently?

I let them all die. I tried and they died. Why be a hero if I can't save everybody?

She started toward home, but remembered she had left her daytime clothes back at school. Careful to avoid the busier routes to her destination, she sang a soft song to take to the sky. The wind caressed her, as if it somehow mourned right alongside her. Her remorse struggled to hang on as she flew. Something about defying gravity calmed her nerves.

At the school, she slipped through the halls, flying out of sight in the shadows, bypassing the alarms. She made it to the dressing room and found her clothes in a pile next to her backpack. As she pulled out her pants from the clothing clump, her Android fell out, striking the floor with a thud. She reached down and found it unharmed. Cursing herself, she went to put it back in the pocket when she saw an alert for an unread text message. Slightly curious, she swiped her finger against the screen to read the message:

Sorry you couldn't make it, Sally. Pizza was phenomenal. Just thought you should know. Natalie

Sally deleted the message. Then she noticed there had been a second message, this one from Caleb. She read it:

Yo, Sally, you missed out on the pizza! Bet you had something important to do as Myna Byrd, huh? Yeah, I know you were the one who saved me from falling that night. You should mask your voice better or something. Anyhow, gotta go. See you at show-time! Oh, thanks for everything, btw. Caleb

Her innards iced over again, a single tear trickling down her face. Was she really going to give up being Myna Byrd because of what happened with Mr. Rauch?

She took a long, deep breath and considered her choice. The Myna Byrd suit landed inside her backpack for her to wear again soon.

A Word from Jeffrey Beesler

Firstly, thank you so much for reading "The Spotlight." It's been a while since I tried writing a short story. Usually, I go for longer-sized works, mostly novella to novel size. Some years have also passed since I wrote a superhero story, thus I'm grateful for the invitation to write for this anthology. My current diversion from the superhero genre is an anomaly, since my adolescent years have found themselves surrounded by the *Superfriends* on TV and *Uncanny X-Men* in comic book format.

I still fantasize about being a superhero, even if my prose finds itself engaged in other activities. Whether it's the sorcerers from my *Mages of Trava* fantasy series, or the road-raging demons in the *Horrors of Helensview*, or even the pregnant men in my *Interstellar Dad* series, I'm always pushing the limits of my own imagination. There's no doubt that I will return to superheroes at some point. It's just a matter of when. I feel that the piece you've just read is the starting line on that path.

My catalog of titles is available at my Amazon page. Thanks again for reading, and have a wonderful day!

JOSI RUSSELL

THE PROBLEM WITH Pirate was that he had figured out he was immortal. Or close enough, anyway. He didn't even hesitate to run into the street after the neighbor's cat now, or pause to consider before he wolfed down a chocolate bar.

"One of these days I won't mend you," Charlotte chided him, passing her gnarled hands over the little dog's collapsed ribcage. She felt the bones knit, the muscles tighten. Pirate's breath came back and his tail started to wag. He gave her fingertips a good licking as he wriggled to his feet, his one good eye gleaming with gratitude.

She could have mended the other eye, could have restored it and his sight perfectly, but there were enough questions from the neighbors about his miraculous recoveries already. They knew he was half blind, and sudden sight would be very hard to explain.

"I'll let you go one of these days," Charlotte said, "you silly thing. Nine resurrections is plenty for one foolish spotted dog."

But she knew as she said it that she didn't mean it. She wouldn't, probably, ever let him go. She'd never been good at that. The black door of death scared her, and she couldn't bear to let him go through it.

Of all people, she should have been the least scared of death. She, of all people, knew it was a swinging door, that it worked both ways. But with all her power over it, she still had no idea what lay beyond it: Heaven? Hell? A vast nothing? She wished, sometimes, for a glimpse, a peek at what lay ahead.

She also wished, sometimes, for a power that could stop it from happening, instead of just reversing it. She knew, through visions she called fades, when a death would happen, but someone actually had to go through it before she could mend them. Sometimes, she wished for the ability to fly, so she could whisk a patient away from their fate. Or for incredible strength so she could stop people from hurting others. Even laser beams from her eyes would be useful in many situations. But she didn't have any of those things. Instead, she had the power to mend. She showed up after the excitement and fixed what had gone wrong. But it had to be done quickly. She'd found that out the hard way when she'd tried to mend her mother. Her aunt had been in the room at her passing, and had carried on for half an hour before she'd finally left and Charlotte had moved to bring her mother back. But it had been too long. She was gone for good.

Charlotte, as a girl, had worked her grief off by doing all it took to figure out exactly how long she had before the death was permanent. Now she let no more than three minutes elapse.

She looked up as Pirate hopped down from the faded Formica table and started crunching at the kibble in his bowl. The house had grown bright while she'd been preoccupied with him. A warm yellow tinge washed over the worn kitchen, lighting up the corners. It had the same counters and cabinets she and Arthur had picked out four decades ago, and in them were reminders of her life with him. His blue mug, an empty tin that had once held his favorite crackers, odds and ends of the life he'd left so suddenly. The kitchen was tidy, and she was proud of that. Arthur had always said she was the best cook and the best housekeeper in three counties. How she missed that man. She pushed away the bitterness that came every time she thought of that last flight he had taken, the crash, and somewhere in the Columbia river, his unrecovered body. That and the fact that her powers had no effect on her own rapidly aging body, were the greatest unfairnesses of her life.

The phone rang, and she knew who it was before she picked it up. Her friend Audrey had pressed her to commit to brunch at the senior center today.

"Not this morning, dear," she said into the phone, "I'll be tending to my mending."

IT'S A BIRD! IT'S A PLANE!

There was a breath on the other end of the phone. Charlotte tried to decide if it signaled frustration or resignation. Audrey confirmed the latter.

"Okay. Well, maybe next week then?"

"It's a date!" Charlotte answered. She checked her watch and hung up. She needed to hustle. She realized that she should not make promises like that. She had little control of the demands her days would bring, and she didn't like disappointing her friend. Charlotte extracted the cookies from the oven— Mason would be over later, and he'd finished off her snickerdoodles yesterday—and double-checked to be sure that the oven was off.

She gathered her purse and snapped open her hand mirror, admiring for a moment, her new glasses with the mother-of pearl inlay that matched her snowy hair. Plucking up the car keys, she tried to avoid Pirate's doleful gaze.

"You can't go today," she said, "You'll get in the way."

He responded with a long, thin whine and a shake of his tail.

Charlotte caved. "Oh, all right. But you're staying in the car."

• • •

The first work of the day would be easy. It was a public tennis court, too late in the morning for much traffic. Her patient was practicing her backswing, completely ignorant of what the next few moments would bring. She was in her mid-twenties,

Charlotte noted, with a long, dark ponytail. Charlotte swung her big brown car into a parking space and stepped out just as she saw the young lady fall. The scene matched Charlotte's fade exactly.

Charlotte heard voices coming around the corner. She slammed the door and rushed through the court gate. Her steps were short and stiff—she wasn't as nimble as she used to be.

She'd need to work quickly, before the voices arrived. This was her favorite kind of job—a young life, full of promise, the sun shining down on the warm expanse of the court, a bird singing overhead. It seemed like the perfect moment to give life.

Though she saw all deaths within a fifty-mile radius, Charlotte didn't save everyone. Usually, she let the very old go, and the very cruel. But this girl, she could tell, deserved it. She would be of use to the world. She was bright and vivacious, with everything ahead of her. She deserved to find love, grow old with someone, have a career, hold her grandchildren. Charlotte gave her those gifts as she eased down beside the still figure. But she also gave her the deathmark. It came with the others, and there was no avoiding it. The process of passing back through death's door cursed the patient to a power of their own. Not Charlotte's same power, but one of a range of physical or mental aberrations that would remain with them throughout their lives.

The thought of it had stopped Charlotte more than once, but she herself had lived with her mending power all her life, and hadn't she been happy? Hadn't she been fulfilled? It seemed, most of the time, a small price to pay for returning.

Charlotte knew what had happened as soon as she put her hands on the girl. Some weakness in the heart, some malformation, had gone unnoticed until now. The girl was dead, of course, but Charlotte put her right again. She called it mending because it wasn't unlike sewing—stitching together what was torn, rearranging pieces until they fit perfectly.

It took just seconds—a defect was an easy mend—still, the voices arrived before Charlotte could slip away.

"Hey," one called, "everything okay over there?"

The girl's eyes were fluttering. Her hand was twitching, reaching for her fallen racquet.

Charlotte made her voice thready, "I saw her fall," she called. "Do come and help!"

Two young men were soon beside her, one assisting Charlotte to her feet, the other kneeling beside the girl.

She left her patient in their capable hands, shuffling more than necessary as she went back to her car, and drove to her next appointment.

That had gone just as Charlotte preferred. A timely arrival, a quick fix, and no need for explanation. As she arrived at the apartment house where her next appointment would be, she saw she wouldn't be so lucky.

Time was running short and there was a door-man. Doormen could sometimes be fooled by her insistence that she'd come to visit a wayward grand-child, but this one, she could tell, was not the type. There was, mercifully, a fire escape down the alley, so she parked her car and tripped up it. The first few flights weren't too bad, but by the time she'd reached the sixth floor where she should find the fader, she had to sink onto the edge of the metal stairs and catch her breath.

A breeze ruffled her hair as she sat. The build-ing was old, but well-maintained. The brown bricks were warm in the midday sun, and she could see out over the little city from here. It seemed peaceful today, even sleepy. The window to her patient's apartment was next to her and she squinted to see past the blinds, but couldn't make out what was inside. She checked her watch. It was time.

From her purse, Charlotte withdrew a handy little tool called the "Springer." She'd bought it from a nice young man in an alley several years ago, and it had served her well. It popped locks open neatly in a variety of ways. This time, she used the standard approach for windows and was soon easing herself across the sill.

"Hello?" she called, but was met only with si-lence. She was relieved to see that she was not too early. That could be awkward. A figure was crum-pled over the kitchen table, his cheek in his cereal bowl. Sticky milk had pooled beside him and was dripping steadily onto the floor. Charlotte reached for a kitchen towel on the table.

She lifted the inert head—as always, slightly heavier than she expected—and washed the patient's face before scooting aside the cereal bowl and swiping the breakfast mess away. Then she laid his cheek on the clean table and got to work.

Charlotte felt a sense of dread as she ran her fingers over his temples and down the thick cords of his carotid artery. Suddenly, the morning didn't seem peaceful anymore. This death was unnatural. Something had ruptured suddenly and violently in this young man's brain. Charlotte knew the inner workings of the human body well enough to know that this didn't happen by accident. She glanced over her shoulder, searching the shadowy corners of the cramped apartment for whoever had done this.

The fact that made her most uneasy, that made her feel weak and nauseated, was that she had seen it before. In the last month, she had revived three—now four—victims of this same unusual death. She could no longer deny that this was intentional and systematic.

When she felt the young man's heartbeat return, Charlotte crossed to the apartment door. She slipped out and walked toward the elevator, carrying the knowledge that somewhere out there was a killer.

• • •

Pirate was barking like crazy when she got

back to her car, and people on the street were casting disapproving glances at her, presumably for leaving him alone. She didn't stop to explain that she'd been trying to make him happy by bringing him.

Charlotte couldn't shake the feeling that somehow, something was going wrong in her cozy city. She found herself glancing worriedly into alleys as she drove by, peering longer than usual at scruffy men on street corners and idling adolescents. She stepped quickly as she dropped off a check at the bank and stopped at the grocery to restock her supply of treats for Pirate. She breathed a sigh of relief as she followed the little dog through their front door and locked it securely behind them.

Charlotte ran through the four similar fades in her mind, trying to recall details. She'd only suspected a connection on the third one, a middle-aged woman. One had seemed odd, two unfortunate, and three a pattern. Now she was faced with the image of the young man in his cereal bowl. Number four. Now it was a true chain of deaths.

Charlotte considered calling the police, but she'd never found them to be willing to listen to a crazy lady who said she knew when people were going to die.

The kitchen was hot now, soaking in the late-afternoon sun, so she opened a window and tried to push the thoughts out of her mind. She jumped when she heard a knock on the front door, and cautiously peered out to see who it was.

Mason. The sweet face of her ten-year old neighbor gazed back at her. She opened the door, feeling a little foolish for being afraid. He buzzed in with a handful of bright petunias.

"Hey Granny, I brought you these!"

In the summer, Mason brought her flowers every afternoon. Sure, they were picked from her own garden, and sure, he knew she'd give him a chance at the cookie jar, but the gesture was sweet anyway. She looked forward to seeing his inquisitive brown eyes peering around her into the living room. She looked forward to the myriad questions he asked: where did she get the umbrella with the parrot on the handle? How did Pirate lose his eye? Why did the skin on her face fold like that? He was open and honest and direct, and she found it refreshing.

She taught him things, too. He'd become a pretty good little cribbage player under her guidance. And sometimes he helped her bake, or weed, or sew a button on. He never stopped talking from the moment he came in, and his voice was a welcome change from the ever-present silence of her house.

Today Mason was excited about a new scooter, so he talked twice as fast as usual. His parents were out and he was in no hurry to get home. He and Charlotte made macaroni and played go fish.

"Got any twos, Granny?" he asked, for the tenth time.

Charlotte was about to send him fishing when

Pirate interrupted her with a flurry of barking at the kitchen sink.

"Settle down!" she reprimanded him. But Pirate barked on, moving along the cupboard doors and finally bristling near the hallway.

"Silly dog," she said, "go fish."

It was then that she felt it. Another fade was coming. She had just enough time to lay her cards down and and grip the edge of the table when the kitchen and Mason and Pirate dimmed around her and she saw a dark figure ahead. She felt pain and fear. The kitchen came back into focus, but its weird, shifting colors told her she was seeing it in the fade. The death would happen here. She heard a cry and focused on its origin. And then, more than ever before, Charlotte felt agony. It was not just the fader's pain. It was her own anguish, too, as she saw that the fader was Mason.

"Granny, Granny. It's your turn!"

She slipped back out of the fade and sat looking at him. His big eyes, his round cheeks. She wanted to throw her arms around him. He was alive. He was safe.

Not for long. Within the hour, he would be lifeless on the worn linoleum of her kitchen floor.

Charlotte stood. She didn't want to scare him, but he had to leave.

"Time to go home, Honey," she said.

"But it's only seven thirty!" he protested, "My folks won't even be home for another hour."

Charlotte thought of him alone in the big colonial next door. She hesitated.

During that moment, when she stilled and tried to think what to do, she heard the squeak from the back bedroom door. She knew who would be there before she turned to look at the hallway, but a jolt still shook her when she saw him.

Tall and lean, with a maniac's darting eyes, the man from the fade stood in her kitchen archway. He was neatly dressed in casual slacks and a polo shirt. Not at all the scruffy type of man she'd been watching out for all day. He was startlingly pale, as if he had never spent time outdoors.

"Sorry to barge in," he said, his voice smooth and confident, "but from the way you bolted that front door I didn't think you'd let me in the usual way."

Charlotte pulled Mason to his feet. She stepped in front of him and spoke to the stranger, "Get out of here." She'd used the tone before, with stray dogs, and it usually worked.

Not this time. It seemed to amuse the intruder, in fact. His youthful face creased in a smile.

"You're spunky," he said. His voice was smoky and too heavy for his years.

Charlotte glanced around at the counters. They were, as always, tidy. No knife, no mallet, not even a frying pan she might grab for a weapon. She glanced at the high cupboard by the sink, but reaching it meant going directly toward the madman. "Why are you here?"

He took a step toward her, "you've been going around undoing my work. Did you think there would be no consequences for that? Did you think I'd never figure out what you were doing?"

"Honestly, I wasn't thinking of you at all."

"Well," he replied, "I suspect that is about to change." He advanced smoothly, and Charlotte scooted around the table, trying to keep it between them. Pirate hopped onto one of the chairs—his usual seat—and stood growling at the intruder.

"But before I finish this, I have to know how you're doing it. Are you messing with time?"

"Excuse me?" She motioned Mason to move behind her.

"Are you changing the timeline? Because if that's it, this is going to be much harder."

"I don't know what you're talking about. Who can mess with time? Time is relentless, unchangeable. Believe me." She waved an arthritic hand at her wrinkled face.

"Well good. You're not a reeler, then. See, that's what everybody thinks about time. But it's more flexible than most people realize."

Charlotte kept him talking, "Tell me one example of when time wasn't rigid. I can't think of any, and I've been around a long time."

"Everyone has felt time slippage, Granny. You look at your watch and you have an hour before your kid's done with practice, so you sit down to read the paper. When you look again, the hour has passed and you're late. Or a meeting has only two agenda items, and it should be over quickly, but every time you look at the clock it has only moved bare minutes. That's not your imagination. That's a time reeler. Somewhere nearby, a reeler is manipulating time."

"Reeler?"

"Like a string on a spool, time can be played out or reeled in."

Charlotte was only half listening. A few more feet and she could make a break for the back door. Mason was moving stealthily behind her, his eyes wide and scared. She took his hand and squeezed it in what she hoped was a reassuring way.

"But I've been on guard for slippage, and I haven't felt it recently. I didn't feel it at Pete Valay's apartment building this morning when you went in and made a joke of all my planning and work."

"You saw me?"

"I saw you leave. And I saw your cute little mutt."

So this was who Pirate had been barking at. The thought chilled her blood. This monster had killed those people, and now he had followed her here. She had led him to Mason.

Charlotte couldn't help herself, "Why are you doing this? What did those people do to you?" She really wanted to know. She'd never met anyone who would willingly take a life, and she couldn't fathom what he must be thinking. Perhaps if she could understand, she could convince him to spare the child.

"That's none of your business," he said.

She made her tone conciliatory. "You're right," she said, "But you just have a very unique," she glanced at Mason, "style, that I've never seen before."

"Because you've never met a reeler."

"And I've never felt the kind of damage you did to those people's brains."

He didn't smile. His jaw tightened, in fact. He wasn't pleased at what he had done, but behind his eyes there was a certain pride in how he did it. She appealed to that.

"It must be a particular gift you have, with time. And you must have figured out a new way to use it. Like I said, I've never seen it before."

"It is new. Most reelers just manipulate time. But the people around them don't know what's going on. They just sense the slippage. Because, well, do you know what the striatum is?"

Charlotte inched past another chair, shaking her head just to keep him talking.

"It's a part of your brain. It does many important things, and one of them is that it helps us know when time is passing, and makes us aware of how much time has passed. Most people sense it in an abstract, peripheral way. Essentially, all I do is make people keenly aware of the reeling of time. It causes an overload of the striatum, a surge of temporal power that shorts out the circuitry. It's quick. Not that painful."

Charlotte was shaking now. He spoke of killing so casually. "Why? Why would you do that?"

He seemed to consider, then answered her question with another question. "You're like me, aren't you? A phenom? Special? Gifted? Super?"

But Charlotte had learned early not to divulge that information.

He nodded knowingly. "You were of *that* era. Where people wanted us fixed. Where whole branches of medicine and psychology formed to figure out what had gone wrong and how to set the human race right again. The special schools, the drugs, the labs," his eyes closed briefly and Charlotte almost pitied him, "they all started then. And decades later, we still haven't progressed that much. We're still hiding out, still covering up what we can do. That's what this is all about, Granny. It's about finding a place, no, *carving* a place for us in society. I'm working on that. Working on setting the balance right and bringing the phenoms into power for the first time in history, as we should be. It'll come too late for you, but maybe it gives you some comfort to know that a better day is coming."

"How am I supposed to feel comfort that you're killing people?"

"I wouldn't if they didn't interfere," he said simply. She sensed he was talking about her.

"Don't fool yourself. I wasn't interfering. You came to my house. I was just playing Go Fish."

The reeler slammed his hand on the table. His

346

patience was running out. "You have been interfering for weeks! You can't keep bringing them back, lady. Didn't you ever think I killed them for a reason?"

"What reason could you possibly have for that?"

His words tumbled out, falling over each other, "They know who I am. They could ruin everything. If anyone finds me, I'll have to go back to the lab." His voice dropped low, "And I won't go back to the lab."

He rubbed a hand across his forehead, "And see, you know now, too. So you've got to go." Charlotte saw his eyes slide away from her face, to the face of the child behind her, "Both of you."

She opened her mouth to argue, but the reeler cut her off.

"But first you have to answer my question. Are you a reeler? Can you manipulate time? Or are you some sort of death angel?"

Her surprise must have tipped him off. She hadn't heard that term for a long time.

"Ahhh. That's it. But don't you have it backward? Are you supposed to be bringing people back?"

It was her turn to talk. She stepped back from the table as she did. "There's no 'supposed to' with phenoms. Not these days. When my parents took me to the doctors, they were told I had a neurological disorder. They were supposed to sedate me. But they didn't. They took me to the country and I grew up free, learning about my powers only from loving parents and careful experimentation. Nobody used me to do their bidding. Nobody stopped me or told me what I could do was bad or scary." She saw in his eyes that their experiences had been very different. "I'm sorry for what you've been through. But have you ever thought what good you could do with your control over time? What remarkable gifts you could give the world?"

Anger flared in his eyes, "It doesn't deserve my gifts!" With the agility of youth, the reeler charged around the table. Charlotte threw herself at him, pushing with all her strength.

The reeler staggered. Her momentum moved them back into the kitchen, away from Mason. But the man recovered, and shoved her to the floor. Charlotte felt pain shoot along her left side.

"Leave her alone!" Mason lunged forward, throwing himself at the attacker. Charlotte tried to stand, but her leg wouldn't support her.

The reeler reached out and put one hand to the boy's forehead, as if holding him off.

Charlotte felt the world sliding by. She knew now what was happening. This was time slippage.

Mason fell. His lifeless body crumpled to the floor, and in front of her was the image from the fade, only this time in full color.

She heard herself screaming. The reeler walked toward her. Pirate leaped onto the table from his chair, then from the table toward the reeler, jaws snapping. Cards fell in a flurry of colors and suits, fluttering to the floor beside her. Pirate received a forceful blow that sent him flying to the corner of the kitchen, where he sat whimpering.

"Stop! Stop!" Charlotte begged, clawing her way toward Mason. She had to reach him in time.

The reeler was reaching out. She felt his hand on her head, the grip of his iron fingers, and she couldn't move away from it. She wondered if her skull would fracture, wondered who would find her here, on the kitchen floor, and when.

She grabbed the reeler's powerful arm, wrenched at him, felt a white-hot pain in her head as time began to slide again.

The reeler didn't seem to even notice her grip. His stared at her, unseeing, and the pain grew more intense. The world itself began to fade, like her visions had been reversed. Through the pain, she became aware of brilliance—an intense light that washed out the everyday world. She was alone in it only a second before she saw someone. The pain grew less as she focused. It was Arthur.

Charlotte reached for him. He looked so good. So happy. She wanted more than anything to be enfolded in his strong arms again. But Arthur didn't reach for her. He shook his head and spoke. Though she couldn't hear him, the three words were as clear to her as if he had shouted.

"Not yet. Fight."

She didn't know how to fight. The reeler was

much stronger than she was. All she knew anymore was mending. Without thinking, Charlotte began to use her power. Just like when she was mending, the warmth flowed to her fingers. Arthur and the light began to disappear. The kitchen eased back into focus. The reeler, his hand, the pain, all came back. She tried to think around the agony. He was stronger than she was. She had no hope of loosening his grip or pulling away.

But if she could mend bodies, could she not tear them, too? *Death angel.* She concentrated, pulling the warmth and energy that flowed through her hands backward, pulling the stitches out opposite the way she would have put them in. She imagined the muscles and tendons and bones under her fingers, and she pictured them ripping. It was just as easy as she had envisioned it would be.

The reeler flinched, then cried out. His arm dropped, useless to his side and he scrambled backward away from her. Charlotte fell back onto her elbow, breathing out the pain—her own as well as his.

"What was that?" he cried. "You're no phenom I've ever seen before."

"No," she spat up at him, "I'm not."

He advanced again, rubbed his injured arm, and retreated. He paced, pain and confusion evident on his face.

"I can't let you touch me. But, but, you have to die," he said. His voice was less sure, less proud, than before. His hand flitted around like an agitated bird. Suddenly, he paused and looked her in the eye, "Unless, unless—you'd join me? Be a part of the revolution?"

Charlotte blinked through the ache growing in her bones. How could he even think she'd consider it? "There are other ways to bring about the changes you want," she choked, "I'll help you find other—"

"No. I don't need any more *help.* I've had more than enough *help.*"

"I understand," she began, but she didn't get to finish. The reeler was lifting one of the heavy oak chairs.

"You'd rather die than join me? Well, okay. But first, you need to be neutralized. You can't hurt me if you're not conscious."

Charlotte had never wanted to hurt anything before, but now a swelling need for survival overtook her. She waited. As the reeler stepped closer, she gathered all her strength. As he raised the chair above her, Charlotte reached out and seized his leg.

All her fear, all her pain, all her anguish over Mason, were wrapped up in that single gesture, and the instant her hands closed around the reeler's ankle, she was tearing loose the knot that held him to mortality.

He cried out and the leg gave way under him. The chair crashed onto the linoleum beside Charlotte as he fell, twisting toward his pain. She pulled back and dodged a blow, then grasped his shoulder as he came at her again.

This time, as she ripped at the structures beneath the surface, she found her way to his heart. She felt time swirling around her—not the smooth whoosh of slippage she had just felt, but a desperate churning of the timeline. He was trying to rewind, trying to move back before she had reached for him. But her grip on him seemed to move her out of time as well. Time spun around her, backward, then forward, then, seemingly sideways. The effect was terrifying. In the vortex, she barely noticed as his breathing slowed.

And then the world returned to its normal pace. She felt his heart stop, felt him slump back onto the floor, felt him writhe away from her and grow still.

Charlotte was left with the body beside her and the reality of what she had done. It was a dark feeling, a smothering pain.

Death angel. She had only heard the term once before tonight. When her parents had taken her to the phenom psychologist. She hadn't known what he meant when he diagnosed that, and when she'd asked, her mother had brushed it off as a mistake.

But this was it. Charlotte had carried with her all this time the power to bring death. She had been using her gift backwards. She didn't know yet how this changed her, and she didn't have time to think of it. She found some strength and, using the upturned chair the reeler had dropped beside her, struggled to her feet.

Mason's eyes were open, but she knew he couldn't see her leaning over him, couldn't hear her speaking to him. She laid her trembling hands on the child's head. She bit back her cry of horror at the realization that she was too late. Her struggle with the reeler had taken more than three minutes. She couldn't bring her young friend back.

Charlotte stood and leaned heavily against the sink. She had once asked her mother if this power was a curse.

"No, no," her mother had reassured her, "it's a gift." And yet, Charlotte had never been able to save the people closest to her. Time and fate seemed always to intervene, and there was no defeating them. They were the constants, the fixed features of her world.

Except.

She looked at the reeler. Except that time was not as fixed as she had believed an hour ago. Time was fluid. Like death, a human could move more than one direction through it.

The reeler controlled the one thing that she needed. Time. She remembered his desperate attempt to turn back the clock. Would he still try? If instead of stopping him, she allowed him to do so, could she save Mason?

But the reeler was a maniac. He was unpredictable, cruel. He didn't deserve mending. And right now, he had no power to hurt anyone ever again. She had stopped him once and for all. If she mended him, what evils would she unleash on the world? Could she bring herself to kill him again, now that she knew the darkness that filled the soul after such an act?

She looked away from the reeler. The kitchen was in disarray. Pirate huddled, whining, in the corner. The cards were scattered across the table and the floor.

Only the bright flowers in their vase sat untouched. They drew her eye like a beacon. For Mason, she had to try.

Charlotte's back protested as she reached for the upper cupboard by the sink where Arthur had always kept his pistol. She'd left it there all these years, mostly as a reminder of him. Now, its weight was reassuring as she lifted it down and checked that it was loaded. Charlotte moved back across the room, toward the reeler. She eased herself down beside him.

His face was smooth in death, with none of the anguish she had seen when he was alive. She laid the gun on her lap, and reached for the reeler's still form. As she touched him, Charlotte felt the damage she'd done. Her stomach turned.

Stitch by stitch, she mended it. As she always had. She knew that if she had found him this way, she would be horrified at whoever had done this to him. She realized how little she had really known of each of her patients. The potential for both good and evil was inside every one of them, and though she had deemed them deserving of another chance, what had she really known? There were some very good people and some very bad ones, but most spent their lives somewhere in the middle, struggling through, both building and destroying. Even the best had the power to hurt, and even the worst, like the reeler, had the power to help.

She felt his consciousness returning, and held tight as time began to swirl around her again.

Pirate took flight from the corner of the room, across the table, returning gracefully to his usual seat. The cards arced back onto the table in a beautiful reversed cascade. The light from outside grew incrementally brighter. The chair righted itself, moved back to the table.

As Charlotte put the last stitch in place, the reeler returned with a jolt. There was deep confusion in his eyes as he wrestled desperately backward through time. Charlotte felt herself slip out of his timestream as he rose and moved across the room.

When time stabilized again, he was just turning away from Mason. The child had just fallen.

The reeler was disoriented. He didn't move as steadily toward Charlotte as he had in their first encounter. He stopped, a hand on the table, and shook his head.

Charlotte didn't wait. With strength born of fear, she fought her way to her feet and leveled the gun at him. The reeler blinked, and Charlotte felt time beginning to flow backward.

"No," she said, using the stray-dog tone again. This time he listened. "You don't want to do that."

"What do you mean?" the reeler asked.

"Go back in time and you'll find yourself dead. I just brought you back."

She was moving now, scooting along with the counter at her back. The reeler looked nervous, and his voice shook as he spoke, "Why would you do that? I'm going to kill you."

"Maybe. But not before I tend to my mending." She passed by him and, keeping her eyes and the gun on him, moved to Mason. She crouched, wondering if she could mend without looking at the child. She had to try. Stretching her aching left hand tenderly across the boy's head, she used her right to keep the gun pointed at the reeler.

"This is crazy. You crazy old woman. You can't beat me."

Mason stirred.

There was a new kind of strength in Charlotte's voice as she responded. It was one born of experience. She found herself liberated from all her fears. Death, that black door she'd feared for so long, simply led into another room. And Arthur was there.

A rush of confidence came from that knowledge. And another from the knowledge that even at her age she had found new skills she didn't know she had. Her power was greater than she had imagined. She didn't have a great strength or laser vision, but she could stop people from hurting others. She could, if she had to, fight again.

"I have already beaten you. And I will again. But I needed you. I needed these moments back and you gave them to me. Thank you for that."

Mason sat up and was still and quiet in his confusion. Charlotte couldn't keep herself from smiling. His brown eyes again shone with questions. He was restored. She touched his cheek, then stood again, groaning slightly.

She kept the gun steady. The reeler's eyes moved around the kitchen. Charlotte expected him to attack again, and was surprised when he stepped backward, toward the door, instead of lunging at her. There was something new in his eyes—fear. He barely looked at the gun. Charlotte realized that he was not afraid of it, but of her.

"This isn't over," he said, as he moved toward the door, "I'll be back."

"I'll be ready," Charlotte replied. He blinked and twisted the doorknob. The golden light of the setting sun spilled into the kitchen, blinding Charlotte for a moment as she watched the reeler fade into its brilliance.

A Word from Josi Russell

Thank you for reading "Fade." As with every story I write, this one was an adventure for me. I love exploring familiar human relationships and conflicts in unfamiliar contexts. My favorite thing about writing superhero stories is that through every hero's story I discover new things about the people around me.

People are always surprising me. "Fade" was born from my strong belief that everyone is more than we see on the outside. In fact, I think that's why we love superhero stories—they allow us to see behind the mask and find hidden strengths we might otherwise miss.

If you'd like to explore more of my work, please visit my website: www.josirussellwriting.com Where you can learn more about my bestselling novels: the Caretaker Chronicles series, The Empyriad Series, and more short stories. If you'd like free stories and updates on my newest releases, please sign up for my Readers' Club!

A Short Word from the Presenter

As a pastor, I often get the chance to present things. "I present to you, for the first time, Mr. and Mrs. Happily-Married." Weekly, I do something called *presenting the gospel*. I present high school and college graduates with Bibles, and new mothers with clothing and diapers for their beautiful new additions. Presenting is a part of my everyday life and I would have it no other way.

There are two things I love to do in (well, there surely are more than that), pastor people and write books. Pastoring is the art of *doing life with people*. Getting to know and love people, despite their faults, personality differences and idiosyncrasies. When I think about melding those together, the result is short story anthologies. What better way to experience camaraderie with other authors than to work intimately together to create something beautiful to present to the world?

To be able to give something to humanity is an honor and a privilege. And this collection is no different. It was with great joy and excitement that I have presented to you, the reader, this collection of short stories. I hope that it has enriched your life, made you smile, and made you think.

If you enjoyed your reading experience, you might also enjoy Volume Two, *World Domination: A Supervillain Anthology*. While you're there, I would encourage you to take a moment and review this book on Amazon. If everyone who loved our books and stories left reviews we would find ourselves in a much different boat. Reviews are the lifeblood of a book—they can make or break an author's career. Even if you didn't love the stories found within, we still want you to share an honest review.

Thank you for your time. We all know how valuable it is. May the God of the Universe bless you.

With Abounding Love,
Steve Beaulieu

Made in the USA
Lexington, KY
27 September 2017